Advance praise for
As the Crow Dies

"Beginning with a body face down in the river, **As the Crow Dies** flies from one unexpected development to another. A pair of unlikely detectives work to find a missing scientist and keep up with a case that threatens their lives and their sanity. Animals with super powers, street musicians, the U.S. president and first lady, and a roller derby matchup all add to the novel's strength and quirkiness. Few authors can combine murder and humor as well as Kenneth Butcher."

—**Anne Hillerman**, *New York Times* best-selling mystery author

"*As the Crow Dies* is a charming, vibrant mystery filled with intrigue that hooks the reader from page one. Kenneth Butcher tells a fascinating tale of murder, animal intelligence, and human foolishness in this wonderful novel that brings the city of Asheville to life. A page-turning follow-up to *The Dream of St. Ursula*. I love this book."

—**Christy English**, author of *The Queen's Pawn* and *Waking Sarah Ann*

"In **As the Crow Dies**, Ken Butcher creates an intriguing mystery that combines a fresh, charming detective duo, the free-spirited vibe of Asheville, NC, and an original plot following a trail of bodies in a race to prevent a crime of international consequence. **As the Crow Dies** takes readers on an exciting ride with more twists and turns than the mountain roads of its setting."

—**Mark de Castrique**, author of *Murder in Rat Alley*, *Secret Undertaking*, and *Hidden Scars*

"No living author writes police procedurals that are sharper or funnier than Kenneth Butcher and *As the Crow Dies* serves up madcap mystery at its most gripping. He sets loose his two military-trained detectives in the foothills of Western North Carolina where they encounter would-be assassins, international intrigue and a menagerie of uniquely gifted animals. Who other than Butcher can introduce cigarette-rolling raccoons, lothario crows and alphabet-reciting mule deer into a murder investigation—and never have readers doubt the truth of every word? *As the Crow Dies* proves as suspenseful as it is entertaining, Appalachia's rollicking rejoinder to Philip Marlowe and Sam Spade: A novel as brilliant and rare as the zany animals that populate its pages."
  —**Jacob M. Appel**, author of *Millard Salter's Last Day*

"Kenneth Butcher's *As the Crow Dies* gives us a crackerjack mystery that begins, like all good murder mysteries, with the discovery of a body—an apparent accident. But the plot then takes us into remarkable territory in which the fantastical becomes true and the detectives find themselves confronting a deadly conspiracy that spreads far beyond the picturesque mountain town of Asheville, NC. Segal, the seasoned lead detective, is recovering from a gunshot wound. In a turnabout of the usual roles, it falls to his partner, Dinah Rudisill, to handle the rough stuff. One of the joys of this fast-paced mystery is watching their friendship develop, as Segal regains his old confidence and Rudisill sharpens her skills, rising to an extraordinary challenge. Both detectives live into the honorable tradition of restoring justice and meaning to a world often lacking in both, and doing so with style and humor. The perfect book to get a smart reader through the pandemic."
  —**Philip Gerard**, author of *Cape Fear Rising* and *The Last Battleground*

AS THE CROW DIES

Kenneth Butcher

An Asheville Mystery

Pace Press
Fresno, California

As The Crow Dies
Copyright © 2020 by Kenneth Butcher
©2020: Kenneth Butcher, Hendersonville, North Carolina
www.kennethbutcher.com
All rights reserved.

Published by Pace Press
An imprint of Linden Publishing
2006 South Mary Street, Fresno, California 93721
(559) 233-6633/ (800) 345-4447
PacePress.com
Pace Press and Colophon are trademarks of
Linden Publishing, Inc.
ISBN: 978-1-61035-361-8

Printed in the United States of America
on acid-free paper

Library of Congress Cataloging-in-Publication Data on file

Acknowledgments and a Note of Thanks

I am deeply indebted to many people for encouragement and help during the writing process, including the whole population of Asheville who make it such a fun and vibrant place.

Thanks to William Greenleaf, who read a very early version of this story and made many helpful suggestions. Also, a very special thanks to Steve Kirk, who not only steered me in the right direction after reading an early draft but also applied his special brand of editing near the end. His patience, thoroughness, and insight have surely made this a stronger book.

Thanks to Marge Cotter for her proofreading and encouragement. Marge passed away last year and is missed by many including myself. Also, thanks to Jen Butcher for proofreading and all kinds of help, including putting up with this whole process.

Finally, thanks to Kent Sorsky and CJ Collins et al at Pace Press for turning this story into a real live book.

To the Princess of Asheville, Lilah Grove

Prologue

Abbottabad, Pakistan

The boy trotted down the narrow lane between cement-block buildings, kicking a worn soccer ball with remarkable control. The sun was just coming up and a heavy dew had formed, settling the dust. It was his favorite time of day. The air was cool and the bigger kids were not up yet. He had the street to himself. He could be who he wanted to be. He practiced a quick sideways kick, a shot on goal. The ball lodged in a niche between two buildings, forcing him to interrupt the rhythm of his trot to pick it up. When the ball was in his hands, he looked at the words written in a language he could not understand. His sister said it was English. The words said, "Made in China," but he had no sense of that.

He thought he was lucky to have the ball at all. Last week, one of the older kids had kicked it over the wall that surrounded the large compound of buildings two blocks away. He did it on purpose, for spite. In less than a minute, a door in the wall opened just enough for a man to roll the ball gently out. The boy had snatched it up and headed home.

Now, he dropped the ball again to continue his solitary practice. A shadow flashed, and the call of a bird made him look up and gasp. It was a large black crow. He watched as the crow glided and then flared its wingtips to settle on the parapet of a building a block away. The building was taller than any nearby and easily visible even from the narrow lane.

As he watched the crow bobbing on the wall, he saw a man approach. Against the red light of the morning sun, it was a silhouette only, just the head and shoulders, but the boy could tell without doubt he was not a local man. It was the shape of the hat that told him this, a smooth cap close to the head with a long bill in front. It was the kind of cap the boy had seen in pictures of American ballplayers in the magazines downtown.

The crow did not fly away but bobbed its head even more and cawed with excitement. The man gave the bird something to eat, and the bird allowed its head to be stroked. The man held up his arm, and the crow hopped on. As the man turned to leave, he stopped suddenly. The boy could tell the man had just spotted him, and he caught his breath. The man held his gaze for a few seconds and then nodded as if to tell the boy that it was okay. The boy could see the man better now in the gathering light. He could see the letters on the man's cap. The boy nodded back, and then the man and the bird were gone.

The boy would remember the man and the crow in days to come, but he would keep his memories to himself. He would remember the letters on the cap, too. *Asheville.*

CHAPTER 1

Vortex

Asheville, North Carolina

Early on another morning a young woman—a true athlete, short in stature, large in hair—skated, perfectly poised and balanced and at peace. Her eyes were barely open. This was a form of meditation, practice, and physical workout blended together, all in one. She called it "feeling the glide." It was an unscripted series of variations on the basic art of roller skating—fast, slow, glide, dip, high on the outside of the oval, low on the inside, all by herself in the cool of the morning around the vortex of the roller derby track. Her name was Dinah Rudisill. To fans of the local roller derby team, she was "the Dinosaur"—Dinosaur Rudisill.

The sound of her cell phone broke the trance. She looked at the screen. It was a call from dispatch, even though she was not yet officially on duty. To the Asheville Police Department, she was Sergeant Rudisill.

The dispatcher described the problem quickly. He ended by saying, "Thought you and the lieutenant might want to go directly there instead of coming in first."

"You think I've got time for a quick shower?" Dinah asked.

"I don't think the guy is going to get any deader than he already is," the dispatcher said, and hung up.

The parking place exactly in front of Vortex Doughnuts was empty, a rare and fortuitous event. Dinah slid her car into it with the ease and accuracy of all her physical movements. As she got out, she did a quick scan of the block, a completely automatic reflex developed from her years as a cop and, before that, her time in the military. She had a reputation for not missing much, and this was one of the habits that accounted for that.

Her scan included the doughnut shop itself. She took a second to check her reflection in the wide expanse of plate glass, pulling a light tweed jacket over the sleeveless white blouse. She decided she liked how the jacket was fitted at the waist and the flare over the hips helped hide her gun. She liked the feel of the new jeans, too; they had a little stretch to them that freed her to move. Her promotion to plainclothes was fairly recent. Before that, it was all uniforms, first military then police. She was learning to dress like a normal person. She lifted her hair off her collar, a mass of brown curls still wet from the shower. She thought the hair was a different story. *I probably never will get this under control.*

She shifted her focus past the glass and into the shop and immediately picked up on an unusual vibe. The place was busy—no surprise for this time of day—but the people, instead of forming themselves into a neat line to look at the doughnuts in the case or ordering coffee, were all looking up and to the left, most with their mouths open. A TV screen there showed the morning news. She pushed the door open with her shoulder and looked around the room before she let her eyes drift in that direction too.

The president of the United States was standing at a podium in the White House. The picture struck her as odd. The podium was set up in a hallway. She thought, *Don't they have rooms for this sort of thing?* Also, the president was not looking directly into the camera but a little to the left, as though he were addressing someone standing by the cameraman's shoulder. Dinah read the body language as reluctant—not completely false, but more like someone making up a story about an event that really did happen but putting some kind of spin on it.

She pushed on in, where she knew she would find Ira Segal at his usual spot. He was there all right, leaning against the high table, not looking so hot this morning. His beloved gray sport coat was folded over the back of a chair. His clothes hung especially loose. She told herself not to worry. He was on the mend, and she was a believer. On the table was a worn paperback book. She took it as a good sign that he was reading Elmore Leonard again. When he brought Hemingway, it usually meant he was in a foul mood. She knew he liked Thomas Wolfe, too, but those books were much too big to carry around all day.

She came up and nudged him to announce her arrival. He looked away from the TV and leaned to whisper in her ear. "They killed bin Laden," was all he said, and they both looked up at the screen again.

Dinosaur Rudisill reached over and picked up Segal's coffee. "No shit," she said, and took a long drink, not taking her eyes from the screen.

The announcement from the president did not elaborate on details of the operation, which was something that would have interested Dinah and probably everyone else in the room. She waited another minute until the president finished and walked away from the camera. She thought that was odd, the way the camera stayed on him as he disappeared down the hallway. It stayed on him a long time, as if the TV producer was just as hungry for details as everyone else and hoped the president would turn around at the last minute and say, "Oh, by the way . . ." But of course, he didn't.

Dinah took another drink of Segal's coffee and said, "Osama's not the only one that died last night."

For the first time that morning, he turned and really looked at her. He appeared to be waiting for her to continue. His blue eyes seemed fully in focus, although they still held a tired look as well. He had that combination of brown hair and blue eyes that made a few ladies at the other tables glance his way from time to time. Women more frequently took him for a college professor than a police detective, an impression that sometimes served him well.

"Good coffee," Dinah said and gave him an innocent smile.

She watched him look at her with a frown of indulgence. "I'll get us a couple to go, and then you can tell me what's going on," he said.

While he went to get the coffee, she finished off his first cup and the last half of a vanilla glazed doughnut as well. She looked at the TV, but the commentators had no further information to share. They just picked apart the president's delivery.

Segal returned with the coffee. She watched him and saw no sign of a limp. His hands were steady holding the cups. She also saw him frown when he realized his doughnut had disappeared.

When they got to her car, she watched Segal set the coffees on the top and clear a place to sit. He picked up the gym bag and a sweaty uniform from the seat and a pair of roller skates from the floor. He placed everything carefully in the backseat, handling them as objects commanding respect and reverence. That was Segal's way.

They drove through downtown Asheville, then down Chicken Hill and into the River Arts District.

"Where are we going?" Segal asked as they reached the bottom of the hill.

Dinah had failed to deliver on her promise to tell him all about it because she didn't know anything other than that a body had been found. "To 12 Bones," she said. "Body in the river, so I assume a drowning."

Segal was silent for a while. Dinah noticed him thumbing the pages of the book, which stuck out of his gray sports coat pocket, something he tended to do when deep in thought. "Coincidence," he said.

It was the kind of shorthand speech that partners used. Dinah knew what he meant by that one word. The president and first lady had picked Asheville for a weekend getaway awhile back and had dined at 12 Bones. Thus, the coincidence. First the president on TV, and now his favorite barbecue joint.

Dinah knew something else, too. In the core of his being, Segal did not believe in coincidence.

North Carolina boasted almost as many barbecue joints as Baptist churches, which was saying something. All it took was a smoker, a little knowledge of the process, and some place to mix the sauces. It was hard to stand out in this crowd, but 12 Bones did. Dinah could tell by the police cars and tape that 12 Bones was about to get more publicity—and this time, not the kind it wanted.

Dinah parked across the street, knowing that Segal preferred to hang back from the scene at first, taking in the big picture. It was the kind of thing she was supposed to be learning from him, one of the reasons they had been paired— she to learn from him and he to lean on her for some of the more physical parts of the job, at least until his recovery was complete.

They got out of the car, and Segal did just that: stood and looked around, so Dinah did too. The scene was complicated. They were at the intersection of Lyman Avenue and Riverside Drive, a broken landscape of old industrial and commercial buildings. The buildings were mostly brick, some painted with fading colors, some windows functional, some broken out, some boarded up. To the north, Riverside Drive continued past buildings and empty lots in much the same character or state of disrepair, depending on how you looked at it. Where the road bent out of sight, it passed under the high Patton Avenue Bridge, which spanned the whole valley that encompassed the River Arts District and the French Broad River itself. Toward the east, she could see the top floors of the Wedge Building, home to numerous art studios and the Wedge Brewery on the ground floor. Toward the west, Lyman Avenue made a sharp turn to avoid the river fifty yards farther on. That's where most of the activity was. In between was a scruffy stand of poplar and sycamore trees and some brush.

Dinah didn't like the complexity of the scene—too many places for people to come and go, too easy to appear out of nowhere and then fade into nowhere, too difficult for her to work out a clear mental map. Hopefully, none of this would matter. It sounded like some poor guy had drowned upstream and ended up down here after following the vicissitudes of the current.

They crossed the street to where a uniformed policeman was waiting for them, clearly anxious to turn this mess over to someone else. He motioned with a nod over his shoulder. They walked that way, through the trees to the river. High in a poplar tree, a squirrel chattered in a loud, long rant, possibly bitching about the scarcity of nuts.

They came to the top of the steep bank bordering the river and looked down. Her years on the police force notwithstanding, Dinah was unprepared for the sight. At the bottom of the bank near the edge of the river, the body of a man floated spread-eagled, turning slowly in the shallow vortex of water. She glanced at Segal. He stood looking as if in a trance. A uniformed policeman waved to them as they stood watching the body turn and turn.

"Thirty-three and a third RPM," Segal said.

Dinah watched as the uniformed cop's eyes got big.

"The speed," he said. "The old record players. It's like watching a record play." He took out a small moleskin notebook.

With a sidelong glance, she caught him writing down the number 33⅓. Dinah knew he often wrote down the first words that came to mind when he arrived at a crime scene. It was more a device for capturing the sense of the moment than recording data.

"Should we pull him out?" the cop asked. Segal nodded.

The cop grabbed the floater by the back of the collar the next time he came around, and Dinah scrambled down the bank to help pull him out. Segal helped, too, when they had the body near level ground.

They all stepped back and looked at the body lying on its back in the grass. Dinah saw that Segal was looking at the guy's shoes for some reason.

"Tan suede desert boots," he said. "They used to call them chukka boots when I was a kid. You still see them around, but they aren't really what you'd call in fashion. I kind of like them. They're more formal than running shoes but still casual and comfortable."

He came around to where Dinah thought he could see the soles more clearly, and other signs or clues that most people missed.

"Slight wear on these," he said, "not new but not ancient either. They would have lasted him a long time." He sighed as if to indicate this was the most egregious part of the scene.

The man's left arm was extended above the head, his right arm flexed to the side, his fingers opened as if in his last moment he wanted to dig up a handful of earth. Dinah didn't linger on the face but stood for some time in silence.

The guy wore blue jeans and a khaki shirt and a ball cap, which was lying next to the body where the uniformed cop had dropped it after bringing it up the bank.

"His hat didn't float away when he drowned?" Dinah asked.

"He was found by a couple of kayakers a little while ago," the uniformed cop said. "They found the hat right beside him, so they fished that out, but they didn't want to touch the body."

Dinah peered downstream and saw a couple of guys still in their flotation vests talking to another officer, who was writing down their statement, all trying not to look in the direction of the body but shooting glances from time to time anyway. She could understand their impulse.

Dinah touched Segal on the arm and whispered, "Crawford's here."

Crawford, the medical examiner, nodded as he brushed by, already with gloves and paper suit in place, all business, saying nothing. Segal and Dinah stood aside, giving him room to do his job.

Crawford circled the body slowly. Dinah was not sure if he was humming softly or talking to himself under his breath.

"He was found right here, but I guess he could have drowned anywhere upstream," one of the uniforms said.

Crawford shook his head. "You seen many drowning victims?" He appeared to size up the guy in uniform first, then turned toward Segal and Dinah.

Dinah blew out a breath and no one answered.

"They don't look like this," Crawford said. He knelt and with care turned the body over. A large entry wound was revealed centered between the shoulder blades. He looked at Segal. "Welcome back to active duty, Lieutenant Segal. Looks like you have a murder."

Dinah couldn't tell if Segal was frozen in thought or just frozen. After a moment, he let her turn him away from the dead man. She had seen more of this kind of destruction than he had, owing to her military experience. She thought of sniper victims in Afghanistan. She knew there was little more the medical examiner would do here.

They approached the uniformed policeman at the tape. "Anyone here that might have seen anything?" she asked in a low tone, possibly out of some combination of respect and superstition. The man nodded toward the porch of the barbecue place, where a thin man in an apron stood with his hands on his hips.

"How about we go talk to that guy," she said to Segal. She could see he was still either deep in thought or in shock at the sight of the dead man and the realization it was murder. She hoped the uniformed guy didn't notice. She knew there were still doubts about Segal in the department, and this was the kind of thing that could get people talking.

Segal touched the book in his coat pocket, then seemed to snap out of it. "Yeah, good idea. We'll talk to the guy." He headed out.

Dinah followed and caught up fast. "Look, Segal, this is looking kind of involved all of a sudden. We got those other cases we're working. Philips and Meyers are on morning shift today. If you want, I could call and see if we could toss this one to them."

He stopped and looked at her and smiled. Her attempt to throw him a rope might have been too obvious. One of her jobs was to protect him, but she realized she might be over-protective. After all, injury or no injury this was Segal. She studied his face for some sign of embarrassment or resentment, but true to his nature she saw none. *He knows what I'm doing better than I do*, she thought.

Another quick scan of the area and Dinah was satisfied they'd done what they could. In the top of one of the scrubby poplar trees, a crow perched, as if keeping an eye on the proceedings.

"There are a bunch of other crows over by the river," Dinah said.

"Yeah," Segal said. "And they set this one as a watchman."

Through the trees, Dinah saw the guys with the stretcher making their way toward the river. She heard the buzz and click of radios. Segal was apparently deep in thought, running his thumb over the pages of the book in his coat pocket in that self-soothing motion she'd noticed so many times before.

"We might as well talk to the guy at 12 Bones since we're here. Then we'll see if we stick with it or not."

The crow raised its beak and let out two caws.

They turned toward the bird. "That bird needs to shut the hell up," Dinah said.

CHAPTER 2

Morning Shift

Segal sat at a table on the porch at 12 Bones talking to the first man on the morning shift. By this time, another employee had arrived, a woman of middle age whom Segal remembered seeing behind the counter in the happier days when he was just a customer. She attended to some of the opening chores, although Segal could see she was upset by what had happened so close by. Dinah was at the next table, carefully removing the contents of the victim's wallet, laying things out on a paper towel per protocol, to blot away the moisture.

The man told Segal what happened earlier that morning. He had parked a little distance away, closer to the river, and had walked up Lyman Avenue as he did every morning. He became aware of loud sounds off to his left.

"Only reason I took a second glance toward the river was the way the birds were acting," the man said. "Crows. Calling to each other like they were upset or excited or something. I was afraid they got into the garbage again, which they do if the night crew don't close up the cans. That's when I saw the kayakers and they called to me, and that's when I called the police."

"You didn't try first aid?" Segal asked.

"I didn't see any point in that. They said the man was dead."

"Did you recognize the guy?"

"I think so, maybe," he said. "It was hard to make out, the way he was turning and turning, but from what I saw and from the way he was dressed, I think he's one of the guys used to come in here pretty often, like once or twice a week—but I haven't seen him for a while."

Segal waited, then asked, "You know his name?"

"Chickey," the man said. "I think that's who he is."

"Chickey?" Dinah asked. "Not Chuckey?"

"No, they called him Chickey. I remember 'cause it was a weird name and I thought most guys wouldn't like it much if people called them that, but this guy didn't seem to mind. There was something about how they said it made it okay. It wasn't like they were using it to put him down or anything."

"You say he used to come in with a group of other people?" Segal asked.

"Yeah, a few, mostly the same people, it seemed like. I think maybe they worked together."

"Creatures 2.0," Dinah said. She held a damp business card between two fingers. "Charles Atley. Job title was Manager, Behavior Augmentation, whatever that is." She flipped the card back and forth and handed it to Segal.

He studied it and flipped it over again. A phone number was written on it in black ink. He showed it to Dinah. He himself did that from time to time. It was not a great way to record things, as he was likely to forget and hand the card to someone else. He watched Dinah write the number in her notebook.

Segal brought his mind to the task at hand. He could see that the man had no other information. "These guys will be out of your hair as soon as possible," Segal said to him, indicating the crime-scene crew outside. "Sorry, your day got off to a bad start."

"Not as bad as Chickey lying out there," the man said. He remained at the table with his arms crossed and his head down, as if the finality of death sat there beside him.

Segal scanned the inventory Dinah had made of the wallet but found nothing out of the ordinary.

"No family pictures," Dinah said.

"That's good, I guess," Segal said.

"What do you think? Should we call in and talk to the captain, or do you want me to check out Creatures 2.0 first?"

Segal pursed his lips when she mentioned their boss. It was a not-too-subtle reminder that the captain didn't want him too extended too soon. But it didn't feel right for him to bow out.

"I'll come with you to Creatures 2.0, whatever that is," he said. "I have a feeling there's not much for us here. We'll stick with the case awhile longer till we know what we've got."

Activity, shouts, and radio garble surrounded the site of the body. Two technicians were searching the area for evidence, but the way they were working—tracking the grass, then moving on—told Segal they weren't coming up with much. At the same time, Crawford and his assistant were wrapping up.

The medical examiner started talking as they approached. "Not much doubt about cause of death here. Bullet wound apparently caused almost instantaneous death. You can tell by the relatively small amount of blood. Heart stopped beating right away."

"No way to tell where he was standing when the bullet struck?" Segal asked. He reflected on what one of the cops had said, that maybe the guy went into the river upstream and floated down.

"I think it happened right here," the examiner said. "Look at this." He led them closer to the river, to the place where the body had been pulled out. A Styrofoam cup floated, moving in little circles. "See, there's a little pool formed by the rocks and this recess in the bank. One of the guys put that cup in, and it just circles and goes nowhere."

Segal could see this was the case.

"Yes, and if you look at those rocks on the other side of the eddy, they're close to the surface. I don't see how the body could be out in the river, then float into this pool," Dinah said.

Segal picked up a stick and threw it into the current a little upstream from the cove. They watched as it moved toward the center of the river, further confirming the point.

Segal glanced at the thicket of trees and bushes, where an assailant with a handgun might have been standing. "I assume you guys are checking in that direction," he said to the technicians. They nodded, but given the thickness of the vegetation, Segal thought they didn't stand much chance of finding anything.

He studied the face of the victim. Considering the violence that made up his last moment of life, Chickey's face held a surprisingly calm expression. *Never knew what hit him*, Segal thought.

"Let's get out of here and let these guys do their work," he said to Dinah.

She brushed her hair aside and shielded her eyes and looked toward the Wedge Building some distance away.

"You see something?" Segal asked.

"Probably nothing," she said. "I'll check it out later."

CHAPTER 3

Creatures 2.0

Dinah drove and Segal held the business card.

"Nine-one-three Oakmont Drive." Segal punched the address into his phone. "That's what I thought. The place is near the Grove Park Inn—in that neighborhood, anyway."

"Whatever they do, they must be making some bucks," Dinah said.

They drove through the heart of downtown Asheville, from the old industrial river district southwest of town through the commercial and historical district and into the oldest and by far most prestigious residential part of town, on the northeast side. The streets there wove up the lower side of one of the mountains ringing the town. The oak trees were large and spreading and the twisted rhododendrons must have been ancient. The houses and buildings ranged from ample to majestic. They were of brick and stone for the most part with ceramic tile roofs and copper gutters. Everything spoke of power and permanence and wealth. Late eighteen hundreds, early nineteen hundreds.

On the edge of this neighborhood, Segal saw a building of more recent construction. Even though it was made of more modern materials it fit perfectly with its surroundings, owing to its color and sense of proportions. A plaque above the address confirmed that they were at Creatures 2.0. Segal surveyed the hills around them as they approached the front door. He surmised they must be on the lower edge of the grounds owned by the Grove Park Inn itself.

Inside the front door, they found a young woman working at a desk. As Dinah took out her badge and approached, Segal sought some clue as to what Creatures 2.0 was all about.

"Who would you like to see?" asked the woman, who introduced herself as Gloria Harden. She wore a short, checkered blue skirt and multiple silver necklaces. Her hair was shiny, long and dark. Mid-twenties. She appeared flushed in her cheeks and throat, not an unusual reaction to the badge.

"Do you know Charles Atley?" Segal asked. He approached the desk.

Gloria's face lit up. "Sure, he works here."

Segal waited to see if she would offer anything else.

"But he's not here right now," Gloria said.

"When was the last time you saw him?" Dinah asked.

"Last night, after work. Some of us went out to eat."

"At 12 Bones?" Dinah asked.

Gloria's eyes went wide. "Yeah."

"And how late did you stay?"

"Not late. I mean, I wasn't late. I was one of the first to leave."

"And what time was that?" Dinah asked.

"About eight or eight-thirty."

"And Mr. Atley was still there?" Dinah leaned in.

"Yeah." She rocked her head back and forth between Segal and Dinah, paling in color. Her voice became lower. "He hasn't come in yet today. Lewis just asked me to call and see where he is. Is that what you're here about?"

"I think you'd better let us talk to whoever is in charge," Segal said.

Gloria hesitated.

"Would that be Francis Elah?" Dinah asked, lifting her eyes from a company brochure she had picked up.

Gloria nodded but still seemed confused. "Francis is away."

"Away where, exactly?" Dinah asked. "How can we get in touch with him?"

Gloria's mouth clenched and she didn't answer at first. "I'm not sure how I can explain that."

"Well, who is in charge in his absence?" Segal asked. He was beginning to get interested in the way this receptionist was reacting to some very basic questions.

"That would be Chickey—that is, Charles Atley," she said. "But like I told you, he hasn't come in yet."

Segal had a rhythm with Dinah. He waited a beat before asking the next obvious question. And sure enough, the Gloria figured it out for herself. "Lewis Abraham," she said, the light bulb going on in her head. "Let me go and get Lewis for you."

Dinah smiled at her, extended a hand and put it on her shoulder. "Better yet, why don't you take us to him?"

Gloria Harden conducted them down a short hall lined with photos, drawings, and paintings of animals. Segal pointed out photos to Dinah, stalling for time, checking the images out as they moved toward a set of double doors. The pictures had a peculiar quality of mood in common. It seemed to Segal as if the animals had all posed with a degree of self-awareness, much as people do. He couldn't decide if it was creepy or funny or what, but it made an impression. Segal saw Dinah raise an eyebrow. She was seeing it, too. Gloria glanced over her shoulder and smiled.

No doubt, Segal thought, she's seen this kind of reaction before.

She rapped softly with her knuckles before pushing the thick oak doors open. As she did, she said in a hushed tone, "This is the central lab room."

Segal stopped in the doorway. His hand dropped to the paperback book sticking out of his coat pocket. His thumb ruffled the pages in an unconscious movement as he took in the room.

It was a large space, well-lit by a wall of windows and a glass door on the opposite wall. There were a number of lab benches and a few cages for mice and other small animals. Most were empty, but Segal made out an owl, a couple of chipmunks, and a small primate of some kind. There were devices that Segal did not recognize with dials, gauges, and digital displays, piles of books, and the occasional hand tool, as well as microscopes and magnifying glasses.

At a large desk to one side, a black man, hair graying at the temples, probably in his late thirties or early forties, worked at a computer keyboard with several monitors.

"Lewis, it's the police," Gloria said in a tone that bordered on apologetic. She wiped her hands off on the sides of her checkered blue skirt.

"Are you here about Francis?" he asked, still not looking up from the computer screens.

Segal shot a glance at Dinah.

"I'm afraid we're here because we have some bad news concerning one of your colleagues, Charles Atley," Segal said. Lewis looked up. His eyes were dark and clear. His complexion smooth and unlined.

There was nothing that Segal could immediately see that indicated Lewis had any knowledge of what had happened to his associate. But you never knew.

"He was found dead this morning." There it was, blunt-force news. Segal had never found any gentle way to convey that message. Perhaps no such way existed.

Gloria opened her mouth and covered it with both hands. Lewis's jowl quivered. His rib cage compressed. He blew out a long, slow breath. "You're sure it was Atley?" he asked.

Segal nodded and gave him time to process the information. Lewis turned slowly in his chair to face away from them, to face out the floor-to-ceiling windows that looked onto a wooded lot behind the building.

After a moment, he said in a far-off tone, "I'm just the computer guy. What am I supposed to do now?"

Before Segal could ask what he meant, a large crow glided to the ground outside the window. It pecked on the glass twice, then made an odd movement with its head, first up and down, then a motion as if it were sharpening its beak against its right wing. Lewis looked up from his reverie, and the bird repeated the window pecking and the movements exactly as before.

"Fuck you, Richard," Lewis said to the bird, getting out of his chair. "This is all I need right now."

Segal looked on, amazed. Dinah glanced at Gloria.

"That's Francis's bird, Richard," she said, as though that explained everything. "Richard says he's hungry. He's asking us to give him some food. That's what those signals mean."

"Only he's bullshitting. Aren't you, Richard?" Lewis said. Whatever emotional stress their visit had stirred up seemed now to resolve itself into anger at the crow. Lewis went on to explain that he happened to know Richard had feasted on a road kill rabbit less than an hour ago. "I was driving in, coming through the pass up on the ridge top, and I saw him drag it off the road. Him and his latest girlfriend started tearing into it," he said. "He can't possibly be hungry. He's up to something."

"How do you know it was the same crow?" Segal asked.

"Oh, it was Richard, all right," Lewis said. "Being big bird on campus with the young females. See, by normal crow society standards, Richard should have called in the rest of the flock, a feast like that, but like I said, he's got to impress the girls."

"I thought birds like that were supposed to mate for life and be monogamous," Dinah said.

Lewis and Gloria reacted with half a laugh.

"That might be true of most crows," Lewis said, "but Richard is special. Bird gets more tail feather than James Bond." He looked at Gloria and they laughed again. Segal viewed it as two friends sharing an inside joke about a colleague. Then the gravity of the moment reasserted itself.

Richard, still outside the window, kept looking in at them. He hopped from foot to foot. Segal saw something in the eyes of the bird he had not noticed before. It was like the pictures in the hall. Maybe it was the influence of what he just learned from Lewis, but Segal felt he saw an intelligence permeating from the crow's dark brown eyes, and into his own. Segal recoiled and shifted his weight, but did not break eye contact with the bird.

"So how did Richard get so special?" Segal asked. "Does it have anything to do with the work here at Creatures 2.0?" He wanted to talk about the murder victim, but he had learned that sometimes it was useful to allow these conversations room to assume their own shape.

"It has everything to do with what Creatures 2.0 is about," Lewis said, appearing to deflate in his chair. "Richard here is our latest and greatest project—or, really, the latest and greatest of our boss, Francis Elah. Selection, breeding, training— Richard is what is possible with someone like Francis." Lewis cradled his forehead in his hand.

"But Francis Elah isn't here right now," Segal said.

Lewis shook his head and closed his eyes.

"When do you expect him to return?" Segal asked.

Lewis shifted in his chair and then with a slight frown, glanced in the direction of Dinah and Gloria. Segal sensed he was reluctant to talk in front of the receptionist.

"Gloria, I wonder if you could show Sergeant Rudisill around the building, and especially Mr. Atley's office. Would that be all right?" Segal asked.

She seemed relieved to have something to do, and Segal nodded to Dinah as the two women left the room. The desk chair squeaked as Lewis got up.

"Given what has happened, we're going to have to talk to Francis Elah. You understand," Segal said, giving no room for interpretation. He turned to Lewis, who now sat on the edge of his desk.

Lewis crossed his arms and shook his head. "That's going to be a problem. You see, I don't know where he is, and I don't have a way to get in touch with him."

Baloney, Segal thought.

Lewis continued. "A while ago some men from the government approached Francis. I don't know what branch. I always thought military, just from the way they acted. That's not too unusual. We've done government projects before, along with our work for the movies and other things. But these guys always met with Francis alone. Francis showed them some things Richard could do, but that's about all I know. Everything was very top secret. Everything moved fast, not how Francis usually operates. Then there came a time when Francis told us there was a job he needed to do. He would take Richard with him. He was not allowed to talk about it, and he would be back as soon as he could. He told us he would probably be gone at least a week, maybe two."

"And when did he leave?" Segal asked.

Lewis turned to the calendar on his desk. "Five weeks now."

"And while he was gone, Charles Atley was in charge?" he prompted.

"Yeah, Chickey," Lewis said. "He was the only one, I think, who could be left in charge, even though he and Francis had been having some arguments."

"Atley didn't like Francis?" Segal said.

"No, it wasn't like that. I mean, Chickey pretty much idolized Francis, even copied the way he dressed and wore his hair and beard. He was like a little brother. But they argued about what to do with the technology. Chickey wanted to publicize more, to expand the whole operation. Francis was not so sure. He was holding back, taking it slow, making sure we understood what we were creating. That was the way he put it."

"And what exactly is the technology?" Segal asked. He looked at the window, where Richard the crow still stood watching them, his beak moving like a person watching a tennis match as they talked.

"I don't know how much detail you want to get into, but it's all about selecting, breeding, and training animals. Actually, selecting and breeding are minor parts of the program. It's mostly training and what Francis calls 'reordering.' That's where our name comes from, Creatures 2.0, like a whole new and improved version of the animals."

"So, it's a little more than teaching your dog to roll over," Segal said.

"More like teaching your dog to roll over and do calculus," Lewis said. Segal raised his eyebrows and Lewis smiled. "Well, not really that extreme, but pretty extreme." He paused. "Let me show you an example."

He got up and went over to a large cage where a rhesus monkey napped. He opened the cage and the monkey woke up, though with little apparent enthusiasm. "Come here, Hollander," he said, and the monkey climbed onto his arm. "Francis doesn't really like to work with primates, but Hollander here is an orphan, and Francis took him in." Then he said, "Hey, Hollander, you want to show the lieutenant here a trick?"

Segal narrowed his eyes, impatient to get on with the investigation.

Lewis removed a small deck of playing cards from a drawer by the cage and brought the cards and the monkey to a lab bench by Segal. The monkey climbed down onto the lab bench, picked up the deck, and began to shuffle it.

Segal could not help smiling. "That's pretty impressive," he said.

When the deck was shuffled to his satisfaction, the monkey deftly fanned out the cards face down on the bench, then looked up at Segal and made a motion with his delicate brown little hand. The curled tail straightened a little along with this gesture.

"He wants you to pick a card," Lewis explained.

Segal did so. It was the jack of diamonds.

The monkey picked up the deck, did a little more shuffling, then fanned it again and held it out to Segal. Segal caught on. He replaced the card near the middle of the deck, then stood with his arms crossed.

The monkey collapsed the cards together and shuffled some more. Finally, he placed the deck on the bench, cut the cards, and nodded for Segal to pick up the top card.

It was, of course, the jack of diamonds.

Segal stood for a moment while Lewis gave Hollander a treat and returned him to the cage. "How did you teach him that?" Segal had never understood how human magicians did that trick, much less a monkey.

"Not so much me," Lewis said. "I'm an engineer. I'm on board for the computer stuff and statistics and monitoring equipment. In fact, before Francis took off, I didn't have all that much to do with the animals. To tell you the truth, I don't have the patience. They tend to piss me off. But it's a small company, and in a small company, everyone does what needs to be done. That was one of Francis's mantras." He looked out the window at the crow. The crow made a motion with his head and left wing. Lewis pressed a button by the window and spoke into a mic. "Forget about it, Richard. Fly away now and come back later. We'll talk."

"He understands when you talk to him like that?" Segal asked. After all, people talked to animals all the time. Didn't mean the animals understood what they were saying.

"He understands, all right," Lewis said, rubbing his forearms, the light in his eyes slowly draining.

It seemed to Segal to be actions that had more to do with disgust than pride.

Out the window, the bird did not move right away but continued watching Lewis. Then he moved his beak without making any sound, turned around, flicked his tail up and down, and flew out of sight.

Segal massaged his temples. "Let's focus on Francis Elah. Francis and Atley are having arguments, Francis disappears, Atley is killed near a place where you guys hang out."

Lewis shook his head. "I see how you're thinking, but no. No way does Francis do something to hurt Chickey or anyone else."

"Did you go to 12 Bones with them last night?"

"Yeah, I was there. It was really kind of a meeting Chickey called. Like, what's the game plan if Francis doesn't return soon?"

"And did you come up with a game plan?"

"Everyone argued, ate some barbecue, drank a couple beers, and left. To be honest, it felt disloyal to Francis to even be having that discussion."

"And Chickey was still there when you left?"

"He went out back when everyone else left out the front. Said he was going to take a leak in the weeds cause there was a line at the men's room. He was feeling bad about the meeting. I guess he tried to do the right thing, but he just didn't get any traction with the staff."

Segal took a moment to absorb this then returned to the main point. "We really need to talk to Francis. There must be some way to get a message to him."

"You don't understand how secret they were about this. I'm telling you, he left nothing," Lewis said, shaking his head. "I asked him if it was a need-to-know kind of thing, and he told me it was more than that. He said we needed *not* to know."

"Who else can we talk to? Family?" Segal asked.

"You can try. He's got a wife and daughter. Emily is the wife's name, lives in the Grove Arcade." Lewis walked back to his computer keyboard, retrieved the wife's phone number and address, and jotted them on a slip of paper. He seemed glad to be wheeling and dealing in the comfortable realm of data retrieval and transfer.

Lewis walked him to the lobby, where they found Dinah and Gloria. Gloria was crying softly, seated again behind her desk, her head down and a soaked tissue to her eyes.

"Thanks again for your help," Segal said. "I'm very sorry for your loss." It was a simple and inadequate statement he had to use from time to time, always aware of how far it fell from making things okay.

Dinah's phone buzzed and she pulled it out and checked the number. It was their boss. She showed it to Segal who frowned and shook his head. She returned the phone to her pocket unanswered.

In the old days, this would have been exactly the kind of case they called him in on. It was looking complex, nuanced, hard to read, at least for anyone else. Now, he had to decide whether or not to hand it off, and he was not ready and thus didn't want to talk to the boss yet.

As they walked down the steps toward the car, he heard the caw of a crow. He craned his neck to see Richard high in a poplar tree, watching them go and cocking his head to one side. Segal felt again a sense of intelligence about the bird. He suppressed the urge to wave goodbye.

CHAPTER 4

Eggs and Bacon

Downtown Asheville had a scrubbed-clean feel about it in the early morning. The air held a freshness and a coolness typical there even in late summer. The city tended to be a late-rising kind of place, so early risers like the man in the green jacket had the place more or less to themselves, which perfectly suited his mood that day. It was to be a day of relaxation, of catching up on little things he had denied himself for the last couple of weeks while he was busy with what they euphemistically called "the Project." This breakfast, at a nice place out on the sidewalk at a table with a linen cloth and glasses of orange juice and ice water, was one such little thing. Soon enough he would feel the pressure of the next phase of the project, but for now, a little pause.

A waitress with straight, dark hair and a tattoo on her arm and a short black skirt put a plate of eggs and bacon and buttered sourdough toast in front of him when his phone, lying on the table, buzzed. At first, he thought to ignore it, but ignoring phones was simply not in his makeup. Either you were the kind of person who could ignore a buzzing phone or you weren't. He picked up the phone, saw the number, and touched the screen with irritation as he put it to his ear. He listened for a second.

"What do you mean, wrong man?" He realized he said this too loudly and checked to see if he had been overheard. He regained his composure and listened to a lengthy monologue from the other end. As he did so, he plucked the napkin from his lap and laid it beside his silverware. As he listened more, speaking only single words from time to time to let the caller know he was still there, he slowly folded and shaped the napkin, one corner at a time. By the time he said "I understand" and hung up, the napkin was in the shape of a flower. The lightness of mood was gone. The irritation with the interruption was gone. He was all business, planning and breaking down the next steps in his course of action. Either you were the kind of person who got to have a nice breakfast at a sidewalk café or you weren't.

His phone dinged announcing a text message. He picked it up and saw the photo attached to the text. He was looking at a thin man in a gray sport coat and a much smaller woman with an enormous shock of curly brown hair standing by a car at the site of the shooting. All he knew of them was what the text told him: *Local complications. Deal with them. Appropriate action.*

The man snorted. *Appropriate action. Living in the world of euphemism.*

He slipped the phone into his jacket pocket and made a sandwich of the toast and eggs and bacon. After he put a couple of bills on the table, he slugged down the glass of orange juice, stood, got his jacket on, and walked away, taking his first bite of the sandwich when he had gone half a block. Checking behind him as he strode away, the waitress with the short skirt came out as he neared the corner, then smiled when she saw the money and the flower.

CHAPTER 5

Aunt Mary Moses

Segal parked in the Rankin Street deck and took the exit onto Walnut Street in downtown Asheville. His phone buzzed, which reminded him he had not returned the captain's call. It was dispatch. This one he took.

"We put out the BOLO alert on your guy, Francis Elah, like Dinah asked," said a no-nonsense woman on the other end. "We didn't have any case paperwork on this, so Dinah said I should go ahead and open a file, which I did."

"Okay, thanks," Segal said. He wondered why the dispatcher was getting into so much detail about paperwork.

"I got to put a name in for primary investigator," the dispatcher said. "I assumed that would be you, but Dinah said ask you first."

Segal stopped walking and thought for a moment. "Yeah, hold up on that till I have a chance to talk to the captain."

"You gonna be in pretty soon?" the dispatcher asked. There were certain positions in the police force where details of protocol were strictly observed, dispatch being one of them.

"Later this afternoon," Segal said. "I have an interview and then an appointment."

"I'll tell the captain to expect you," the dispatcher said.

Segal winced at the mention of his boss. He did not look forward to that conversation.

He continued his steep climb up the hill that led from the parking garage to Haywood Street. He had not taken ten steps before he heard a plaintive chord from a squeezebox and a unique voice carrying a melody above it. It registered as Old English, and he knew perfectly well who he would see when he reached the top of his climb. It was Mattie, sitting on an instrument case with her long legs stretched out in front—long legs with at least three layers of stockings torn in different places, long legs coming out of cut-off jeans and ending in knee socks bearing bright horizontal stripes and disappearing into combat boots. She gave him an abundant smile as soon as he rounded the corner. He already had a matching smile on his face.

She launched into the next verse of a song heard rarely, if ever, outside the south of England, at least not in this century, Segal thought.

God bless Aunt Mary Moses
And all her power and might, oh.
And send us peace to England
Send peace by night and day, oh.

He was even with her now and beamed as she sang the chorus:

Hal and Tow
Jolly rum below
We were up
Well before the day, oh.
To welcome in the summer
To welcome in the May, oh.
For summer is a-coming in
And winter's gone away, oh.

He let the last chord from the squeezebox trail off before he stepped in and gave her a hug. It had been a while since he'd seen her. Street singers were good people for detectives to know, but for Segal, Mattie was special. He had helped her out in the past, and she had not forgotten. She stood, rising well above his own height as they pulled back to get a good look at one another, as old friends do. She slipped the book out of his coat pocket with a flourish and looked at the cover.

"Ah, Elmore Leonard, the Great One," she said.

Segal nodded and grinned.

"The thing I like about Elmore Leonard novels is that, in the end, everybody gets exactly what they deserve," Mattie said. "I mean, *exactly.*"

"That's right," Segal said. He had not thought of it like that, but it probably was one of the things that drew him to those books.

"Where's that sexy partner of yours?" she asked.

"Dinah's around. We're working on something right now," he said. It made him think of the reason he was there.

Two girls came up, walking side by side. They passed, but before they turned into Malaprop's Bookstore, past the big plate-glass window with posters announcing authors who would be visiting, one said to the other, "Check that out." She was staring across the street.

A man walked slowly up the sidewalk, a priest in a black suit and black hat. His hands were clasped behind him and he bent forward, apparently deep in thought and looking not to the right or the left. Following him at intervals of about two feet were eight pigeons walking in a line.

Segal watched with Mattie and the two girls, amazed and amused, as the man walked on up the block toward the Basilica of St. Lawrence. When he got to the intersection, he proceeded into the crosswalk without any apparent hesitation or any sign of checking to see if the light was in his favor—which, it so happened, it was. All the while, the pigeons followed right behind. It reminded Segal of a black and gray version of a mother duck and her ducklings. When the man got to the front door of the basilica, the pigeons scattered as he opened the door and entered, never checking behind, never acknowledging the birds in any way. The show was over.

One of the girls said, "Was that some kind of miracle or something?"

"No, those pigeons were trained," the other girl said.

"The priest trained them?" the first girl asked.

"No, some guy who lives in the Grove Arcade did. That's what I heard, anyway."

The girls pushed on into Malaprop's.

Segal shrugged his shoulders at Mattie, who shrugged and grinned in return.

"Just part of the downtown morning show," she said.

Segal was still trying to wrap his mind around what he had seen.

She grinned at him and said, "This is Asheville, Segal."

Yes, this is Asheville. He was thinking of the whole case, more than the little two-species parade he had just seen. He promised to buy Mattie a coffee next time he saw her. He was heading for the Grove Arcade to interview Emily Elah, Francis's wife.

Maybe she will know where the mystery man is.

He walked around the bend in Page Avenue, which took him by the old Battery Park Hotel building and to the north entrance of the Grove Arcade. He looked at the two stone statues of winged lions guarding the door. Mattie's words came back to him: *This is Asheville.* Those lions were about as Asheville as Asheville could be.

The Grove Arcade took up an entire city block and was a masterpiece of what Segal thought of as Art Deco/Egyptian Gothic architecture. The outside was ornate, clad with glazed tile and gargoyles, as well as the winged lions. The outside perimeter was filled with restaurants and shops, kicking into action for the day.

Segal pushed through the glass doors between the sphinxes and stopped to take in the sights inside the vault of the arcade. It was bright and tall and full of the sounds of commerce. All along the ground floor of the inner arcade were shops of various sizes and types. A unique kind of ceramic tile that resembled carved stone covered the walls.

Various fittings and trim pieces were made of well-aged bronze. Segal's favorite features were the spiral stairways leading to the upper stories. They corkscrewed in and out of the side walls in a way Segal had never seen anywhere else. A handrail encircled the mezzanine, which hosted offices. An identical one ran around the third floor, which was where the apartments, including the one he was looking for, were situated. At the top of the structure was a ceiling formed by a bronze framework that held panes of glass, the source of the white light filling the vault of the arcade.

The spiral stairways, whimsical and inviting as they were to spectators, were gated off and no longer in use, so he proceeded to the central structure, which housed the elevators. He found the elevators required a special code for operation. Nonresidents had to call one of the residents' numbers, listed on a placard nearby. He found the number for the Elahs, keyed it in, and got no response. *Pretty good shield from the outside world,* Segal thought.

He turned and saw a security guard making his rounds. He showed the guy his badge and told him he was looking for Mrs. Elah.

The man held up a finger and moved to where he could look down the length of the central vault. He grinned. "That's what I thought," he said. "This time of day, she's out with their little girl, Suzie, getting some sun by the window at the end of the hall."

Segal followed his gaze. He saw them there in front of a large half-circle arch of window, silhouetted against the northern light, a slim lady and a girl in a wheelchair. The girl held her head to one side, resting her cheek on her palm. On both sides were the silhouettes of palms and ferns of a small but lush indoor garden. The slim lady had a phone to her ear.

A dark feeling invaded Segal's core. For an instant, he relived the time that he had been in a wheelchair. It was not that long ago. And for a time, the doctors had told him he might be in it for good.

"This way," the security man said, and led him to the elevators. Segal entered, and the security man reached in far enough to key in the code.

The elevator deposited him in a third-floor vestibule. To his left was a small common area with some rocking chairs and a couch and a coffee table with a collection of magazines and paperback books. It was like a shared living room. He imagined the residents getting together there for a glass of wine in the evening or perhaps sitting on the couch and reading, taking a break during the day. Now, the chairs and the couch were vacant.

He swung right and went around the central column, spotting the mother and daughter at the end of the hall. From this perspective, the arched window was even more beautiful, suspended as it was between the arcade below and the skylight above. The sounds of the arcade drifted up, forming a tinkling and murmuring background music.

Segal moved toward them along the wide carpet, the doors and windows of the apartments to his left, the bronze and steel railing to his right. He glanced down into the arcade, across to an identical walkway on the opposite side, and upward to the curved and riveted steel beams that supported the glass ceiling. *It's like living inside a work of art.*

He walked with the thick carpet silencing his step. The girl was turned sideways to him in her wheelchair. Her eyes were closed, and he noticed that she held the tip of a fern leaf in her left hand, rubbing it lightly between her fingertips. He thought she might be around eleven or twelve, but it was hard to judge. The woman had her back to him, looking out the window and talking in short bursts into the cell phone clamped to her ear. Segal slowed so as not to sneak up and startle them. He finally came to a stop about twenty feet away and waited.

After a moment, the woman made an impatient turn, one hand on her hip and the other holding the phone to her ear. She nearly swiveled into a chair, saw Segal, and gave out a startled breath.

In spite of his precautions, he'd rattled her.

"I'll have to call you later," she said and hung up. "What part of the government are you from?" She crossed her arms and shifted her weight to one leg, sticking out a hip. It stopped Segal in his tracks. Most people didn't take him for a cop. He withdrew his badge and held it out to her. She was of medium height and had straight black hair. The bangs were trimmed razor-straight above her eyes in what Segal thought of as the Cleopatra look—a look he found exotic and intriguing.

The girl opened her eyes but did not move her head or any other part of her body. She simply stared at him. The corner of her mouth turned up in a crooked grin.

"My name is Ira Segal. I'm with the Asheville Police Department," he said. "You, I presume, are Emily Elah."

She made no answer but shifted her weight again. It reminded Segal of a boxer circling in one direction, then shifting to another. He knew those moments could conceal surprises in and out of the ring.

Finally, she said, "What are you after, Mr. Segal? I need to get my daughter to therapy soon."

It gave him a chance to acknowledge the girl, at least with a nod. The window behind her offered a view of the basilica. "Did you see the line of pigeons walking behind the man in black?" he asked in a friendly voice as he bent closer to her face with its crooked little smile and loose curls falling down on either side.

With the same unreadable expression, the girl reached out and placed her palm on Segal's cheek. She held it for a long moment until it seemed her appraisal was complete. Her smile widened a little.

Segal barely breathed as she did this. For him, it was a remarkable exchange of feeling.

"That was one of my husband's little projects," Mrs. Elah said, "done for Suzie's amusement. She likes to come out here and watch them walk to church every morning." She stopped and continued to glare at Segal, waiting for him, he supposed, to get to whatever had brought him up there.

"Are you familiar with Charles Atley?" he asked.

She frowned. "He works with my husband."

Segal saw no special reaction in her face or manner. He was close enough to smell her floral perfume when he leaned in. Speaking in a whisper, he said, "I'm afraid Mr. Atley was found dead this morning."

Mrs. Elah recoiled. "Dead? Are you sure? How?" She made no effort to lower her voice.

Segal turned toward the little girl, who did not react or give any indication of being upset. "You knew Mr. Atley pretty well?" he asked.

"Chickey? Yes, I knew him. He worked with my husband for a long time. Sure," she said. "What about Francis? My husband? Have you heard anything from him?"

"Actually, Mrs. Elah, that's one of the questions I wanted to ask you. Whether you could help us get in touch with your husband, Francis."

She withdrew a step and narrowed her eyes. "So, you're another person from the government looking for Francis."

Now it was Segal's turn to step away. He pulled his badge out and showed it to her again. "Mrs. Elah, as I said, I am with the Asheville Police Department, which is, I suppose, part of the government, but I don't know about anyone else looking for your husband. We did find the body of a man identified by his driver's license as Charles Atley. His card took us to his company, Creatures 2.0, and from them we found out that your husband cannot be accounted for. You can understand why we need to speak with him. They claim they do not have a way to get in touch with him, and we were hoping that you do."

"They still say they know nothing about where he is?" she asked.

Segal heard mostly suspicion there, but a little hope as well. "Can you tell me anything about the project that took him away?" he asked.

"Oh, the Project," she said, raising her hands. "The big, important Project."

He followed her gaze as she shook her head, down toward the arcade, where happy people came and went.

She continued. "He said it was top secret. He was sworn to secrecy, and even if he wasn't, I would not want to know where he was going or what he was doing, only that there was a lot of money involved, enough to help out with our daughter and the operations she needs. Then he packed up a few things and left with that crow of his, Richard." She blew air into her dark bangs. "Said he would be out of contact for a while, but no matter what, we would be okay. We would be taken care of. How are those for words of encouragement? I remember Suzie wanted to watch out the window, to see him come out of the building onto the street like she always does. There were a couple of guys waiting for him with a car. Everything about it looked dangerous to me. It felt very bad to see him go, very wrong."

Segal inhaled and sized up Suzie in her wheelchair. It was hard to tell from her face how much of this she was picking up. But as soon as he turned away, he heard her say something. He swung around and she said it again. "Richard?" She was moving her head side to side and up and down as if expecting to see the bird.

Her mother came to her. "No, honey, Richard is not here now. This gentleman and I were talking about him, but he's not here." She went behind the wheelchair and pushed it toward their apartment down the hall. "I'm sorry, Mr. Segal, I really do need to take her home. Too much light at one time can give her headaches."

As Mrs. Elah leaned into the chair and started walking, the little girl reached out for him. She wrapped her hand around two of his fingers, and willingly Segal followed. He was amazed at the intimacy of the little gesture, at how good her hand felt there. He sensed it was a blessing of some kind, and he was filled with a rush of emotion, more emotion than he had allowed himself to feel in a long time. In that moment, he felt he would do anything for this little one.

Emily sighed. "I'm sorry I can't help you get in touch with Francis, and I'm very sorry to hear about Chickey. Do you have any idea yet what happened to him?"

Suzie has apparently softened your mood as well, Segal thought. He shook his head. "I'm sorry. It's too early to know, but I will be in touch."

The little girl raised an arm when they got to the door of their apartment. To Segal, they all seemed identical, save for the numbers on the doors. He wondered if that was how she knew which one was her home, or if she was picking up on some other cue. He had no idea where she was on cognitive or reading skills.

When Emily opened the door, Suzie continued to hold his hand.

Emily stepped in, slid the girl's hand off of his, and said, "We have to let the man go, honey. He has things to do."

It brought Segal out of the trance the little girl had put him under. He did have things to do, yet he felt compelled to offer them something. He said, "It seems she likes the bird. Would you like me to see if someone from the company could bring him over for a visit?"

Mrs. Elah's eyes widened. "What do you mean? Richard is with Francis."

45

Segal explained how he had seen Richard at Creatures 2.0, but she shook her head.

"You must be mistaken, Mr. Segal. There's no way Richard would leave Francis for very long. No way."

Segal said nothing, surprised at her certainty on this point.

She turned to enter the apartment but then waited. "Will you let me know if you find out anything about Chickey or Francis?" The hard edge was gone now. He noticed the little girl was looking at him as well.

He started to explain that he might or might not stay with the case. But instead, he nodded and said, "Sure."

CHAPTER 6

The Wedge

B y the time Segal returned to the ground floor of the Grove Arcade, his phone was buzzing. He looked at the screen and saw a picture of a *T. rex* outlined against a sky of pink and gray. "Miss Dinosaur Rudisill," he mumbled.

"Better get over here," she said when he answered.

He checked the time. He could probably make it before his appointment. "On my way," he said, and hung up.

He started toward the door when he noticed the security guard who helped him before. He approached close enough to lean in and speak in confidence. "Hey, do me a favor. Give me a call if you see anything strange going on with the Elahs, anyone snooping around or acting suspicious." He handed the guy his card.

By "over here," Dinah meant the Wedge Building, one of the tallest of the old industrial buildings in what was now called the River Arts District. When Segal got there, she was waiting on the loading dock, trying to brush some dust off her white blouse and jeans without much success.

"This place is a maze," she said as she led him through the narrow halls, up a number of stairways, past art studios of every size and description. She had told Segal she was going there to check out a hunch.

When they reached the top floor, his leg was hurting, and he was still in a weird mood from seeing the little girl in the wheelchair. But he was determined to give no sign of distress, even to Dinah. She took out a pair of gloves and handed them to him. She put another pair on herself before she gently knocked on an old wooden door. Inside, a crime-scene tech was busy dusting the doorknob for fingerprints. He pulled the door open for them and they squeezed by.

"No luck, sergeant," he said. "Some smudges from gloves, but no useful fingerprints."

"Let's keep looking," Dinah said.

The room appeared to be a small studio not currently in use and not particularly clean. Segal saw a desk and a bookcase with some papers and a couple of magazines. A few sketches in sanguine and charcoal were tacked to the wall. They looked like quick studies, not finished work.

Dinah stood behind him. "Do you smell it?" she asked.

He took a deep breath through his nose. "There is something," he said. "Very faint."

"Some kind of gunpowder or propellant," she said, and immediately he knew she was right. "Like someone fired a gun in here." She went on. "This was my hunch. There was something familiar about that scene this morning. It reminded me of sniper victims I saw overseas."

Segal knew Dinah had served in both Afghanistan and Iraq, but she rarely said anything about the experience except for specific references like this, and only when it was of immediate practical importance.

"Over there, when we were moving into a new area, especially in a city, our snipers found high vantage points to cover the area ahead of our movements, scanning for anyone who might be a threat. At the scene this morning, I saw two places that would work like that: this building and the overpass. I figured the overpass would be too public. But in here, a guy could set up and wait."

Segal appraised the room with renewed interest. It was private, all right—not exactly homey, but private. He walked over to the window, which faced southwest—great view of the river, the street, the railroad tracks, and, farther on, 12 Bones and the place where the body was found that morning. "Be a hell of a shot from here," he said.

"Not for a military sniper," she said. "Those guys are good. It starts with their eyesight, which has to be outstanding. Then the training is legendary. Those guys have to be some of the toughest just to survive it."

Segal gauged it again. It was a hell of a distance in his eyes, but he trusted Dinah knew what she was talking about.

Dinah continued. "Look where the dust has been disturbed. Here, on the window sill. Here, on the floor in front of the window, where the guy would have knelt. Here, where the chair was moved closer to the window, then scraped backward." As she spoke, she moved around the room pointing and acting out the movements she described.

Segal saw what she meant, including the marks on the floor made by the legs of the wooden chair with a seat woven from cane.

Dinah flipped open a small pocket-sized notebook. "I talked to some of the people who work here when I came in. A couple of them did see a guy in the hallway last night who they didn't recognize, a guy with a backpack. But people are in and out of here all the time, and they didn't think too much about it."

The theory made sense to Segal but didn't exactly take them a giant leap forward without some hard evidence. He tried to imagine himself sitting there in the dim light of the evening. He sat on the chair as the man might have, the window a few feet in front of him. He saw the two marks on the sill where the supports for a sniper's rifle might sit. He imagined seeing a person over by 12 Bones. He moved to a kneeling position, as he imagined the sniper might have done. It felt right. It made sense. Still kneeling, he let his gaze fall downward and across the floor. And there, under the bookcase, a glint of metal caught his eye. He leaned over and with a pen coaxed the object out. It was a bullet, but not like any he had seen before. It was long and tapered and had odd marks on the end. The large brass shell suggested a powerful charge. Dinah came over and let out a low whistle.

"I was just thinking it would be good to find an empty shell casing," Segal said.

"If he fired from here, he would have been aware of the shell casing and would have picked it up to leave no evidence," she said. "I think maybe that bullet fell out of his pocket or his pack and he didn't realize it was gone. He didn't realize he was leaving it behind."

Segal dropped the bullet into the plastic evidence bag Dinah held out, then while he was still kneeling, he decided to check out more of the room from that low perspective. Near the feet of the chair, he saw a piece of drawing paper. It was folded into the shape of some kind of bird. Segal picked it up. "What's this?"

"This was an artist's studio," Dinah said. She took the folded paper from Segal with great care. "Looks like an origami swan." She returned it to him.

"A swan," Segal said.

He delicately unfolded the paper. It appeared to have the same kind of abbreviated sketches as the other pages tacked to the wall, and it was clearly the same type of paper. He imagined the guy sitting there in the chair, waiting, passing the time, maybe picking up a scrap of paper and folding it to keep his hands busy. Segal understood that impulse. He refolded the paper and studied the shape again.

"Cormorant," the evidence tech said. He came up behind Segal and looked over his shoulder.

"What?" Segal asked.

"I used to be into origami. That's a cormorant, not a swan. A swan has a longer neck and it doesn't hold its wings out like that."

"Good to know," Segal said, struggling to stand. He knew these guys were all about detail, but sometimes it became tedious. "So, we're looking at a sniper's nest, you think." He managed to get vertical, wiping his hands on his pants as he turned to Dinah.

"The bullet looks like the ones I saw snipers use over-seas," she said. "I mean, the size and shape and the way the point is made so the bullet will fragment when it hits its target. And I'm saying this is the kind of place they are trained to seek out."

"So, we're going from accidental death to murder to military-style assassination all in three easy leaps," Segal said. "We're moving right along."

"Yeah, and not in a good direction," Dinah said.

Segal noticed her downcast eyes. It was an unusually pessimistic comment for her to make.

"These snipers are some of the most dangerous people in the world, Segal. If we're right about this we're going to have to hunt one down and capture him and I don't think he's going to like it."

Segal stood with his hands on his hips. All the while, he was hearing Emily Elah's voice in his head, asking, *What part of the government are you from*?

CHAPTER 7

Dr. Gold

Segal trudged up the stairs of the building where Dr. Gold kept her office. The building was an Art Deco classic with lots of white and black tile inside and frosted windows on the office doors. When he got to the top of the stairs, he realized his thoughts were totally on the case, trying to put the pieces together. The effort of the climb had not entered his mind. He did feel some discomfort in his bad leg, but that was something apart from his core now, not part of his definition of himself.

He also realized he was not thinking much about his appointment. Dr. Gold was a psychologist who specialized in PTSD. From time to time, Segal would tell her he didn't think he had PTSD, and she would say, "Good."

Her door was closed, indicating that she was with another patient or was otherwise occupied and not ready to see him yet. A chair was by the door, but he chose not to collapse into it as he had on earlier visits. An oil painting hung on the wall.

He had seen it before but never really examined it closely. Now, he found it inviting. The warmth and the unusual contrasts of the colors reminded him of Vincent Van Gogh. And the subject resonated with Van Gogh as well.

It was a field of wheat in midsummer, golden yellow against the green of the grass and the cedar trees. In the foreground, a peasant girl lounged on the grass beneath a tree. She reclined, slightly, and her dress was pulled up, exposing one of her legs from the knee to the bare foot. She watched several figures in the background harvesting the wheat with scythes. All pretty standard fare, but something pulled him closer. Something triggered the idea that there was more here to learn.

He leaned in. The first thing he noticed was that the peasant girl was no peasant, she was Jackie Kennedy, and what he had taken for a scarf tied around her head was really a pillbox hat. Then he noticed the figures swinging the scythes in the wheat field; metallic robots right off the cover of a 1950's science fiction magazine.

"It's by an artist down in Hendersonville named Colebrook," said a voice beside him.

He'd been too focused to notice Dr. Gold had opened the door. "Why do you think he painted it?" Segal said. "And for whom?"

She gave him a generous smile. "I've been wondering how long it would take you to notice that painting." She held the office door open, and he stepped inside. "You seem different today."

The comment surprised him. She usually concentrated on questions rather than observations, especially at the beginning of their sessions.

"We got a case this morning. The death of a man," he said.

Dr. Gold said nothing. She sat down behind her desk, looking like a proper if elderly school girl with her salt and pepper hair turned up neatly on each side and her navy-blue sweater. She picked up a pen and poised it over a yellow pad of paper. Segal took this as a sign for him to continue, which he did.

He left out the part about the suspected sniper, but he did talk about Francis Elah and what little he knew about the animals he trained. He paused. Dr. Gold clicked her pen and wrote. After a moment, he continued. "I met his wife and daughter. It seems like they really need him."

Dr. Gold lifted her pen. Her eyes were bright blue. "And you're the primary investigator on this case?"

Segal understood the concern behind the question. Dr. Gold had explained to him many times about triggers. In his case, the threat of violence or the perceived threat had the potential to shut him down.

Segal gave a long exhalation and slouched in his seat. "I don't know. They didn't know it was a murder when they assigned it to me. I'm not on record as the principal yet. It's a decision I have to make, and I have to make it pretty soon."

"And you want to know what I think." Dr. Gold smiled. Her lower lip went crooked in a goofy kind of girl way. "You asked me two questions about that painting in the hall. You asked for whom it was painted. The short answer is the artist painted it for me. He's an old friend from long ago. Another way to answer that question is that he painted it for you, or at least people in situations like yours."

Segal mind went a hundred directions.

"That painting has been hanging there all the time you've been coming to see me, and this is the first time you really looked at it. Until now, you've been too tied up with your more immediate problems to notice." Segal started to say something defensive.

Dr. Gold held her hand up. "I'm not being critical. It's a perfectly natural response. But something made today different. Something called you forth."

Segal sank in his chair and thought.

Dr. Gold continued. "The other thing you asked me was why he painted it." She paused and smiled. "He never told me. In fact, he never says anything anymore. In the days when he was talking, he did answer it in a more general way. He told me that in ways we don't understand, we don't pick our paintings, our paintings pick us."

Scratching. More scratching. Segal followed her pen. He worked on what Dr. Gold had said to him about the paintings.

She clicked the pen a few times. "I would say sometimes things reach out and take us by the hand to get our attention. If you feel something reaching out it could be a sign that you're ready."

Segal thought of the little girl's hand wrapped around his fingers, a detail he had not included in his account to the good doctor. This was not the first time he looked at Dr. Gold and wondered if she was not at least a little psychic.

He stood. "Thanks, doctor. I need to get to the station."

She sighed and nodded, even though he was cutting the session short. He stole one more look at the painting before he shuffled down the stairs. He pulled out his cell phone. "Dispatch," he said, and when the no-nonsense woman answered, he said, "You can go ahead and fill out that paperwork."

CHAPTER 8

Boss's Office

Segal picked up on a vibe right away when he got to the police station. Everybody had heard about the case. Something like this, the news traveled fast. Everybody gave him a look while trying not to give him a look. He knew they were all wondering what he was going to do with this.

He passed the desks of Philips and Meyers, the other detectives Dinah had mentioned, the ones who would catch the case if he decided not to take it. They were solid guys, but like most in their position, they relied on people talking to solve cases. So far, in this case, no one was talking, including Richard the crow. In the old days, this was exactly the kind of case that would be handed to Segal when guys like Philips and Meyers hit a brick wall. Segal figured out how to get over, under, around, or through the brick wall. At least he had. Now, Philips and Meyers nodded to him as he walked by. He knew they were waiting for some clue about what he was going to do. Segal nodded to them and walked on to the boss's office.

If there had been a black typewriter on the desk instead of a computer keyboard and monitor, Segal could have convinced himself he was in the 1940s. His boss was even wearing suspenders and a tie that was substantially wider than recommended by current fashion. Generally, when Segal or anyone else came into the office, it took at least a few beats for the boss to disengage himself from the papers on his desk and acknowledge the visitor. But not today. Today, his boss crossed his arms in his chair, appearing to study Segal from head to foot as soon as he tapped on the doorframe and entered. Segal stopped in front of his desk and met his eye. His boss was one of the few people with whom he could exchange a great deal of information in such a nonverbal way. When, by mutual consent, the stare-down was finished, Segal dropped heavily into a chair and exhaled. His hand went to the paperback in his coat pocket, and he thumbed the tops of the pages.

His boss nodded and asked, "From what book of wisdom are we drawing our inspiration today?"

Segal tossed him the worn paperback.

"*City Primeval*, by Elmore Leonard," he read on the cover. "I suppose that could be Asheville."

"Feels pretty primeval today," Segal agreed.

"I got the paperwork on this drowning victim turned murder victim you pulled this morning," his boss said. "Lists you as the primary investigator."

Segal understood everything behind this short sentence. He understood that he got the assignment because it was thought to be a simple one. He understood that he was supposed to be in a period of transition—a transition between convalescence and a resumption of his normal life, if he had ever known such a thing as a normal life. He understood that his boss was concerned that the case was quickly blowing up into something much larger than a routine accidental death. He understood that his boss was asking him if he was okay. He understood that this was a genuine personal concern, combined with a concern for the department and for a timely and accurate resolution of a serious crime.

Segal's response to this complex and multilayered statement was a nod.

"You're okay with this?" his boss said. It was a question without much of an inflection at the end.

"I'm okay with it," Segal said, not fully meeting his eye. "I mean, I don't think I'll need to run any marathons or climb a mountain to solve it."

"You will let me know if you need any help," his boss said, emphasis on the "will."

Segal knew perfectly well his boss was concerned with more than his physical fitness. The visits to Dr. Gold were part of the deal allowing him to return, a part his boss insisted on. "Dinah Rudisill is helping me. Dinah is good."

"Dinah Rudisill is better than good," his boss said. He unbuttoned one of his sleeves and began rolling it up.

Segal cleared his throat. "Yeah, she's a lot better than good."

"Well, it looks like you're getting some additional help, whether you need it or not." His boss slid a paper across the desk.

Segal glanced at the note, which declared without wasted words that someone named Jerome Guilford would be there later that day to discuss the search for Francis Elah. More interesting was the origin of the message.

"Office of Naval Intelligence?" Segal said.

From across the desk, a shrug.

"How did they even know we were searching for this guy?"

His boss took a few files and stacked them. "How does anyone know anything these days? They probably have a search function set up on the internet looking for any mention of Elah's name, would be my guess. You put out a BOLO notice on Francis Elah, they know about it."

"But Naval Intelligence?"

"Dinah told me Francis Elah was working on some kind of secret project for the government. So now I guess we know what part of the government that was."

Segal sighed, taking in the implications. In the first place, he had trouble imagining what kind of project would link the navy with a guy who worked with animals—in this case, a crow. Did crows even fly over the ocean, or was the ocean reserved for seagulls? But even putting this aside, how was it they wanted in on the search for the guy? If his big, secret project was with the navy, then why didn't the navy know where Elah was? If they didn't know, who the hell did?

"Is it true what they say about military intelligence being an oxymoron?" Segal said.

"If I were you, I'd keep doing what you're doing on your investigation, and when you meet this guy, Jerome Guilford, be real polite. For instance, keep the oxymoron stuff to yourself. Maybe he'll explain the whole thing."

Segal nodded and smiled. Some sixth sense told him it was not going to be that straightforward.

"And Segal," his boss said, "I meant what I said about asking for help. This is looking pretty weird, and you haven't been back that long. This isn't about you proving something. This is about getting bad guys and keeping people safe." He held his eyes steady.

Segal didn't blink.

Segal found Dinah at her computer. She glanced over her shoulder when he walked up.

"I've been looking up stuff here about Francis Elah and Creatures 2.0," she said.

Segal pulled up a chair beside her. He had to push some of her hair out of the way to see the screen.

"Like, here is an interview on that morning show about two years ago."

Segal watched the screen. A thin man in his late thirties sat across the table from a woman with bright features. The man had slightly long and unruly brown hair. Segal's attention was drawn to his eyes, which had a warm, inviting effect while at the same time emanating intelligence and authority.

Interviewer: So, considering all your work with animals, I wondered about your name, Francis. Were you named for Saint Francis, and do you think that may have influenced you to work with animals?

Francis (laughing): That's a wonderful theory. I never made the connection, but that's really good. No, the fact is my mother was a big fan of the Minnesota Vikings, and she named me after their quarterback, Fran Tarkington. She named me Francis, and she named our Labrador retriever Tarkington.

Interviewer: Was your Labrador your first training subject? Is that how you got started on your path?

Francis: I was very close to Tark. At first, I guess I did the same kind of training everyone does with their dog—"Sit," "Stay," "Come," those commands. But what I think was more important for me was that I really studied him. I watched him for small signs and movements and reactions. The more I watched, the more I picked up on really small details that were easy to miss. If you can pick up on those subtle reactions, you can respond to them yourself, and you're in a position to persuade the animal to do things you want them to do, sometimes things that are difficult to teach them by conventional techniques.

Interviewer: Some people think you have a special, almost psychic connection with animals that allows you to do the things you do.

Francis: I don't believe in psychic connections.

Interviewer: Then you think you can teach other people how to do the things you do?

Francis (laughing): I think it should be possible, but so far, I haven't been able to get very far with it. It takes an enormous amount of work up front before a person is in a position to do anything with the techniques. Most people are not prepared to put in that much work before they get any payoff.

At that point, the camera panned to a wider shot. A gray squirrel walked into the room and across the table. It offered the interviewer a peanut M&M, derailing an interesting line of questioning. The interviewer accepted the M&M. The squirrel pressed the palms of its hands together and bowed in a way that reminded Segal of a Buddhist monk. The interviewer bowed back. The camera stayed on the squirrel as it turned and walked slowly away.

"Pretty interesting guy," Segal said. He was looking at the frozen image of Francis Elah on the screen, thinking there was a special quality about him, a poise and charisma that came from being perfectly comfortable in his skin. He thought of Emily and Suzie Elah and could easily imagine the three of them together.

"Maybe he trained squirrels to hand out poisoned M&Ms to the Taliban," Dinah said.

"Maybe if we find him, we can ask him about it," Segal said.

Dinah turned toward him.

"I mean find Francis, not the squirrel," Segal said with a grin.

Dinah shoved away from the computer. "Listen, Segal. Thanks for keeping us on this case."

"Yeah, well, I hope you're still thanking me when we get deeper into it," he said. "Speaking of deeper, check this out." He handed her the paper.

Dinah looked at it. "Office of Naval Intelligence?"

"I know," Segal said. "What could someone from Asheville, in western North Carolina, have to do with the navy? Especially someone who works with animals."

"I don't know," Dinah said, "but these are serious guys, Segal. Naval Intel was how the whole military intelligence business started, and they have a reputation for being interested in everything that happens everywhere."

"Even up in the mountains, away from the water?" Segal asked.

"You're forgetting the marines and the navy SEALs. Those guys can be sent anywhere at any time to do anything. You think the navy is going to trust some other outfit to look after their marines and SEALs?"

Segal thought about that. As usual, he would defer to Dinah on anything military, but it did get the cogs turning in his brain. "You made me think of a guy I used to know, Andrew Roche. He was into training dogs for the army or the marines, I forget which. I haven't seen him for a while, but I heard he's out at the VA hospital."

CHAPTER 9

Raccoons

Dinah arrived first at the VA hospital. She sized up the front registration desk and the patient waiting area, wondering if it was such a great idea for Segal to be in this place of pain and broken lives. Patients gabbing in their rooms. Tears. A lot of misery. They were deep in the case now, and it was not a good time for him to relive the bad old days.

One of the new people in the police department had asked her what Segal's story was, anyway.

"He's got no story, that's his problem. It was one of those things you couldn't see coming and it didn't make any sense."

"Sounds careless to me. Guy gets himself shot and everyone walks on eggshells around him," the new guy had said.

"I'm going to pretend I didn't hear that," she had replied in an even voice, "and I'm going to advise you not to say it to anyone else."

She saw Segal push open the door and walk in. He looked okay, at least for now.

"Are you kidding me?" Andrew Roche said. "Of course, I know Francis Elah. I mean, everyone in this business knows him or knows of him. But I know him personally."

Segal sat next to Dinah on a couch in one of the lounge areas in the VA hospital on the east side of Asheville. Andrew's brown eyes were full of light. He had a farm boy's face—clean- cut, a scatter of freckles—and he seemed glad to see Segal and even happier to meet Dinah. Segal thought Andrew would probably have been happy for a visit from just about anyone. A long recovery was a lonely road.

"Have you seen him recently?" Dinah asked.

Andrew's face lost some of its radiance. "No. I was hoping he would stop by, but I haven't seen him."

"Did you ever work with him on any government projects?" Dinah asked.

"Do you mean the raccoons?"

"Raccoons?" Segal said.

Andrew laughed. "Oh, man, you didn't hear about that? It was a crazy idea. I mean, it would have been crazy for anyone but Francis. He had this idea that he could train a raccoon to assist a doctor during surgery. You know, they have those tiny little delicate fingers, and they can do intricate movements with them."

"Are you serious?" Segal said.

"Francis was. He convinced some people in the government that it might be possible, and he got a grant. He was working right here in the Asheville VA hospital. This started before my time here," Andrew said.

"So, how do you convince the first person to let a raccoon operate on them?" Dinah asked.

"They were years away from that step, I think. First thing was a demonstration that you could, with a high degree of confidence, train a raccoon to do some complex task over and over again. They did that, but as far as I know, that's as far as the project got."

"So, what did Francis teach the raccoon to do?" Segal asked.

Andrew looked up at the clock and said, "In a couple of minutes, you can see for yourself."

The lounge began filling with patients and a few staff members. Someone said, "There she is," and they turned to see a raccoon approach from the outside. She disappeared behind an apparatus affixed to the wall of windows, and then everyone turned to a TV monitor mounted high on the wall.

Segal watched the monitor along with the others. Dinah was riveted on it, too. The raccoon paused a moment. She looked up and down, sniffed the air until she appeared to be satisfied she was alone on the porch, then wiped her hands with her tongue. Afterward, she first sniffed the box on the right, then approached the box on the left.

"She does that every time," said Andrew. "She checks to see if she can get into the reward box without doing the task first. I don't know if she doesn't like to do the task or if she resents the manipulation the whole setup represents. Hope springs eternal, I guess, even in a raccoon."

At the box on the left, the raccoon reached up and pulled a black lever. A door opened beside the lever. The raccoon reached in and pulled out a package of cigarette papers. She moved over slightly and pulled a second lever. A second door opened, and the raccoon reached in and pulled out a small cloth pouch with a yellow drawstring. The group watched silently as the raccoon worked one of the papers loose and set it on the ground. She loosened the drawstring and, holding the pouch in both hands, spilled a little tobacco onto the paper. Grasping the filled paper with her tiny, dexterous fingers, the animal proceeded to roll a cigarette. When it was time to lick the paper to seal it, the raccoon looked directly into the video camera as she ran a pink tongue along the seam, then twisted the ends closed. She held the completed cigarette in her hands and rotated it slowly as if inspecting for flaws.

She scampered over and opened a third door with a third lever and placed the finished cigarette inside. She walked quickly along the box, replacing the unused tobacco and papers and closing all three doors by flipping the levers up. The instant the last door shut; a bite-sized Snickers bar was ejected from a slot in the box on the right.

"Francis said it was important to dispense the treat immediately," one of the men said.

"She likes those little Snickers bars, huh?" Segal asked.

"Who the hell doesn't?" Andrew said.

The raccoon seemed to know exactly how to tear the wrapper off the little candy bar and did not need to use her teeth. She disposed of the wrapper in a small trash container and then began to eat the treat in several unhurried bites. She chewed slowly and gave every indication of savoring each morsel. It made Segal wish he had one of his own.

Andrew flipped a separate lever on the inside wall and pulled out the freshly minted cigarette. "Better than the Marlboro Man," he said, admiring the craftsmanship.

"You're going to smoke that?" Segal asked.

"One of us will. Hell yes. We are all God's children here at the VA. From the lowest to the highest, we hold none in contempt."

"You're not worried about rabies or bubonic plague or anything?" Dinah asked.

"Hasn't done anyone any harm yet," Andrew said. "And besides, I would put that raccoon's personal hygiene up against most of the guys here."

Segal thought of the animal's spotless fur, then looked at the guys milling around the lounge and could not disagree.

A guy in a wheelchair came by, and Andrew handed him the cigarette, which seemed to make his day.

"So, you were saying you know Francis Elah pretty well?" Dinah said. She went to work on her notebook.

"Yeah, I've known him for a long time," Andrew said.

"When he got involved with his military work?" Segal asked, checking out Dinah's chicken scratches.

"Yeah, I saw him a little then."

Segal jerked his head up. Dinah stopped writing.

Andrew smiled. "Let's go to my room," he said. "I might have some pictures I can show you."

They followed him down the hall with Dinah in the lead to a room that held several beds, all currently empty and neatly made. It was not difficult to spot Andrew's little corner. Around his bed were several pictures of German shepherds. In some, Andrew himself, dressed in camo fatigues, was kneeling by the dog.

"These are beautiful dogs," Dinah said. She moved from one picture to another, her finger tracing each animal in the photo.

"They're the best," Andrew said. "Powerful, fast, absolutely fearless, and absolutely faithful."

"Intelligent?" Segal asked.

"They're intelligent in their own way."

The answer surprised Segal. He expected something more pro–German Shepherd.

"You got to understand, animals are intelligent in different ways than we're intelligent," Andrew continued. "I think that's what Francis really tuned into. He can work with an animal for a while and really understand what they know and what they don't know, what they pay attention to and what they ignore. At least that's what I took away after talking to him."

"You mean talking with him in Afghanistan?" Dinah asked.

Segal was reminded that Dinah had been in Afghanistan herself and she must have recognized the terrain in the pictures.

"Yeah, that's what I was going to show you. I think I have some pictures here in my scrapbook." Andrew moved to the footlocker by his cot. When he flipped it open, Segal was surprised to see how perfectly neat and organized the contents were, unlike any storage space he himself had ever used.

Andrew removed a thick black binder, shut the footlocker, and slid it away so he could sit on the edge of the bed and use it as a coffee table. Dinah sat beside him. Segal looked at the two of them there and thought there were very few guys who wouldn't tell her everything she wanted to know. Most cops, especially detectives, cultivated an edge of intimidation. Even when they were talking to someone who was trying to help, it was there, below the surface. Segal didn't have that and didn't want it. He was glad to see Dinah didn't have it either—no need of domination for domination's sake.

Andrew started turning pages, most containing pictures of dogs, mostly German shepherds, some by themselves, some action shots of dogs jumping over barricades, some posing with servicemen kneeling by their sides. Presently, he stopped and put his finger on a glossy photograph.

"There, that's the one I was thinking of," he said.

Dinah leaned in and Segal followed. The picture showed Andrew Roche dressed in army fatigues standing beside Francis Elah. Francis was dressed in a khaki shirt and blue jeans and a ball cap. The two men had their arms around each other's shoulders in the universal pose of brother-hood. A German shepherd was standing by Andrew, and on Elah's outstretched arm was a large crow. The two men and the dog were all beaming full smiles at the camera. The crow was in profile with its beak wide open, perhaps in mid-squawk.

"You guys look really happy," Dinah said.

"Oh, man! You cannot believe how good it was to see him. I mean, you're over there, everything is strange and dangerous, and then out of the blue someone from home shows up. Especially someone like Francis. It was great." Andrew seemed to brighten again remembering.

"This was in Kabul?" Dinah asked.

"Yeah, I was there on my second tour, or maybe my third. It all kind of flows together after a while." At this point, he stopped, and a tiny shadow crossed his face like a cloud passing over the sun. His hand shook. It was the first glimpse they had of the illness that was keeping him in the facility. However, he quickly regained his composure and continued. "Francis was there only two or three days, but still it was great."

"I can believe it," Dinah said.

Segal studied the picture. As he often did, he focused past the main subjects at details in the background. In the distance, he saw a clear line of mountains with a few clouds. Nearer to the camera were some tents and military vehicles. Closer still, behind and to the right of the main subjects, was a woman in profile. She had dark hair of medium length pulled together and sticking out from underneath a military cap. However, she was not in uniform. She wore dark glasses and seemed to be in conversation with an officer, yet her glance appeared sideways at Andrew and Francis.

"Who's the lady there in the background?" he asked.

Andrew blinked at the picture. "A mystery lady. Very good looking, but she didn't mix with us. She came in on the same flight as Francis. Didn't wear a uniform but seemed kind of military anyway. Know what I mean?"

Dinah nodded and shifted a little.

Segal didn't understand exactly what he meant but took him at his word.

Andrew continued. "I noticed her talking to a couple of the officers, including a guy who was there with some kind of special forces squad. Whatever she was talking about, they seemed to listen closely. She talked to Francis, too. Hell, she even talked to the Cormorant guys, and nobody talked to them."

"Cormorant?" Segal asked.

"Private military subcontractors," Dinah explained.

Segal waited. She did not elaborate on why it was unusual for the others to talk with them.

"Did Francis ever say anything about her or about what he was doing there?" Segal asked.

"No. Of course, when I first saw him, I was surprised as hell and asked him what he was doing there. I mean, I had a hard time figuring Francis with anything military. He told me how great it was to see me and kind of changed the subject to what was happening in Asheville. I gathered that whatever brought him there was something he couldn't or didn't want to talk about. You steer clear of things that are not your business in that kind of situation, so I didn't bring up the subject again, and he didn't volunteer anything else about his project or about the mystery woman." He tapped the photo with his finger and added, "I figured she was in military intel of some kind or another."

He turned the page to another picture. This time, the mystery lady had her glasses off and appeared to be clearing something from the corner of her eye. She was also turned more toward the camera, so Segal got a better view: slim figure, high cheekbones, heavy eyeliner.

Next to that picture was one of the German shepherds alone. Segal glanced at Andrew's face and picked up on the tension and sadness. Dinah had filled him in a little on the situation. From talking to some of the staff, she learned that the dog had not made it back from Afghanistan, killed in the same explosion that almost killed Andrew. Segal thought it was time to change the subject. "What can you tell us about the company, Creatures 2.0? Do you know any of the people there?" he asked.

"Well, I knew Chickey, if that's what you mean. That's a shame, what happened to him. I never worked with him, but I'd run into Francis and the gang once in a while out for beers or something."

"Did Chickey ever seem like he was arguing with Francis? One of the guys at the company said there were some disagreements," Segal said.

"No, I never saw anything like that. Chickey was more like a little brother to him. He idolized Francis, dressed like him. Even started wearing his hair kind of sticking out of his ball cap like Francis does."

Segal had his cues with Dinah. He gave her room.

"Is there any chance someone could mistake Chickey for Francis? I mean, at a distance or maybe in poor light?" she asked.

"Sure. They were built pretty much alike," Andrew said. "You could easily make that mistake."

"You mind if we take a couple of these pictures with us to make copies?" Dinah said.

"I promise I'll bring them back."

Andrew beamed, seeming more than happy for her to have a reason to return.

As they got ready to leave, Dinah paused and held up a finger. She flipped back a couple of pages in her notebook.

Segal waited on her. She usually had facts scratched in the corners of her pages.

"Got it," she said. "I did a reverse search with the name associated with the number written on the back of Chickey's card. Do you know someone named Lucile Devroe?"

Andrew got another grin on his face. "Now you're talking about another one of my favorite people. She works over at the Biltmore Estate. Kind of a student of Francis. Good lady."

The intercom crackled. A scratchy voice interrupted them. "Andrew Roche, report to physical therapy. Andrew, P.T."

Andrew's face darkened for a second. Then he smiled an apology. "The master's voice," he said.

Segal looked at him, thinking how small and vulnerable he looked, how all he had been through registered in his figure if you only knew how to look. And Segal knew all too well how to look.

CHAPTER 10

Perfect Brown Shoes

Segal did not know what to expect from the guy from Naval Intelligence. In the first place, he didn't even know if he would be wearing a uniform or not. Were guys in Naval Intelligence actually in the navy, or were they civilian support staff? Would this guy have a military bearing like a navy SEAL who got a desk job? Or would he be more like a computer analyst, some back-room kind of guy who pored over data and looked at satellite photographs through a magnifying glass?

As it turned out, the guy reminded Segal of the lawyers he saw in the courtrooms and the restaurants around Pack Square. He was dressed in a good suit. The suit fit him, and more importantly, he fit the suit. He was one of those guys who lived in his suit. Segal never felt exactly right dressed like that himself. He did okay with a shirt and tie and sport coat, especially since the pockets of sport coats seemed designed for carrying a paperback book. A suit, on the other hand, never had the desired effect, or at least that's how he felt. A suit felt false on him. He felt like someone had dressed up a barnyard animal as a joke.

But Segal's eye was drawn even more to the guy's shoes. They were a medium shade of brown and highly polished. They looked solid and substantial without being stiff or uncomfortable; perfect and unlike any shoes Segal had ever owned or even seen in the stores around Asheville. He had seen this kind of expensive shoe, but always on guys from New York or D.C.

Segal took all this in before he and Dinah entered the conference room at the police station, bringing with them their files and notebooks. The conference room had a long window in one wall with Venetian blinds that could be closed for privacy. Right now, the blinds were open, so Segal could see the man sitting with his chair pushed away from the conference table. He had one leg crossed over the other, allowing Segal to make his observations of the perfect shoes. Dinah turned toward Segal and rolled her eyes.

The guy read something on a phone with a plus-sized screen. He had a smile on his face. He put the phone down immediately when Segal rounded the corner with Dinah in the lead and entered the room. He rose and extended his hand.

"Lieutenant Segal and Sergeant Rudisill," he said. "My name is Jerome Guilford. I was sent by ONI. I was just reading about you." He held up the phone with his other hand.

So, this was Naval Intelligence, getting information from Google on a cell phone. Segal could imagine what kinds of postings the guy was reading—news reports about Segal's incident from two years ago, a classic standoff with people pointing guns at each other, just like in the paperback books he read—only this one didn't end like they did in the books. Nobody got what they deserved that time. What he would not be reading about was all that Segal had lost, nor about the long period of convalescence and rehabilitation.

But to Segal's surprise, Jerome Guilford was not checking *him* out, at least not at the moment. The navy man touched the screen and a YouTube video of the Blue Ridge Roller Girls was activated. The whole team showed up in the video, but the focus was clearly on Dinah—or, as the crowd was shouting, "Dinosaur."

Segal grinned. It was little wonder the camera followed her. For one thing, she was the jammer, and for another, she was clearly faster, more agile, and by any measure better than anyone else on the track.

"You got some moves there, sergeant," the navy man said and gave her a smile. "I see you've got a bout tomorrow tonight. I may have to stop in and see you girls in action." He scratched his nose and gave Segal his profile. Then he reached for a box of tissues and whispered as if to himself, "I doubt there's much else happening in Asheville," before he sneezed.

Dinah's expression did not change.

That's right, Segal thought. *Don't rise to the bait.* He knew she was used to the YouTube stuff. Given her notoriety on the track and the number of people recording the matches, she dealt with it. She'd also been a runner and a gymnast in school and in the military, but she was a modest person and didn't like to talk about it. He remembered her interview comment for the department when someone asked her about her athletic accomplishments. Her only answer was that she was "pretty comfortable with the physical part of the job."

The next words out of his mouth are going to be about her size, Segal thought.

"I have to say, you're smaller than I thought you would be," the navy man said.

Dinah remained silent.

Segal watched for her "tell"; little splotches of color along her collar bone. There were none. She wasn't fuming. Mad maybe. No fangs yet.

He swallowed; an awkward moment. No one said anything.

Finally, Guilford blinked. "So, I heard you're looking for our guy, Francis Elah. You think he might have been involved in a murder here in Asheville."

Dinah was writing. She'd deflected confrontation, propping her legal pad on her knee, taking notes under the table.

From Segal's viewpoint, Guilford could not see what she was writing.

Segal could see it. "OUR GUY." The word *OUR,* was underlined.

Segal cleared his throat. "A body was found yesterday, Mr. Guilford. It has been identified as Charles Atley, a.k.a. Chickey." He opened a folder and slid out a picture of the victim at the site where he was found. Guilford did not pick it up or study it. Segal had the impression he'd already seen the photo through whatever magical route Naval Intelligence gathered its information.

"And you have reason to think Francis Elah may have been the shooter."

Dinah wrote, *shooter.*

Segal picked up on it. They had not told Guilford the man died by gunshot

"We don't have any specific reason to think he was the shooter," Segal said. "We don't really know what to think. We find this man dead, murdered—Charles Atley, that is. We find from the contents of his wallet that he works for a place called Creatures 2.0. Then we find out that the head guy at Creatures 2.0, Francis Elah, Chickey's boss, is missing. No one seems to know where he is. We heard Francis and the victim argued before Francis went away on some mysterious project, so maybe Francis snuck back in town and took care of business."

Guilford nodded. He reached for another tissue.

"On the other hand, we are also told the victim looked like Elah and dressed like him, too. So maybe it was a case of mistaken identity. Maybe Elah was the intended victim and Charles Atley was in the wrong place at the wrong time with the wrong appearance."

Guilford blew his nose a second time.

"Then again," Segal said, "maybe Francis Elah had nothing to do with the incident either way. Maybe it's a coincidence that Francis went missing at the same time strange stuff happened here."

More honking.

"No matter what, we need to find Francis Elah," Segal concluded.

"And what were you told about the project that took Francis Elah out of town?" Guilford asked, high-tossing the tissues, missing the wastebasket against the wall.

Dinah stopped writing.

Segal glanced at her, then spoke. "All we were told, by the people at Creatures 2.0 and by Elah's wife, was that he was going away on a project for the government. They knew he would be gone and out of contact for a while. They expected him home by now, but he has not shown up. We didn't even know which branch of the government he was working for, at least not till you walked through the door and informed us."

Guilford played with a paperclip on the desk. "Well, with all due respect to what I am sure is a very competent Asheville law enforcement team, you should not draw too many conclusions from that. ONI gets involved with a lot of things."

"Actually, we were hoping you could tell us something about the project, maybe something that could help us out," Dinah said.

Guilford's paperclip was now a spiky strip of metal. "There is very little I am at liberty to divulge about the project, for reasons of national security. I can tell you we are searching for Mr. Elah, too. Mr. Elah went AWOL on us. We need to find him."

Pissed at the games, Segal reclined in his chair. Dinah bit her lip. Segal checked her above her collarbone and saw one red patch.

"And we believe Mr. Elah took some things when he disappeared, things that belong to the government."

Segal and Dinah waited again.

Guilford must have sensed hostility. He threw his hands up. The paperclip bounced off the desk. "Look, this much I can tell you. You should consider Francis Elah a dangerous person. Very dangerous. You find him, we need to know about it. In fact, if you think you know where he is, don't try to apprehend him. Inform me. I will put a team on it."

"And what about Chickey?"

"Who?" Guilford asked.

Dinah pressed her palms on the desk and leaned in. "Mr. Atley."

"I appreciate your problem with the death of a local man, but what's at stake here is bigger than that."

Segal forced his brows together. "You know, Mr. Guilford, I'm having a hard time."

"You are?"

"Yes, sir. Squaring what you just said with the interviews we've done so far. Elah appears to be a creative individual. Not a combat type."

Dinah grunted.

Guilford glared. "You don't believe Francis Elah is a dangerous man? Try telling that to Charles Atley."

Segal declined to respond but held Guilford's eye.

"What I'm trying to tell you is to take this seriously. Don't be fooled. People could be in danger. A lot of people. Francis Elah may seem innocent to you, but I happen to know he has been in the company of some very violent people in a very high-pressure situation. You have to realize people change. Especially when they're cornered."

Segal did not respond.

Guilford's face colored. He sat deeper into his chair. "What are your plans for Creatures 2.0? Surveillance?"

Odd question, Segal thought.

Dinah furrowed her brow.

83

"We hadn't made any plans for surveillance at Creatures 2.0," Segal said.

Guilford paused, then said, "Let me see your folder."

Segal obliged and passed it to him.

The ONI man helped himself. He leafed through the photographs and the short list of objects gathered as evidence at the scene of the crime. When he got to the contents of the victim's pockets, he ran his finger carefully from word to word.

Segal glanced at Dinah. She saw it, too. "This is all you found?" he asked.

Segal scratched his forehead. "What exactly are you looking for? Maybe we could keep our eye out for it."

"I'm afraid that's classified."

"From your investigation so far, is there anything you can tell us that would help us find Elah?" Segal asked.

"I'm sharing as much as I can, lieutenant. Up to this point, there is not much I can tell you. The fact that you were looking for him brought me over. That's it."

This got Segal's attention. "That reminds me, Mr. Guilford. We were surprised at how quickly you showed up. Surely, ONI doesn't have an office here in Asheville. Was it you who questioned Mrs. Elah?" Segal was thinking of the big federal building on Patton Avenue. It housed a number of agency offices, more than he could keep track of.

"Some of our people have contacted Mrs. Elah in an effort to gather information. Not me personally, not yet." Guilford pursed his lips as if trying to come up with more for them. "You see, I'm a different type of information gatherer. I guess you could say I find ways to persuade people to share information they might otherwise not choose to share. That is one of the reasons I was brought in."

"Like enhanced interrogation," Segal said.

"Waterboarding," Dinah said.

Guilford looked at her. His nostrils flared. "Waterboarding is a very crude method of enhanced interrogation, and as it turns out not all that effective. It has a bad reputation in some political circles. There are much more effective methods if"—he raised and wagged his right index finger—"you're willing to get creative."

There it is again, Segal thought. *The only way to solve a problem is to pressure someone else into solving it for you.* He had seen this all too often.

"Well, we've interviewed Mrs. Elah and some of the employees at Creatures 2.0, and they seemed genuinely concerned for Francis Elah."

"I'm sure they were. In my experience though, somebody always knows something. Meanwhile, I'm interested in any hard evidence you've gathered."

"We've got no real evidence concerning Francis unless you count Richard. Some of the employees, maybe Mrs. Elah also, believe that if Richard is here, Francis must be nearby."

"Richard?" Guilford said, his Adam's apple bobbed. He leaned forward in his chair. "Are you talking about the crow? What do you know about Richard?"

Dinah jotted a note.

Segal wondered if they had just handed Guilford the first piece of information he didn't have before they entered the room. "Yeah, we saw Richard, over at the Creatures 2.0 lab," he said.

"And you're sure it was Richard?" Guilford asked. It seemed more a challenge than a question.

"Well, there was a big crow. And then they told us the crow's name was Richard," Segal shrugged. "Didn't seem to be too much question in anyone's mind about it."

Guilford sat back and exhaled slowly. "Richard," he said softly. "And did he have anything with him?"

"Did the crow have anything with him?" Segal asked.

Dinah frowned, then jotted another note.

Guilford shook his head and said, "Never mind." He reached for his phone and then stopped. Instead, he got up. "Listen, I've got to get going." He handed them multiple business cards. "Call me with any developments." He went out the door and then appeared again. "The bout is at eight tomorrow night?" he asked.

Dinah was up. She nodded.

"And you'll both be there?"

"I wouldn't miss it for the world," Segal said, and gave Dinah a sheepish grin, having missed all her other bouts lately.

Segal watched through the Venetian blinds as Guilford strode off with great purpose.

"Well, that tweaked something way up inside his butt," Dinah said. "I don't like him."

"I don't like him either."

Dinah bopped him on the arm. "Since when did you get so judgmental? Usually, you give everyone a pass."

"For him, I'll make an exception. He sure does have nice shoes, though."

"Pretty much perfect."

Segal sat at the table and Dinah followed suit. Through the window, he saw their boss walking down the hall, holding a cup of coffee in one hand and the ever-present sheaf of papers in the other. When he got to the door of the conference room, he looked down the hall, presumably watching the ONI guy exit stage left.

He came in and said, "Well?"

"I think he wants to find Francis Elah even more than we do," Segal said. "Other than that, he didn't say much."

"We liked his shoes," Dinah added.

The boss crossed his arms over his chest. "Well, I'm glad you liked his shoes. I guess that's something to build on because you have to work with him on this."

"Copy that," Dinah said.

Segal's phone rang. He answered and listened. "That was one of the security guards over at the Grove Arcade. He sounded kind of shaken up, and there was a strange noise in the background."

"Like what?" their boss asked.

"Like an Alfred Hitchcock movie."

CHAPTER 11

Aerial Combat

inah drove. Segal watched the landscape and the skies above. She parked on Grove Street and called in their location to dispatch. He got out and winced a little. A shiver ran through him. Bum hip.

A crowd huddled on the sidewalk, looking up at the roof of the Grove Arcade. Some stood across the street for a better vantage. Several dining at the sidewalk tables around the arcade stood and shielded their eyes with their hands or their menus.

They're wondering if they should run, Segal thought. He didn't know what to tell them.

The scene reminded him of his days growing up in the country. Crows sometimes ganged up on an owl or a hawk. You heard the noise before you saw anything. The sky would fill with angry, loud cries and black shapes darting back and forth. He remembered one such scene centered on a great oak tree. When he came upon it, the crows were still gathering, several of them sitting in the highest branches, sending out the call to arms. More and more arrived until they had critical mass, and attack ensued. Sometimes one at a time, sometimes in twos or threes, the attack birds darted in, while the others in the branches kept up the alarming and confusing din.

It was like that at the Grove Arcade. Dinah hurried across the street, her hand high with the video on her phone recording. Segal moved to the entrance where he saw the guard who had called him. His first concern was for Emily and Suzie Elah.

The guard wiped sweat off his face. "They're okay," he said. "They're in their apartment, and I asked one of our guys to stay outside their door."

"When did this start?" Segal asked.

"They came home a little while ago. Emily…I mean Mrs. Elah, called me 'cause she was spooked out. When she came in on the street level, she looked up and saw a man she didn't recognize near her apartment. When she and the girl got off the elevator, he was gone, and the door to the steps was closing. She was scared to go into the apartment. I came up and checked it out. No one was there. She checked around. Didn't see anything out of place or missing. I came down. We checked the surveillance video, didn't see anyone come out of the stairs on ground level. That's when all hell broke loose on the roof."

Segal scanned the top of the arcade. The crows were even more agitated than before. "That stairway you mentioned. If you go up from the apartment level instead of going down, does it lead to the roof?"

"Yeah, there's a service door up there."

Segal called to Dinah, who continued to film as she came over. The three of them pushed open the brass-plated doors into the arcade. Although the sound was not as sharp as outside, the calls of the crows echoed off the tile walls and glass windows in an eerie reverberation. People ran by, bug-eyed, staring up at the glass ceiling where dark shapes could be seen darting back and forth. The birds also cast shadows on the walls and floor of the arcade vault.

A horror movie for sure. "Where are the stairs?" he asked.

The security guard led them to a stairway entrance on the other side of the arcade. He reached for his keys, fumbled them. Dinah pushed with both hands and the gate swung free. She ran through and started taking stairs two at a time. Segal was close behind with the security guard in the rear. Dinah touched the gun on her belt and thumbed open the restraining straps. Segal followed suit.

Inside the stairwell, light and sound muted for Segal. His injured leg was stiff at first, and after he had run up three flights the pain set in for real. He willed himself not to limp or slow down. He had declared himself back in the game, and he was sticking with it. It felt good to be more worried for the safety of the people around him than for himself.

At the top, the security guard pushed past and reached for the lever to open the door. Dinah laid a hand on his shoulder and whispered for him to wait. Segal took cues from Dinah. She, then Segal would go through the door first. She got into place. Segal nodded, the guard swung open the heavy door and Segal ran after Dinah out into the blinding light of the roof.

Dinah pointed for them to break off slightly. She would go east. Segal west.

He found he was on a catwalk that encircled the central tower of the building, situated several feet above the roof of the arcade proper. Some crows flew around, but the noise and intensity of motion had diminished. No signs of blood or attack. Segal told the guard to stay put and watch the door.

Segal motioned to Dinah to move along the catwalk. She walked forward in a well-balanced crouch while he moved the other way. As he advanced, he looked around the roof but saw no sign of Mrs. Elah's intruder, if indeed he had come up this way, nor any sign of anything special that would have triggered a crow battle. He turned the corner and moved up the side of the tower parallel to Page Avenue. The view over the city was great, and likewise the mountains to the east. *One day*, he thought, *he would hike those mountains again.*

When he rounded the next corner, he saw Dinah at the opposite one. She was walking slow, breathing easy. They met in the middle and scanned over the roof with the glass skylight in the center. Segal realized he could see the entrance to the Elahs' apartment. *Nothing fishy there.*

Dinah put a hand on his arm. "Look," she said, pointing to the parapet on the far end of the building.

There, Segal spotted a man climbing over. His hands grasped the lip of the parapet, his cold eyes looked right at them as if in challenge. The man held there for a second, lowered his head, and after another second released his hands and was gone.

Immediately, two loud caws made Segal jump.

Dinah yelled, "Duck!"

A large crow swooped down; Segal ducked but not fast enough. The crow grazed his cheek. It was followed by an even larger crow in hot pursuit. Segal felt a trickle of blood. The pair of crows kept close to the central structure. The lead crow appeared to use the structure as cover to shake its tormentor, without success. The first crow dove toward the roof of the arcade as if it might land and instead, pulled up. The move, obviously intended to fake the larger bird into crashing, backfired. The one in pursuit struck the lead bird with beak and claws at the same time. It rode the other bird down. Together, they glanced off the skylight and landed like a bundle of black rags on the gravel of the roof. The crow riding on top struck once, then twice, hard into the back of the other bird's head.

Before it could finish off its adversary, two smaller crows swooped in to the rescue. They were no match for the larger bird, yet were able to force it to leave their comrade and focus on them. The first crow got unsteadily to its feet, hopped a couple of times, and managed to flap its wings and get airborne. Segal watched it rise to the roof of the central structure above them. The crow spread its wings for a landing, soon disappearing over the roof. By the time Segal slowly turned one eighty to the arcade, the big crow had chased off the rescuers and got airborne. It rose quickly with powerful thrusts, circled the building, searching, it seemed, for its prey.

It took no time for the big crow to spot the other bird on top of the central tower and make a dive. Soon the two crows reappeared in violent struggle.

The crows then separated and disappeared from sight.

Segal waited. He stood tense, his mouth open, breathing hard. Dinah came to his side and put a hand on his arm. He relaxed his stance and started to speak, but just as he did, he heard a scuffle above. He leaned back only to see the head of the large crow spying down at them. When the head withdrew, they heard more scuffling, then saw an object being pushed over the edge. The object hurtled toward them and fell like a heavy bundle at their feet.

It was the body of the murdered crow.

Segal could only stare. The dead crow was crumpled, the back of its head wet with oozing blood. There was a small plastic band around one of the legs.

"The band," Segal said. His hip was killing him.

Dinah reholstered. "Somebody's pet or science project." She fished in her jacket pocket and pulled on a pair of latex gloves. The gloves were difficult. She pulled on the latex fingers and struggled.

Dinah crouched and put the bird on the ground. She spread the wings, and the head fell limp to one side. "Big crow pecked this one's brains out."

Segal heard a sound above. The larger crow was at the edge of the roof. It opened its beak and shook its head as if to fluff its rumpled battle feathers. It seemed to Segal that its eyes glowed with intelligence and something else. Vengeance? The crow picked up something with its beak, then with a hop launched into the air and began to fly, it seemed to Segal, a little uncertainly.

The large crow was joined by one other, and somehow Segal could tell this was support, not pursuit. The birds headed northeast.

"I think that was Richard," Dinah said.

"I think that was Richard, too," Segal said. He remembered what Elah's wife had said about the bird not being far from Francis. "If it is Richard…"

"…Creatures 2.0," Dinah said.

The birds flew off into the sunlight. At that point, Segal heard another sound to his right. It was more crows, presumably the remnants of the opposing flock. They were perched on the parapet and on a wire and antenna mounted to the roof. They all seemed to be watching Dinah hold their fallen comrade, Segal thought.

"Weird," Dinah said.

Segal agreed. There was something unusual about a couple of them. Something was attached to their heads. They reminded Segal of those stupid headset mics that singers sometimes wore. The crow on the highest part of the wire gave a loud call, and they all, bounding into the air, rose up, then paused in midair and began to plummet toward them.

Segal yelled to Dinah, "Run!"

The crows were a wall of black missiles. The sky screamed.

She took off with the dead crow.

Segal did his best, gaining speed even as the crow screams threatened to overtake him. He felt wings bash his head and the threat of more stabs from beaks and feet. He almost went down, stumbled and righted himself.

The door to the rooftop was suddenly near. Dinah and the security guard reached out and pulled him through. He ran his hands over his shoulders and head to make sure no birds were clinging to him, then collapsed against the wall. They slammed the door shut and for a moment Segal could hear banging and scratching against it. When the sound stopped Dinah opened the door a crack and held her phone, videoing the entire flock of crows as they rose and flew southwest, directly opposite the direction the first two crows had headed.

"What the hell is going on here?" It was the security guard, whom Segal had left guarding the door. He was sweating bullets, pale as a plastic dinner plate. "Are you guys okay?"

Segal nodded and caught his breath. "Dammit," he said, checking his head for more wounds. He led the way outside. It was quiet, like the feeling after the passing of a storm.

"Jeez, look at this," the guard said. He ran his hand over the exterior of the steel door, fingering the deep dents and gouges. "I didn't know birds could do this kind of damage."

Dinah called in for backup.

"Richard," Segal huffed. "I'm going to the lab. See if Richard shows up there."

Dinah tossed the bag with the dead crow. He caught it one-handed.

She went for the stairs, then turned. "You're okay to split up?"

Segal knew her orders from their boss were to back him up. He staunched the blood on his forehead with his hand. Motioned for her to go.

Segal drove downtown, bending and craning his neck from time to time, never seeing any sign of the birds. He'd tossed the bag containing the dead crow onto the passenger seat. Bloody-pink smears coated the inside of the bag.

When he entered the Creatures 2.0 building, Gloria, the receptionist was there. She wore an even shorter skirt than the first time he met her. This one was red.

"Is Richard here?" Segal asked.

If Gloria was surprised to hear him ask for the crow by name, she showed no sign of it. If she was surprised at the fresh cut on his forehead, she showed no sign of that either. She only nodded.

"Take me to him," he said. Gloria led him across the lobby toward the back of the building and into the large laboratory they had visited before. She pushed open the door, and he saw Lewis and another man; one-twenty, six-foot, brown hair, brown eyes, Segal thought. Richard the crow was on a lab bench, allowing the tall man to examine him while Lewis gently held the crow's feet.

Lewis didn't seem surprised to see Segal. "Richard here got his ass kicked, lieutenant," he said by way of greeting.

"You should see the other guy," Segal said. "In fact, you can see the other guy."

Segal held up the evidence bag containing the dead crow. He tossed it on the lab bench. Lewis and the tall man didn't flinch. Studied the bag, studied Segal.

Is that normal or not for them, Segal wondered. What's going on?

Gloria was still at the door. "You saw Richard do this?" She seemed more upset by this than when he had told her about Chickey.

Lewis sighed. "I told Francis stuff like this would happen," he said. "Pump up the intelligence in these animals and you don't know what they're going to do." He softened his face toward Richard and resumed dressing the crow's wounds. "Give us a minute, lieutenant, while the doctor here finishes up."

Segal obliged. Soon, the doctor seemed satisfied with the condition of his patient. He pulled his hands away, smoothed the feathers at the back of Richard's neck, then pulled off his surgical gloves and tossed them in the waste can by the bench.

"Gloria, why don't you show the doctor out," Lewis said.

The room emptied.

Segal wondered about Lewis. Richard was another matter entirely.

"So, you saw this going down?" Lewis asked.

Segal told him about the clash of birds above the Grove Arcade, culminating in the fight to the death that Richard won. Then the crow attack on Segal and Dinah. Lewis sat on a stool and put an elbow on the lab bench. He fingered the evidence bag with the dead bird. Segal opened the bag and gently pulled the body out far enough for Lewis to see where Richard had done his damage.

"Is this normal crow behavior?" Segal asked. "I mean, I've seen crows attack other birds, but I never saw one attack another crow."

"It happens," Lewis said. "Not a lot, but it happens. Could be a squabble over a female, or over territory or a food source. Thing is, the fights are not usually to the death. One crow chases another one away. I don't think this was a natural fight. Seems more like it was staged."

"Staged?" Segal asked. "You say this because Richard actually killed the other crow?"

Lewis paused, then seemed to come to a conclusion. "I'm saying so because it's Richard, and because Richard brought this with him when he came." Lewis opened a drawer in the lab bench and withdrew a plastic bag of his own. He opened it and slid the contents onto the bench. It was a small black device with a wire loop and a tiny lens.

Segal picked up the device and cupped it in his hands. He thought immediately of the irregularity he had noticed about the heads of the other flock and he remembered seeing something in Richard's beak when he flew away. "What is this, exactly?"

Lewis shifted his feet while seated. He glanced right and left before he leaned forward and spoke in a low voice. "This is getting me into a real touchy area here. I mean, I know I got to help you find out who killed Chickey, but this is some stuff I was sworn to secrecy on. Government stuff."

Segal nodded. "I understand. I won't share this with anyone who doesn't need to know about it."

Lewis rubbed his throat and seemed to be working up the courage to speak. "Okay, when the government guy first came to talk to Francis, he brought one of these with him. It's a little video camera and transmitter and recorder. It's meant to fit on the head of a bird, a crow in this case. It transmits more or less what the bird sees. Obviously, it had something to do with the project they wanted Francis to work on. That's when Francis pulled me in on it. He decided to do the project, but he wanted to modify the device so it worked better for the bird. Like I told you, I'm more of a computer and electronics guy than an animal trainer."

"What were they trying to do?" Segal asked.

Lewis shook his head. "They never told me. Francis said I didn't want to know. Thing was, Francis didn't like the way this thing fit on the bird. It bothered the crows—probably too tight on their heads or distorted their balance sense—and they would try to lose it. Richard is definitely intelligent enough that he would have ditched it."

Segal picked up the device again, truly feeling the weight of it in his hand. Light, compact. He held it up and studied the scale against Richard's head, trying to gauge how the thing would fit. Richard gave him a squawk and took a sideways step, as if to say, *Don't even think about trying to put that thing on me.*

"So, is this the design you and Francis came up with?" Segal asked.

"No, that's the original version. Government issue. Here's our version. Richard was wearing it when he showed up a couple of days ago." Without getting off his stool, Lewis leaned back, opened a drawer in the lab bench, and extracted a lighter and what appeared to be a more streamlined version of the device Segal held.

Lewis handed it over.

Even to Segal's untrained eye, the Asheville version was a clear improvement. He sat still for a moment, holding the two devices, trying to let the information and its implications soak in. He looked at Richard, then at Lewis. "That's what you meant by staged. You think the crows that Richard fought—the ones that attacked us when we were on the roof—were trained by someone and sent there for a specific reason, or at least to relay pictures of something. Like a drone, or more like a living drone."

Lewis nodded. "Here's another thing I'm not telling you about." He picked up the dead crow and pointed to the end of its beak. "See this? This guy's beak has been reinforced with some special composite material. Makes him a killer. Same with the tips of the claws. That's another thing the government wanted to do with Richard, but Francis wasn't having it."

Segal thought about the cut on his forehead and the marks on the door. No one had mentioned the cut. Not Gloria, Lewis or the doctor. Segal pointed to his head. "Should I be worried? No poison tips or anything?"

"No." Russel smiled. "Nothing like that. As far as I know."

Super, Segal thought. If Segal could believe what Lewis was telling him, and he saw no reason he shouldn't, the scenario was strange indeed. Someone sent trained crows to the Grove Arcade, for possible observation. Or attack? The obvious thing to observe was Francis's apartment and family, maybe to spot Francis if he showed up. Richard was there, too. Maybe he was there to watch over the family as well, then he ran into this other flock. But who sent Richard? All this went on in plain sight in downtown Asheville, and no one noticed a thing until a full-scale crow war broke out. Even then, if Richard hadn't killed that other crow and brought back the camera, the fight would have been over and the humans would have shrugged their shoulders and gone home. Just some random act of nature.

"Do you think Richard wanted you to know the other trained birds were there?" Segal asked. "I mean, is he capable of that kind of thinking?"

"I wouldn't put it past him," Lewis said. "Our bird, Richard, is capable of stuff that would blow your mind."

Segal thought about this, still holding the cameras, one in each hand, weighing them back and forth as if on the scales of justice. He looked more closely at the government-issue one, holding it close to his face. His expression suddenly changed as he looked at the lens. "Hey, you don't think this thing could still be transmitting, do you?"

"Oh, snap!" Lewis grabbed it from him in a panic.

CHAPTER 12

Freeze Frame

The image on the computer screen jostled around chaotically before blanking. The young technician leaned forward and moved the cursor over a command at the edge of the screen labeled *Signal strength*. The number beside that label changed to zero. The young man made a nervous, self-soothing gesture of rubbing the palm of his left hand over his crew cut. He clicked the update button, with the same result.

He glanced at a worktable set up in the room. In contrast to the state-of-the-art computer station, it was an old room, originally the dining room of the house. At the table was another, larger man in a green golf shirt. The man in green seemed intent on a square of ivory paper in front of him, manipulating it with surprising delicacy, given the size of his body and his hands.

"We lost signal," the technician said.

The man in the green shirt gave him no response. He rose and walked into the kitchen.

The tech heard coffee being poured. He glanced out the window. Across the backyard, an odd platform had been affixed to the trunk of a walnut tree by the alley.

"The birds have not returned," the tech said.

"You better let the colonel know," the man in green said, coming back in from the kitchen with his steaming cup.

The technician checked his watch, then pulled out a cell phone and punched in a number. "Colonel, we lost bird signal just now," he said. He listened to a question on the other end. "No, I don't think it's the battery. It didn't fade out. It went out all at once. Either the device failed, or someone turned it off." He listened, said, "Yes, sir," and hung up. "The colonel said he would be here in a minute."

He turned to the computer, using the keyboard and mouse with great speed and precision. He reviewed the video recording he had been watching. Most of it was jumbled movement, difficult to follow. Occasionally, he halted on a frame and studied it more closely, cropping and magnifying part of the image. After that, he clicked some other controls.

Across the room, a printer came to life. When it spit out five sheets of paper, he got up from his chair and retrieved them. He took them to a whiteboard that covered the opposite wall and put them up with Scotch tape. He backed up to take in the impact of his work.

At that point, the backdoor opened and a third man joined them. He was not a large man. His build was trim and fit and he held himself poker straight. He wore a khaki shirt, dark slacks, and hiking boots. Like a uniform without being a uniform. He moved with authority directly to the board. The technician stepped aside to give him room.

"We have a few new photos, Colonel," the tech said, stepping back to the board.

A new picture of Lewis Abraham, a close-up of his face and shoulders, was taped up under the heading "Creatures 2.0." Under it in small, neat letters the tech wrote the date, the word *Source*, and a number. There were already a couple of older photos showing Lewis getting out of his car and going into the lab. They were labeled with his name, earlier dates, and different source numbers.

In the same section of the board, the tech taped up the new picture of the Creatures 2.0 receptionist, Gloria. This one was a full-body shot of her looking surprised; lips open, eyes wide. She had her hands raised, which, the young man noticed, also raised her skirt. Under his breath, he muttered "Damn" as he added a date and source number.

On a section of the board labeled only with a question mark were pictures of two cops. Their full names were taped beneath the photos. The first cop, Segal, was standing with his hair disheveled, looking down and to the right. The second cop, Rudisill was caught in midstride of a sprint, giving the man a great view of her athletic thighs in action. "Double damn," the tech said to himself.

Finally, he hung up the last picture, a close-up of Segal and Lewis at Creatures 2.0. He pointed to the pictures one at a time, as though putting together the sequence. The significance hit him all at once.

The tech said, "Colonel, I think the camera has been compromised."

The man in the green shirt swore softly.

The tech said, "This looks like a selfie. This guy is holding the camera in his hand."

The colonel was holding a photo of his own, this one apparently cut from a magazine. He raised his hand and flicked it back and forth as if air-drying the image. The colonel approached the board and picked up the marker. He erased the question mark above the pictures of the cops. In its place, he wrote, "Local Complications."

Then he took the picture in his hand and taped it up near, but not exactly under, the Creatures 2.0 section. He connected the picture to the label with a dotted line. The photo showed a glossy image of an attractive woman with wavy hair. On her raised arm was a crow, which was eating from her other hand. Under this picture, he wrote the name Lucile Devroe, date unknown, source "Public."

"New lady?" the tech asked.

The man in the green shirt said nothing but studied the board and sipped his coffee.

"We found a reference that she's a trainer who worked with Elah," the colonel explained over his shoulder. He pursed his lips, seeming to assess the board with the satisfaction of a person who had magically fit together three pieces of a jigsaw puzzle.

On the extreme right of the board was the word *Countdown* in large block letters. Beside that was the number seven, which the colonel erased, replacing it with the number six. Below, perhaps for even more emphasis, was a list of dates. He crossed off yesterday's date.

The man in the green shirt scowled. "There are getting to be a lot of pictures on that board," he said.

The colonel only nodded.

"Maybe we could get rid of some local complications. Clear the field a little," the man in green said.

The technician watched the colonel as he seemed to consider. He understood the intuition guiding the colonel and the man in green, like a chess master having a feel for the board without a precise picture of how the game might play out.

"Maybe," the colonel said. "It would have to be the right kind of situation. Target of opportunity. We may have to."

"What about this new lady, Lucile Devroe?" the man in the green shirt asked.

"Let's find out more about her," the colonel said.

The man in green grunted from the table.

CHAPTER 13

Biltmore Estate

"Let's find out more about her," Segal said.

He held a picture of Lucile Devroe. It was her number on the back of the card they had found in Chickey's wallet, so she was on his list of people to interview. After they found out from Andrew Roche that Lucile had worked with Francis, she moved to the top of Segal's interview list.

Dinah grinned and said, "I see why you offered to take this interview. She looks like a Hollywood movie star from the 1940s."

Segal frowned. "I'm not looking for love in all the wrong places."

"Maybe you should, Segal. It might improve your outlook on life."

Segal turned into the Biltmore Estate entrance and drove through the stone-and-brick archway. Passing through this portal, he left the modern city behind and moved smoothly along the narrow lane. It took him through thickets of ancient rhododendrons growing on both sides of the road, allowing occasional glances of the Swannanoa River on the right and open fields on the left. Segal lost track of the number of stone arched bridges he crossed, mounted over creeks and drainage ways.

He came to a building used as an information center and for ticket sales. It had been built recently, in harmony with the other structures on the estate, adhering to the conventions of the Arts and Crafts tradition. Beyond that, uniformed guards stopped cars, asked for tickets, and gave directions. Segal stopped, rolled down the window, and showed his badge. "I'm meeting one of your people at Antler Village," he said. He hated saying that name out loud because it was so out of character with the elegance of the rest of the estate. It reminded Segal of one of those cheesy Christmas villages that department stores set up at the holidays. Even though he'd visited Biltmore many times, he still allowed the ticket taker to give him directions. The place covered eight hundred acres, and the winding access roads were complex.

He drove through another forested area of large oaks and poplars, through wide meadows where Black Angus cattle grazed, and through fields where hay was almost ready for cutting. It was hard to believe he was five minutes from the center of Asheville.

He drove up a short incline and though a wide gate in a stone fence and found himself looking at the Biltmore mansion off to his right. He took in the view of the elaborate stone building across two hundred yards of perfect green lawn.

This view was familiar even to people visiting for the first time because the mansion had been the setting for several popular movies. It was a castle in light-colored stone, built in the late 1800s, ahead of its time. The center entryway had a smooth façade leading up to lacy masonry work at the eaves. The slate roof was sharply pitched and fitted with copper flashing, eaves troughs, and spouts. To the left of the center structure was a series of diagonal lines corresponding to the flights of the grand stairway inside. To the right of the entry was Segal's favorite feature, a large conservatory built from panes of glass set into a copper-clad frame. As impressive as these details were, the sheer scale of the building and grounds and the spectacular setting with the gardens and fountains in the foreground and mountain ridges in the distance made it more majestic still.

Segal eased the car away from the main house and drove past the formal gardens and onto the winding roads toward his meeting place.

Antler Village was a stupid name, but the buildings and layout were beautifully done and fit seamlessly with the rest of the estate. It had a couple of restaurants and a shopping area constructed next to one of the old stable buildings, which was now used for demonstrations of various farm and village crafts. More to the point, it also had a small farm and next to the farm an ice cream shop, which was where the meeting was arranged.

Segal recognized her immediately. Lucile Devroe did look like a movie star from the forties, as Dinah had said. She seemed very much at home where she sat. He could easily imagine her as one of the summer guests at the estate in its high society days, mixing with the writers and artists and Wall Street tycoons and politicians. Part of the impression was her hair, light brown and curled slightly under at the shoulder. Then there was her clear complexion. Yet, the whole was more than the sum of the parts. She possessed an aura of complete comfort with who she was.

Seated as she was on a bench beside the ice cream shop, her eyes appeared focused toward the little farm area. She was wearing khaki shorts and a light khaki shirt with the emblem of the Biltmore Estate on the sleeve. Her shoes were clunky—couldn't run in those, Segal thought—as he realized that somehow instead of detracting, they drew more attention to her long legs, which were crossed.

As he approached up the walk, she turned her gaze from the farm and toward him. Her face lit up in a smile as she uncrossed her legs and stood in one fluid motion. She said, "You must be Lieutenant Segal. I'm Lucile Devroe." She extended her hand, and he met it with his.

He needed a beat or two before he could get words to form in his mouth. "Thanks for meeting me."

She smiled wider. "Buy me an ice cream cone and I'll tell you everything I know."

This gets better and better, Segal thought.

"I met Francis when I was in grad school. He came to the conferences and meetings sometimes, but he never presented or published papers. I remember him always surrounded by people or sitting in hotel lobbies talking one on one with important men and women. My advisor introduced us, and I remember he talked to me about my research project. He asked some really good questions, questions no one else asked and that had never occurred to me either." She was looking at a bowl of fudge ripple ice cream as she talked, swirling a wooden spoon around on the top of it. She put a small spoonful in her mouth and closed her eyes.

Segal was thinking he could understand Francis or any other guy taking time with this lady, research or no research. He tried to steer himself around the business at hand. "I've been told he was good at what he did."

"You're speaking of him in the past tense," she said. "Is there something I should know?"

"No, you're right. I'm sorry. I guess I mean he is good at what he does, or he was good before he left, anyway."

"Have you seen the raccoons at the VA hospital?" she asked.

Segal nodded and smiled.

"Do you have any idea how far advanced that kind of behavior modification is, especially in only partially controlled conditions?"

"Partially controlled conditions?" Segal asked.

"Most trainers maximize the control they have over the animal. They confine it in a cage or on a leash. They control the animal's source of food and water so it is dependent on the trainer. They do everything they can to command the animal's complete attention. Francis didn't do that. He didn't want to command its attention. He wanted to earn it. Even in the presence of the normal distractions of life. It was one of his guiding principles. The work you want from the animal has to make sense—make sense in an economic kind of way, he meant. The animal has to get a fair return for what it is being asked to do. Otherwise, the whole deal doesn't make sense, and you're fighting an uphill battle."

They each took a spoon of ice cream while Segal digested that thought. "So, in partially controlled conditions, the animals can come and go as they want?" he asked.

"Come on, I'll show you the training station for my flock of crows," she said.

Within moments, they were riding in a golf cart, cutting through a narrow path to a place near the greenhouse and the formal gardens. She explained that part of her compensation for taking care of the little farm was the opportunity to continue her animal research on the estate. She stopped outside the stone wall of the gardens. Across a few yards of lawn, a forest grew. On the edge of the forest, an oak tree stood out from the rest. About ten feet above the ground was a wooden platform affixed to a forked branch. On the platform were a couple of boxes and some kind of apparatus. As they waited, several crows appeared, some sitting on the platform, some on the branches, and one, presumably the lookout, in the topmost branch of the tree. One of the largest of the birds on the platform called out. Lucile put a whistle in her mouth and issued a short tweet, then gave a hand signal, and the bird flew down to the cart. She reached into a bag of cat food in the rear of the cart and held a piece out to it. It ate from her palm while keeping a sideways eye on Segal.

"So, this is a place you use for training and testing?" Segal asked.

Lucile nodded and gave the bird another signal. It flew to the platform.

"And all this you learned from Francis?"

"The basics, yes," she said. "We did a lot of Richard's training here."

"Did you ever work directly on government projects with him?" Segal asked.

"He occasionally brought me in on projects to help out. It was not so much to help with the direction of the project or anything like that. He was always in the driver's seat. But he knew he could count on me to carry out test protocols without letting other stuff get in the way of the experiments, and he knew I could keep good notes and write up accurate reports."

Her remarks reminded Segal that he had taken no notes of his own yet. So far, this seemed more like a social call than a police interview. *Get your head in the game,* he told himself. He pulled out a small notebook and a pen and managed to write down the date, but then Lucile did this Hollywood move of brushing her hair behind her ear with one hand, and he put the notebook down.

"How much do you know about his latest project, the one that took him out of town?"

"Out of the country is more like it," she said. "That's what I heard, anyway. I don't really know what he was working on or where he went. Some of his guys said it was top secret. The last time I actually worked on a project with him was with the mule deer."

"Mule deer?"

"You know about deer?" she asked.

Segal shrugged.

She started the cart up and they did a half circle and went in the direction of Antler Village. "Well, the deer you see around here, in North Carolina and the rest of the eastern U.S., those are white-tailed deer. The mule deer comes from out west," she said.

"What's the difference?" Segal asked.

"The biggest difference you would notice is the size of the ears. The mule deer has much bigger ears, which is how it got its name."

Segal nodded knowingly, even though the truth was he had never noticed that mules had big ears. He was not even sure he could pick out a mule in a lineup that included horses, ponies, and donkeys.

"So, what was the mule deer project about?" he asked.

"Maybe we should go to my office. I could show you some pictures." She had a Mona Lisa smile on her face.

Her office turned out to be in a converted room in the old stable building on the hill above the petting farm and Antler Village. The brick walls had been left bare, and the heavy poplar beams of the ceiling were exposed as well.

She walked to a stand-up desk near the center of the room and took a key out of a drawer, which she used to unlock one of the several filing cabinets. Segal watched her cross the floor in a lovely, fluid motion. She let her fingers walk through the tops of some files, then pulled one out. From the manila folder, she withdrew a file with a plastic cover.

"Here is the subject himself," she said. She flopped the file on the desktop.

Gazing up at Segal was a head-and-shoulders portrait of a deer mugging directly into the camera. The word that jumped into his mind was *stupid*, which was what he wrote in his notebook beside *mule deer*. Its mouth was open, and it was ever so slightly cross-eyed.

"Is it an intelligent animal?" he asked.

"I never saw much evidence of intelligence, unless resistance to training can be considered intelligence," Lucile said.

"I suppose that depends on what Francis was trying to train the deer to do," Segal said.

"Recite the alphabet."

Segal recoiled and saw that Mona Lisa smile breaking into a wider grin. He choked down a response, eyed the folder and saw the stupid deer face.

"What could possibly be the motivation for teaching a mule deer, or any deer, for that matter, to recite the alphabet?"

"It was to settle a bet. This guy called Francis and said he had met him at a conference. Francis didn't remember him. Apparently, the guy and a friend of his had been arguing about the intelligence of different animals, and his friend was saying that the mule deer was on the low end of the scale, and the guy, who was a hunter, disagreed. So, they ended up making this bet, with the guy betting that a mule deer could be trained to recite the alphabet. I'm guessing drinking was involved."

"What did Francis think of this?" Segal asked.

"He thought it was pretty funny. Still, he didn't want to do it. He told the guy he was booked up on other projects. The guy kept pressing him for a monetary quote. Finally, Francis quoted a price that was five or six times higher than his time could possibly be worth, thinking that would make the guy go away. Instead, the guy took Francis up on it. Turns out, he was one of those internet billionaires. Money was no object. So, the guy had the mule deer trapped and sent out here."

"And I take it Francis signed you up to help with the project."

"Yes, but only in a minor way. Like I told you, he preferred to work with animals who were free to come and go, but that was not practical in this case." She ran her delicate finger over the picture of the mule deer and shook her head. "If you turned that thing loose around here, it's hard to tell where he would end up. The farm on the Biltmore Estate was a good compromise. The pastures are pretty open, so the mule deer had quite a bit of freedom."

"Plus, it's close to downtown," Segal said, nodding. He understood what an ideal location Biltmore was for this enterprise. "How did the project go?"

"At first, not so well. The subject had problems adjusting after the move. He seemed nervous and depressed."

Segal wondered how depression manifested itself in a mule deer and thought it better to stay quiet. He didn't want to take the story down that sidetrack.

"Anyway, then we realized it was rutting season and maybe he was pining away for a girlfriend. We had some white-tailed does here but no female mule deer, so we sent for one out in Colorado."

"And that worked?" Segal asked.

"Not exactly. By the time the female mule deer was delivered, the male had started mating with some local white-tailed deer. Apparently, once he got a taste for white-tailed deer, he lost interest in female mule deer. I mean, who can really blame him?" She flipped the pages of the report to another picture, which Segal took to be the female mule deer Lucile was talking about. "Look at the face on that thing," she said, shaking her head.

Segal did so, trying to recall other deer or pictures of deer he had seen. He did not perceive why this one would be considered especially unattractive either by the male mule deer or by Lucile.

"Okay, so the mule deer was presumably happier once he had some girlfriends. Did things go better then?"

"I guess so," Lucile said. "I wasn't active in the training sessions. Watching them from a distance it at least appeared to me like the mule deer was responding. He did seem less jumpy and nervous."

"And did he ever recite the alphabet?" Segal asked.

"Personally, I never heard him get past the letter *C*. Even then, it took a lot of prompting. He was trying for *D*, but I don't think he ever made it."

"No kidding? You mean he could say *A, B, C, D*?"

"Like I said, he was struggling with *D*." Lucile slid off the high stool, which had been doing a great job of displaying her legs, and opened a laptop computer. After some keyboard and mouse work, she found a video clip. "Check this out," she said, clicking on the play arrow.

On the screen, Segal saw the mule deer shaking his head, first up and down, then side to side. Then a man's arm entered the screen, presumably Francis's, holding a morsel of food between his fingers. The mule deer licked his lips. Francis said the letter *A* in a clear and patient voice. The mule deer repeated the vowel in a guttural way. It reminded Segal of the early versions of computer voices, understandable but not remotely human, devoid of any inflection.

The mule deer was rewarded with the morsel of food, which he sucked down with disgusting relish—much action of the tongue and lips. The process was repeated for the letters *B* and *C*. Then the mule deer stuttered trying to say *D*. He turned and flicked his tail at the camera and walked away.

"That's amazing," Segal said.

"You think so?" Lucile clicked away at the computer and snapped it shut.

"You don't think so?" To Segal, the whole thing was remarkable.

"That deer had a bad voice and a bad personality," she said.

Her time with the mule deer clearly had not engendered much affection for the animal. "I thought scientists were supposed to be neutral observers, above the fray," Segal said.

"Who told you that? And what about policemen? Do you treat all of your suspects and witnesses the same?" She uncrossed her legs and slipped off the stool again.

Her question and action got Segal's attention for sure. He leaned an elbow on the stand-up desk, and Lucile took up a similar stance on the other side, meeting his eye.

"What happened with the project?" he asked.

"Never finished," she said. She released her gaze. "Francis was called away on whatever big project was going on that took priority over everything else. I took care of the mule deer for a while, but then one of the volunteers left a gate open overnight, and he escaped along with some females and a white-faced Hereford calf we were training for the petting zoo. We found the calf up by St. Paul's church grazing by the holly bushes, but the deer were long gone. I think the internet billionaire settled his bet with a partial payment based on a copy of the video you just saw. I doubt we'll be training any more mule deer anytime soon."

"And you haven't heard from Francis since he left?" Segal asked, finally getting to the question he really wanted to ask.

Lucile shook her head and bit her lip.

"And you would tell me if you had?" he asked, fixing her eye again.

Before Lucile answered, there was a knock at the door. Dinah entered. She stared at Lucile, stared at Segal, back and forth, her shoulders squaring.

Picking up on the vibe, Segal thought.

"Sorry to interrupt," Dinah said. She smiled at Lucile, then tilted her head once in Segal's direction.

Somethings up.

"I got a ride over with a friend after practice."

"This is my associate, Dinah Rudisill," Segal said. Dinah crossed the room and shook hands with the taller woman.

"Dinosaur Rudisill?" Lucile asked.

Segal was always surprised when his partner was recognized by the adoring public, although by now he shouldn't have been. Also, he would not have guessed that Dr. Lucile Devroe was a devotee of roller derby. This lady got more interesting by the minute.

Dinah smiled demurely. Then she seemed to get an idea. "If you're interested, I've got an extra ticket to the bout tonight," she said.

Lucile nearly snatched it from her hand.

Dinah gave Segal a grin. "The lieutenant is going to be there, sitting behind the team bench. Maybe he could save you a seat."

Segal hesitated before he said, "Sure."

"You can thank me later," Dinah said as they walked down the hill to Segal's car.

Segal started to protest. Then the image of Lucile Devroe came to mind, and he had to be honest with himself and smile. "At least I won't have to sit there with only Jerome Guilford to talk to," he said.

Dinah grinned. Segal thought she looked quite pleased with herself. Then her expression changed.

"Oh, yeah, I have news from ballistics. That bullet you found in the studio at the Wedge, like I told you, it's designed to fragment when it hits its target. They recovered fragments from the victim, Charles Atley, and those fragments are from the same kind of bullet."

"So, we know where and how," Segal said. "Now, we have to figure out who. And why."

CHAPTER 14

Dinah on Skates

That evening Segal went downtown. In the pocket of his coat was a copy of *The Great Gatsby*, more for the Jazz Age vibe than anything else. It was the same paperback copy he read in high school and many times thereafter. He emerged from the narrow passageway that led by the library and out to Haywood Street. The streetlights were coming on, and the air was cooling, although the pavement retained some of the heat of the day. Groups of people moved around and he immediately felt that sense of anticipation and fun that Asheville exuded on a good night.

He turned right toward the civic center, where clusters of people milled around, getting ready to go inside for the roller derby match. A large banner with girls on skates hung over the entrance, right next to the sign for the Thomas Wolfe Auditorium. He heard music. When he drew nearer to the entrance, he saw his favorite street singer, Mattie, this time with other musicians, in the midst of a rocking street ballad. She was one of those players who could lead or blend in as the mood and the piece spoke to her. She smiled and nodded as he walked by. He knew the friends and family of the team members would save him good seats, but he was anxious to arrive early anyway. He made a quick scan around. Across the street was the basilica, and a little farther was the north end of the Grove Arcade. *The center of Francis Elah's world*, he thought. And there by the winged lions was the gently sloping roof that had allowed the man to get away that morning. Asheville being Asheville, no one had taken particular notice of a man climbing off the roof of a building.

He felt a tap on his shoulder and there was Lucile Devroe. She wore a light cotton dress, looking even better than when they had met at the Biltmore Estate. She gave him a wide smile and immediately put her arm through his. He got a wide, stupid grin on his face and guided her through the door.

Inside, a carnival atmosphere was in full swing. They stopped by the stand in the lobby for beers and a bag of popcorn. The crowd was already noisy when they walked into the arena. The home team was warming up on the track, and he stood with Lucile at the upper rail, taking it all in.

Segal saw his partner right away and pointed her out to Lucile: Dinah, a.k.a. Dinosaur, skating around the track. Segal took a mental snapshot as she whizzed by. The skates seemed like natural extensions of her legs. Both were covered with some sort of stretchy spandex material in an iridescent cobalt blue. She glided with her body upright, hands stretched over her head, back arched. From this, she lowered into a crouch, going into the turn at incredible speed. She was always in perfect balance. She was always in perfect control, and always with that crazy hair flying out behind. Gravity and centrifugal force were her friends. And in addition to controlling her own movements, she was in effortless control of her team. A glance here, a nod there, or a quick hand gesture, and the formation of girls skating in a pack opened or closed around her as she wished. Often, Segal could see no sign at all, so it seemed like they communicated by access to some communal roller derby mind. Even though she was by far the smallest one out there, she was clearly in charge. From the rest of the team, she got the respect of a drill sergeant—which she had been for a while in the service—combined with the affection big girls reserve for their little sisters.

The crowd started chanting, "Din-o-saur! Din-o-saur!" She let that go on for a few rounds and then acknowledged it with a wave to the stands. Then she flipped around and skated backward around the loop before swooping into the infield and raising her hand to call the team to surround her. The fans loved it. The team formed a huddle, put their hands into the center, and chanted something Segal could not understand, then ended with a loud war cry, bringing their hands up together. They retreated to their chairs as the visiting team took the track for its warmup.

"Looks like she really is the star of the show," said a voice beside Segal. He turned and saw the Naval Intelligence guy. Jerome Guilford had changed from his suit to jeans and a golf shirt, but he still had those perfect brown shoes on. Segal had no choice. He introduced Lucile.

"Lucile Devroe," Guilford said. "I've heard about your work."

Lucile knit her eyebrows together.

"The lieutenant and I are working together on a case," Guilford explained.

Segal waited. He had no easy way to deny or explain, not in this atmosphere. He had hoped the guy would not show up. Here he was. Segal led them down to their seats close to the floor, where they would have a good view of the action. They settled in time for the two teams to line up for the start.

"How come Dinah is behind the other girls if she's the leader?" Guilford asked.

A girl sitting in front of them turned and answered. "See the star on her helmet? That means she's the jammer."

Segal saw the star and another on the helmet of the girl beside Dinah, presumably the jammer for the other team.

The girl continued. "The jammers try to get through the pack of the opposing team and pass them. That's why they start behind. Don't worry. The Dinosaur won't be back there for long."

The whistle sounded. When the jammer of the opposing team accelerated toward the pack, her first try was rebuffed by a double block from two of the big girls on Dinah's team. Meanwhile, Dinah made a start at a gap between two of the opposition's blockers, pulled up short and, to everyone's surprise, swerved to collide with the opposition's jammer. Bent on retaliation, she made a move against Dinah, who was too quick. She ducked under her opponent's arm, which sent the other girl off balance and into the center of the track. When the blockers from the opposition glanced over their shoulders to see what happened, they opened up enough for Dinah to dart through the pack untouched.

"Girl's got finesse," said Guilford. "I'll have to remember that."

It was the kind of jackass comment Segal expected from the guy. He shrugged it off. The action was too good for him to dwell on it.

The crowd went wild when Dinah broke through. She was all business now, switching into high speed to lap the pack. Now that she had passed the pack once, she could begin scoring points every time she passed a member of the opposing team. The other jammer recovered and worked her way through the pack as well, in time to avoid embarrassment and extra points if Dinah lapped her.

The home team continued to build its lead as the opponents regained composure and assembled effective plays and formations. Dinah ended the jam by putting her hands on her hips. Only then, when the whistle sounded, did she allow herself to relax and acknowledge the fans, including a big smile and wave at Segal and Lucile.

Segal yelled and clapped with renewed pride in his partner, reminded of how good she was. That one little push of provocation she gave the other jammer, in the beginning, set off a whole chain of events, and since she was the instigator, she was one step ahead the whole way. *Not a bad plan, if you can pull it off*, he thought.

The second jam began. This time, Dinah skated a more traditional strategy. Problem was, the opposing team had a better idea now of what it was up against. One of the big girls, in particular, seemed to have it in for her, throwing increasingly aggressive blocks. After Dinah passed her a couple of times, the girl got frustrated and threw an elbow that connected squarely with Dinah's jaw and sent her skidding onto the track. The referee somehow missed this blatant infraction, so the big girl got away with it. And to make matters worse, one of Dinah's teammates, a girl from West Asheville, sought revenge with a major hit, which did draw a penalty. The crowd erupted in booing and whistling. By this time, Dinah had regained her feet. She put her hands on her hips to bring the second jam to a close. The action was rough around the edges, but her team still extended its lead.

It was then, during the break in the action, that Segal noticed that the Naval Intelligence guy, Guilford, was gone. He looked up to the mezzanine and saw him walking toward the exit with a cell phone to his ear. Segal assumed he had taken a call and was getting out where he could hear well enough to have a conversation.

Segal swiveled around when something else caught his eye. The street singer, Mattie, was standing at the edge of the mezzanine with her elbows on the railing. Next to her was another familiar silhouette, Emily Elah. Segal did a double-take. After all, Emily Elah was not the only Goth woman in Asheville with straight-cut black bangs. But it was Emily. She was talking earnestly to Mattie, who looked straight ahead and nodded almost rhythmically, a serious look on her face. Mattie had a cup of beer. Not so Emily. Her hands were free to gesture, which they did.

Segal studied the scene, trying to read body language. He paused, sipped his beer, thought hard about Mattie and

Emily. It probably didn't mean anything, at least not anything to do with the case. This was Asheville, and he shouldn't be surprised when two women turned out to know each other. And why shouldn't Emily Elah come to a roller derby match, especially since it took place almost on her doorstep? He wondered who was watching the little girl. Probably no one. The girl was likely okay on her own, especially in a place as secure as the Grove Arcade.

Then the whistle blew for the beginning of another jam. Lucile held his arm in excitement. He admired her profile. She seemed to be having a great time. A moment ago, he was totally into the match, but now he was distracted. He scanned for Guilford and saw him walking across the mezzanine level. Guilford apparently was ending a conversation because he said a couple of words into this phone, then slipped it into a pocket. Halfway down the stairs, the phone must have buzzed again because with a look of irritation he answered, spun around, and headed up the steps.

Segal wondered what was going on, then told himself there was no reason the phone calls had anything to do with his case. At that point, his own phone vibrated. He saw it was the department dispatcher. The crowd erupted as Dinah sailed through the opposing pack, and he had to ask the woman on the other end to repeat herself. He listened for a moment and said, "On my way."

The match was only a few minutes from its end. Segal apologized to Lucile. Lucile said she understood, said she would be fine.

Segal saw a shadow of disappointment cross her face.

As the first jammer to clear the pack, Dinah could have given the sign to end the last jam at any point simply by putting her hands on her hips. However, that is not what she wanted. She was feeling the joy of the action and had no wish for it to end. More importantly, she knew the crowd didn't want it to end, so she let the jam clock go until time was called.

When the final whistle blew, she and the rest of the team raised their fists in the universal sign of victory. They waved to the fans as they took a couple of leisurely laps. On the last lap, Dinah noticed that Segal was gone but Guilford was present, standing and clapping with the rest of the crowd. He said something to Lucile. She tucked her hair behind her ear and seemed to be doing her best to ignore him. The last thing Dinah wanted was to be alone with that jackass after the match. She felt a twinge of irritation with Segal for putting her in that situation, but she was feeling too good to give any energy to the emotion. One of the big blockers clapped her on the shoulder, and she skated off to the locker room with the rest of the team.

The locker room was a mess of uniforms, skates, fishnet stockings, and women in every phase of dress and undress. The noise level was higher than normal, which, given the nature of this team and the echo in the room, was saying something. Dinah headed for the showers wrapped in a towel, after packing the locker with her gear, street clothes, and her uniform, damp with sweat.

When she returned, she checked her phone by habit as she dried her body. She saw two messages. One was a missed call from dispatch. Second was a text message from Segal: *Murder at Creatures 2.0. Get here ASAP.*

CHAPTER 15

Tobacco and Mint

Suzie sat alone in the darkened apartment in the Grove Arcade. She had declined her mother's offer to go to the roller derby. She liked it, but tonight the civic center would be too loud and crowded for the way she was feeling. Anyway, sometimes she wanted to be alone.

Her mother left an hour ago, after making her a bowl of spaghetti. Suzie ate half of it, selectively mining out the little meatballs and subsequently sucking noodles one by one through pursed lips and licking the sauce off her mouth. It took her a long time to eat this way, but she savored every bite and felt each of the ingredients, the way her father had shown her. It was what he called "conscious eating," a form of meditation, opening up to the experience with gratitude for the food and the people who prepared it. The recipe was his, and her mother made it for her from time to time, knowing it made her feel close to him now. She stopped eating when she felt satisfied and left the unfinished bowl on the table.

Her eyes were tired from the activities of the day. She had spent too much time in strong light and looking at a computer screen. It made her head hurt, as it often did. She wheeled into the bathroom, held a washcloth under the faucet, soaked it with warm water, and wrung out the excess.

She wheeled down the hall, past the kitchen area, and into the big living room. From outside the door, she heard activity in the arcade below, as she always could this time of day—people talking, children's voices, a trace of music, sometimes a strange noise like the clang of dishes being stacked. This was her home, and the sounds were a reassuring and familiar background. Now, to get rid of the headache, she wanted to relax, to let go. She found her iPhone, plugged in the headset, selected music, and put the warm cloth on her eyes. Her current favorite was a Celtic mix put together by one of the best street musicians in Asheville, a big girl named Mattie. When she thought of Mattie—her size, her strength, the sweetness and power of her voice—she imagined being like her and could feel some of the strength flowing in her own body.

She took three cleansing breaths, then settled and let the music take her away. She felt she could almost understand the weird Celtic words, as if through some inherited memory passed on by her ancestors. By and by, her breathing slowed and her mind entered a deep state of relaxation and renewal. Soon, at the edge of this waking dream, she became aware of a sensation. It was a smell, so delicate at first that she dared not move or alter her mind in any way, lest it disappear. Even before she knew what it was, she understood it was something she very much wanted. And the smell began to form itself into recognizable components: a trace of mint, a sweet undertone of tobacco, the warmth and moisture of perspiration. It was the smell of her father when she pressed her cheek to his chest, before he left on this project and before that, going into her past as far as she could remember.

As the recognition registered fully, she thought she felt a gentle touch from behind her chair. She felt his arms wrap around her. She felt him nudge the earphone aside and whisper, "I'm with you, baby girl, we have to wait a little longer." She thought he hugged her in silence for a time, and she put a hand on his arm. There was no need to say anything else. He held her for a moment, and then it was time for him to go.

CHAPTER 16

Second Crime Scene

On the dark and quiet street, rotating blue lights of police cars were visible from blocks away. To Segal, it evoked the memory of many such scenes before his injuries: the moist night air, the cluster of neighbors standing a respectful distance, wondering what was going on, police radios snapping on and off, sounding like a foreign language. It brought back his early days on the force. It brought back his early days as a detective, being the central actor in scenes like this, the one who stepped into the void, who took charge and made sense of things and resolved the wrong and restored the peace so badly disturbed. Back then, he felt pride in his role—not a boastful pride, but a kind that centered him and focused him on his task. Now, it was different. He felt the excitement, also the exposure. He had to be up to the challenge. More than anything, he felt apprehension and was keenly aware that it had been his decision not to put a more robust guard on this building to protect the people inside.

Only one officer was posted outside Creatures 2.0 when he walked up. He nodded to the guy as he hurried past, then stopped and turned to him. "Who called this in?" he asked.

"We did," the guy said, which Segal understood to mean him and his partner. "We got this neighborhood on our patrol route, and this place was on the worksheet to keep an eye on. We were cruising the block and saw flashes from inside the building."

"Flashes?"

"Yeah. The building was mostly dark. I didn't think about it at the time. Now it seems kind of strange. I mean, no security lights on outside. Anyway, I think that's why the flashes got our attention. They weren't all that bright. We both thought gunshots—you know, muzzle flashes."

"Did you hear gunshots?" Segal asked.

"No, we didn't hear anything," the officer said.

Segal considered this. From up the block, with the building closed, maybe gunshots would be audible, maybe not. Also, there was no security alarm reported. He would have to check on that.

He went on in. Plenty of lights were on. By the receptionist's desk, another officer stood stock still, arms across his chest as two people from the medical examiner's team fussed around. He saw legs. His heart sank in his chest. At the far end of the desk, Gloria's body lay on the floor. Segal's first thought, when he came around to where he could see was, *How small she looks in death*. That's what he wrote in his notebook: *Small in death*. She was dressed in a white blouse and a short, dark skirt, sheer hose on her legs. She had no shoes on her feet. Segal ducked his head and saw a pair of dark flats under the desk. It looked to him as though she'd been working, had stood and come around the side of the desk, and been shot twice, once through the heart, once a little lower, the blood showing dark red against the white blouse.

He looked at her face. *A beautiful young flower,* he thought. He wrote that in his book, too. Segal filed away such unbidden thoughts. Sometimes the immediate reaction held meaning, sometimes not. The enormity of the death seeped into his core. His heart raced and his face felt flushed. He wished he had not brought *The Great Gatsby* with him that night. Anything else.

"Two entry wounds, one exit wound," the tech closest to him said. Segal struggled to concentrate on what the man said. "We'll have at least one bullet."

Segal nodded. The comment brought him to practical matters. He saw another tech across the room examining a mark on the wall, probably the impact of the bullet that passed through.

Two more officers came in from the hallway that led to the rear of the building. "We did a preliminary search to see if the perpetrator was still on the premises," the second of the original officers said. "We found nothing and saw nothing disturbed."

"Good," Segal said. These guys had done things by the book and by good common sense. The first two would have called in right away and waited for backup before making a search. Too dangerous to do otherwise. "How long between seeing the flashes and you entering the building with backup?" Segal asked.

The cop thought for a moment. "Five minutes, probably a little less," he said.

Segal thought, *Reasonable response time, but plenty of opportunity for the shooter to get away.*

He walked down the hall and into the laboratory where he had met with Lewis and where he had first seen Richard. He flipped on the lights and stood in the doorway. There was a door on the opposite side of the room, easy egress out the back of the building, as he expected. Behind that was a sizable stand of trees that would make it easy for the killer to slip away into the neighborhood and beyond.

He walked slowly around the room, trying to remember how things were arranged before. It was tough. Most of the equipment was strange to him. He went over and sat on the same stool he had used when Lewis showed him the crow cams, the one the government originally came up with as well as the redesigned one. He opened the drawer and did not see either one. He opened a couple of others in case he was not remembering correctly. Nothing.

He went to the lobby and out the front door without examining the body again. He pulled out his phone, called the station, and asked for dispatch. "I want two more cars if you can spare them. I want them cruising the neighborhood around the crime scene."

"We'll clear the ones from the civic center," the dispatcher said.

It reminded Segal that half an hour ago he had been there himself, along with half of Asheville and Jerome Guilford and Lucile Devroe. He pulled out his notebook and found the number for Lewis Abraham. "I need you to send a car to pick this guy up," he said and gave the dispatcher the name and number. "Has Dinah checked in yet?" There was a pause. "Never mind, here she is." She was coming up the walk. Her wild shock of hair was pulled out of the way, still wet.

"How bad is it?" she asked without preamble.

"Gloria, the receptionist," Segal said.

Dinah closed her eyes. "Oh, no."

He noticed Guilford. "I see you brought our buddy."

Dinah turned to see Jerome Guilford talking outside the tape with two other men, one burly and one slender. Then he ducked under and came striding up. He grinned, extending his hand to Dinah. "Congratulations on your victory tonight," he said.

Dinah gave him a stone face.

"We can talk roller derby some other time. We have a homicide here," Segal said.

One of the crime scene techs came up to Segal. "We checked the security cameras and alarms. Both disabled. Either it was a professional job or someone who knew the system."

"Yes, I believe the last time we talked, you explained how you were not convinced Francis Elah was much of a threat to anyone," Guilford said, shifting his grinning countenance to Segal. "I guess he would have known how to disable the security system in his own lab."

Segal decided not to rise to the bait. He led them into the building, where they could observe for themselves.

Guilford brushed past him and began visually scouring the room before stopping at the body on the floor. "Any bullets recovered?" he asked the tech.

The tech twitched his nose as if wondering who the hell he was. Segal nodded that it was okay to talk to this guy. The tech held up an evidence bag with the bullet recovered from the wall.

Guilford asked Segal, "Anything missing?"

Segal hesitated, deciding not to share his suspicion that the crow cameras might be gone. After all, he was not supposed to know about the cameras in the first place. "We're not sure yet. We've got one of the staff coming in to check for what's missing. Or not missing."

"Let me know," Guilford said. "And try to take better care of this one. This place is running out of people." He scratched his hair, finger-combed it into place.

Segal thought about the two men he had seen Jerome Guilford talking to when he came in. "Guilford, were any of your people watching this place?"

"What?" Guilford paused with his hair.

"You've been searching for Francis Elah. I thought maybe you'd have this building under surveillance. Maybe your guys might have seen something useful," Segal said.

Guilford stood up straighter. "We are not in the habit of disclosing the whereabouts of federal agents."

Segal watched him walk away, brown shoes shining as good in the car lights as they had in the office.

"How's that for a non-denial denial?" Dinah asked.

"Did you tell him about this?"

"No," Dinah said.

"Me neither. That means someone else told him. Like maybe one of his own guys. Either that or they're monitoring the dispatch calls. They probably monitor everything."

"I don't like him," Dinah said.

"I don't like him either," Segal said.

They continued to watch as Guilford ducked under the police tape like a boxer leaving the ring. As he did this, they saw a woman approach. It was Lucile Devroe. She was stopped at the tape barricade by a uniformed officer, who spoke to her. Segal caught his eye and motioned for him to let her through. Dinah raised her eyebrows.

"Back at the civic center, I might have mentioned I was coming here," he said. He let the statement, in all its lameness, go at that.

"No one will tell me what's going on," Lucile said when she reached them. She surprised Segal by putting her arms around him and laying her head on his shoulder.

Segal returned the embrace.

Dinah was astute where Segal was concerned. She saw something working in his eyes, a smoky intelligence few else could read. The smoke was low. He was troubled, or tired; a sign that she had better take over. "Miss Devroe? Did you know Gloria Harden?" she asked.

Lucile pulled her head off Segal's shoulder. "Did something happen to Gloria?"

Segal's eyes went cold. She fell into him again, and Dinah wondered if it was a bit too dramatic.

"Listen, Lucile, it's really not a good idea for you to be here right now." Dinah pictured the spectacle of the body being wheeled out on a stretcher, which for many people was the most disturbing vision in an incident like this. She also thought of reporters showing up.

Lucile stood upright and wheezed out a breath, her face drained of color. "Do you think I'm in danger?" she asked.

Segal opened his mouth, closed it.

Dinah filled in the gap. She explained that it was true, after all, that people who worked with Francis Elah were not doing well lately. And although Lucile was not an employee of Creatures 2.0, all had to be cautious who were dealing with the company.

"I don't want to go home, at least not right now," Lucile said in a hushed tone.

Dinah spoke up. "Lieutenant, let me suggest you take Miss Devroe someplace where she will feel safe. I can stay and oversee things here." Segal started to protest, but Dinah gave him a look of assurance. "I'll call you when Lewis gets here. Meanwhile, the scene is in the hands of the techs. It will be all right. There's not much to do until Lewis is found."

Segal nodded and led Lucile away.

CHAPTER 17

Rules of Recovery

Segal emerged from sleep, called forth by a sound. He left the nether world with a dichotomous range of reluctance and also a profound sense of contentment. The contentment arose from a cellular level, or maybe someplace even deeper. The sensation calmed him as he had not been calmed in a long time.

He could tell from the level of light that it was still night, but past that he had no sense of what time it was. The covers were warm, the bed infinitely comfortable, and he felt no impulse to move. Then the message tone on his phone sounded—the low beat of African drums—and he realized a similar tone had called him from sleep.

He slipped out of bed and walked to the kitchen of his apartment, where the phone was charging. He did have a text. It was from Dinah, who had taken charge of the operation and waited for Lewis Abraham to surface. The message on his phone read, "Found Lewis, on his way here now."

Good, he thought. *Wonder where the hell he's been.* He looked at the time on the phone. It was 3:45 A.M. His eyes drifted to the little corkboard on the wall. A page torn from a memo pad was secured there by a thumbtack. Written across the top of the pad in perfect script was a list penned by his therapist:

Dr. Gold's Rules for Speedy Recovery
Get plenty of sleep
Limit consumption of caffeine
Do not identify closely with crime victims
or anyone else involved with police cases

He looked at his cell's clock, which had advanced to 3:46 A.M. He needed to go in and help Dinah and would not sleep anymore this night. *Check.* The smell of coffee seemed eminent. He wondered when Vortex Doughnuts opened. *Check.*

He peered down the hall toward the bed, where Lucile Devroe slept like an angel, one arm extended above her head in a pose from a Renaissance painting. *Double-check.*

It had started earlier that night at the crime scene with Lucile's vulnerability and fear and the death of Chickey and now Gloria, two of her friends and former colleagues, killed in the span of two days.

But no, he thought. In reality, it had started from the instant he laid eyes on her at Biltmore. As Dr. Gold would say, *we know.* That is, Segal clarified in his own head, we sometimes know everything we need to know just by looking at another person. We see, but we pretend we don't and move though life powered by the stories we make up. *Well*, Segal thought, *there's nothing like death to push aside pretense and make us look at reality.*

Lucile had said she didn't want to spend the night at home alone. That was partly emotional, partly practical, too. Once in his car, they drove straight to his apartment with no discussion. Once there, he got as far as getting a cover and pillow for himself to use on the couch, but when he found Lucile in his bedroom, her cotton dress had dropped to the floor, and a second later she was in his arms. It was the end of pretense between them, and the couch had not been needed.

The hell with it, he thought. So far, his recovery had not been all that speedy. Besides, Dr. Gold had also advised him on the importance of relationships, citing studies that showed a strong correlation between happiness and close ties with other people. Didn't matter. He'd needed Lucile and she'd needed him.

He dressed quickly and silently, wrote Lucile a note, tore it up, and wrote another, more intimate. He started to pick up his coat and thought about the paperback in the pocket. *Sure, as hell don't need* The Great Gatsby *right now,* he thought, meaning he did not need a story about an obsessive love affair that went tragically wrong, including the death of an innocent woman tangential to the main conflict. He removed it and went to the small bookcase on the wall. "The *Great One,*" he whispered under his breath. He pulled Elmore Leonard's *Freaky Deaky* off the shelf and smiled. He recalled that the plot included a detective falling in love with a girl involved in a complex crime. As usual with the *Great One,* the story ended with everyone getting exactly what they deserved, although Segal could not immediately remember exactly what that was.

He managed to get out the door without waking Lucile. He took the soundness of her sleep to be a good sign. No doubt, she deserved it as much as he did.

He rolled up at Creatures 2.0 a little after four. The crime-scene tape was still in place. That and a single squad car were all that remained of the outwardly visible police presence. He walked to the front door and thought how quickly the world moved on, how for most people, even those who knew the victim, the events of last night would be a bump in the road from which they would quickly recover. They would go on with their rhythm of meals and work and coming and going. Gloria would not. *That's the way of the world*, Segal thought. *But not for us.* He knew that for himself and Dinah, there would be no moving forward until they resolved this. He wanted renewed stakes in the game, and this was the game.

He went through the lobby and checked beside the desk where the body had been. It was clean. There was no chalk outline on the floor and no requirement for one in the age of digital photography. It occurred to him to find out what had kept Gloria working so late. However, there was little on the desk, and when he tapped on the computer's keyboard, he found he needed a password to log on. Voices came from the lab and he moved toward them.

Lewis wore a tuxedo, minus the tie. He stood hunched, searching through a filing cabinet. Dinah sat on a stool at one of the lab benches with a small notebook. She used her pen in a lazy fashion, he assumed drawing pictures on the page opposite her latest notes, a habit she had picked up from him. That and the habit of writing down short bursts of first impressions. His notebooks were like illustrated haiku, more triggers for discussion later rather than recordings of fact. Both acknowledged him by pausing their tasks. Dinah winked. Lewis resumed with the file cabinet.

"You're making me feel underdressed tonight, Lewis," Segal said.

"Seems while we pursued the lowly sport of roller derby, Mr. Abraham here focused on more refined arts," Dinah said.

"I happened to be at the opera," Lewis said low key.

He's trying to make it sound unpretentious. Segal raised his eyebrows.

"What? A black man can't go to the opera?" Lewis asked.

True, it was easier to picture Lewis at the Orange Peel or one of the other music venues downtown than the opera, yet Segal was not about to admit that. "And the opera lasts till three in the morning?" he asked.

His fingers continued to work through the file drawer. "I've been over this with the sergeant here. I met someone there, a lady, and we spent some time together after the performance. She and I both would be in a world of trouble if it came out, if you know what I mean. I really don't want to involve her in this unless it's absolutely necessary."

Segal could relate.

"You may already be in a world of trouble, Lewis. I don't know if you noticed, but two of your coworkers were killed in the last two days. A third is missing."

"Yeah, I noticed," Lewis said. "I came in as soon as I got the message. Your sergeant here asked me to see if anything is missing. That's what I'm doing."

"Do you know what Gloria was doing here so late?" he asked. "It looked like she was working on something out there. I didn't see anything on the desk."

"Yeah, I noticed that, too," Lewis said. "That's what I was checking the file for. She was consolidating all the documents related to Richard, his training, habits, flight patterns, feeding rituals. Some of it was already in the computer system. Most of it though was in hard copy here in the files. She was supposed to scan any hard copies we had. It was a big pile. Not sure how far she got. I'm looking in here. No Richard documents. That means she could have taken them all out, but then, like you said, I didn't see any around her desk either."

Dinah scribbled in her notebook.

Fast this time. She's penning impressions. Good. "Anything else missing?"

"The crow cam's gone," Lewis said.

"You mean the government one or the new and improved version you and Francis made?" Dinah asked.

"The old one, government issue," Lewis said.

"The new one's still here, then? It wasn't taken?" Segal asked.

"Not exactly."

Segal waited. Dinah paused.

He exhaled sharply, then confessed. "I put it on, Richard. When he was here. Earlier today."

"You what?" Dinah narrowed her eyes.

"Why'd you do that, Lewis?" Segal asked. Heat filled his chest. He was surprised and exasperated. It was one more way the events in this case seemed to be spinning out of his control. What was Lewis up to?

Lewis huffed in a breath. He stood upright, cheeks holding air before he let it out. "You want to find Francis. And I sure as hell want to find Francis. I mean, I'm left here all alone dealing with this stuff. The cam was here, so I figured, why not? Maybe we get lucky. Maybe we learn something."

Dinah raised an eyebrow.

Segal had to wrestle with it. He inhaled and exhaled. "You know what, Lewis? That might be a good idea. What do you think, Dinah?"

"Good."

"That might be the best idea any of us has had all day."

Dinah returned to drawing, slow lazy strokes. "Only next time you have a great idea like this, Lewis, check with us first."

CHAPTER 18

Like a Rolling Stone

The predawn light filtered through the big windows of the lab. Segal looked at his watch. "There goes the night," he said.

Lewis was gone. Segal considered their next move.

"How is Lucile Devroe?" Dinah asked. "Did you get her settled down and find her a safe place to stay last night?"

"Uh, yeah. She's okay, she's safe," Segal said, a little too quickly. He felt the overwhelming need to take a drink of coffee.

Dinah watched his face for a moment. "Oh, brother. I'm not even going to ask."

Segal avoided her eyes, thinking about what to say, then realizing there was nothing he could say, nothing he needed to say. Dinah probably understood this stuff better than he understood himself.

"So where is she going to be today?" Dinah asked.

"She'll be out at Biltmore at work. She should be okay there. Later, she's got a movie shoot. She's supposed to do something with her own trained crows. I think it would be good to be there. She said it's a vampire movie."

"I may have met the director of that movie at a party a couple of weeks ago," Dinah said. "Maybe I'll touch base with him before we go out."

"I'll check in with Emily Elah. Let her know about Gloria. See if she's heard anything else," Segal said. He walked over to the windows. The air held a light mist as it so often did in the early morning hours in the mountains. The light bore scant color; everything was gray.

"Might be worth a look around outside now that there's some light. I know the guys checked it out with flashlights. Tough in the dark."

Dinah slid off the stool she was perched on and followed him to the door. Segal could tell by the way she moved that she was hitting a wall of exhaustion. She had worked yesterday, skated in the Roller Derby, and then stayed up all night managing the crime scene.

"Why don't you head home and get some rest," he said. "I already got some myself."

A grin crept onto Dinah's face. "Did you, Segal? Did you really get some? Rest, that is?"

Segal started to say something.

Dinah held up her hand. "It's OK. I'll just patrol with you a little and then go home and grab a couple hours sack time."

Outside everything was damp from the mist and the heavy dew. They took a couple of steps on the soft ground and Segal held up his arm to signal a stop while they scanned for footprints. But the grass was too thick and, in any case, if they spotted a print they wouldn't know if it belonged to the assassin or one of their own officers who had been out last night.

Segal heard a rustling in the tree branches ahead and ducked as if he might be dive-bombed by a crow. But it was just a couple of chickadees and a nuthatch at a feeder that hung nearby. Segal glanced at Dinah to see if she noticed how jumpy he was.

The first trees they came to were white pines with a carpet of brown needles on the ground beneath them. Here and there were decaying stumps of ancient hemlocks which had died and made way for this new growth. Between the trees and stumps, Segal could make out a slight path leading uphill. And there on the brown pine needles was a knife, a combat knife, loose in its scabbard with a little glint of blade shining out.

Segal approached and bent down for a closer look. Dinah's hand went to her pocket.

"Damn, I don't have any gloves," she said.

Segal stood up and thought in silence for a moment. "They'll be back for it," he said. It was the first thought that jumped into his mind, and then he worked out why it must be so. "They'll realize it's gone and come back for it. If it's the kind of professional outfit we think it is, they'll have to. They can't leave something like this behind. Probably has fingerprints and maybe even other ID. They'll come soon, at first light." He was thinking about leaving it as bait in a trap.

"Sooner than you think, Segal," Dinah whispered. She was facing up the path and drawing her gun at the same time. Segal saw a figure outlined in the mist, forty yards up the hill above them. He felt a flood of adrenaline as he reached for his gun, too. Dinah raised hers.

"Police," she yelled. "Hands up where we can see them. Now!"

The figure made no sudden movement which would have ignited an immediate response from Dinah's gun. Instead, he made a calm underhand pitching motion and stepped off the path and out of their view. Segal stood amazed for a moment. He heard a thud and then saw a dark object bouncing and rolling down the steep path toward them.

"Grenade!" Dinah yelled.

Segal felt her yank his sleeve and pull him to the side of the path before diving with him behind one of the huge hemlock stumps.

He heard the grenade roll a little way past and he had time to count to four before the blast and the sound of shrapnel slamming into the trees around them and into the dense damp wood of the hemlock stump. The blast seemed to shatter his eardrums. *The stump saved us.* By the time he dared put his head up, he saw the man running downhill and skidding to a stop to pick up the knife, before running back up the hill. He moved with impressive speed for someone his size.

Dinah jumped up to give chase, but Segal said, "No, this way." He pointed into the woods at right angles to the path. "There's nothing up that way but there's a side street over here. They must have a car waiting there."

Dinah took off running but then slowed to wait for Segal as he caught up.

"Go ahead," he yelled. "I'll be right behind you."

She took off, bobbing and weaving around trees and ducking low branches. Just as Segal had said, in a hundred yards or so she emerged onto a side street he could barely make out. She pulled back a little into the cover of the trees. Segal caught up to her, panting from the run. A van pulled up and stopped a little uphill from them and their man came trotting out of the woods toward it.

She stepped out and took careful aim. "Stop! Police!" she yelled.

The man reached the van and slid open the side door. He turned at her voice, and this time his hand went quickly to his waist as if to draw a gun of his own.

Dinah did not hesitate. She fired at the center of the man's body and he was knocked backward. He fell partly into the open door and Segal could see the hands of another person inside pulling him the rest of the way in. The door slid shut and the van screeched off. Dinah kept her pistol trained on the vehicle but there were houses across the street from it now and Segal knew they dared not fire.

Dinah pulled out her cell phone. "We need assistance. Shots fired. We're on—what the hell street is this, Segal?" Segal told her but by that time a siren blared and flashing lights approached. "Never mind," she said into the phone. "A car's coming. They must have heard the blast."

The police car screeched to a halt.

Segal pulled his badge out. He ran toward them with its face in full view. "We need you to secure the site behind the lab building," he shouted to the officers who got out. One leaned in and shut off the siren. Segal quickly described the location in more detail and what to look for. "And we need your car," he said.

The two officers looked at each other.

"It's OK," Dinah said. "We'll take good care of it."

"Siren or no siren?" Segal asked as he jumped behind the wheel.

"No siren," Dinah said. "No use telling them exactly where we are."

"Right. I'm taking a shortcut to Charlotte Street, maybe make up time on them." Segal was thinking his knowledge of the city might well be his only advantage in this chase. He careened onto Charlotte Street and turned left toward downtown. It was still very early so the street was nearly deserted. Segal drove like a werewolf.

"Up there, Segal. Turning right," Dinah yelled.

He caught a glimpse of the van turning onto a side street. Segal sped up even more and screeched around the turn onto the same side street.

"I never saw you drive like this, Segal," Dinah said.

"No one ever threw a hand grenade at me before." Segal did not let up. "We're going to get these guys." The side street went level for a way, then angled down, allowing the van to disappear from Segal's sight. By the time he came to the downhill slope, he caught the van turning left onto the next large street.

"Left turn," Dinah said. "Headed for the center of town. I expected them to jump onto the highway."

Segal cursed under his breath. "What the hell are they doing?" At the bottom of the hill, he paused for a garbage truck rolling ponderously by. When he got going, the van was out of sight. A few blocks farther on was another highway entrance.

"Highway or downtown?" Dinah asked.

"I say downtown. If they wanted the highway they would have stayed on the other street."

Segal followed the road under the highway and into the main downtown section of Asheville. There was no way to know for sure which way they went so he went straight, slowing at intersections so Dinah could check the side streets. They still had the roads to themselves, except for a few trucks making early morning deliveries to restaurants and bars.

Dinah yelled, "Stop," at the intersection with Walnut Street.

"They're trapped," Segal said, angling the police cruiser to block the street.

From where Segal sat at the intersection, Walnut Street ran up a steep hill to their right. At the next intersection, at the top of that hill sat a stake bed truck, like a farm truck used to move bales of hay. But instead of bales of hay, this truck was loaded with kegs of beer from one of the local microbreweries. It blocked the narrow street. Below this, the van was pulled off to the left into the exit space of a parking garage.

"That is our van, isn't it?" Segal said.

Dinah nodded. She was on her phone calling for backup.

He watched for a moment to see what the van would do. No movement. He made a decision, turned the engine off. "Let's go." Opening his car door, he slowly eased out, drew his gun. Dinah followed.

He heard a door open but could not see what was going on. They each ducked for cover on opposite sides of the street expecting the guy to come around the other side of the van shooting.

Instead, a man took a few strides up the hill, then vaulted up onto the bed of the beer truck and opened the back gate. At first, Segal was confused, thinking the driver was about to make a delivery. Then the man took out a combat knife and cut the nylon strap securing the kegs tilted inside the truck bed. Slowly, the kegs tipped and rolled off the truck. In seconds an avalanche formed. The street swelled with runaway beer kegs, jumping, colliding as they crashed down the steep pavement picking up momentum.

"Look out, Dinah," he yelled, but she was way ahead of him. She had pressed herself into a doorway, and Segal did likewise on his side of the street. He watched helplessly as the lethal metal cylinders careened by, slamming into their borrowed car. Each time Segal tried to lean out another hundred-and-thirty-pound missile came rolling and bouncing by.

The first one to hit the cruiser demolished the right front panel and set off the airbags. The second hit front center, breaking the radiator and creating a fountain of coolant. The third and fourth bounced on one of the others and caved in the windshield, landing in the front seat as the others piled on.

When Segal sensed that the last keg had come to rest, he emerged to look around. The van was still there, just off the street, but the driver's door stood open now. Segal suspected they had abandoned ship. He was about to say as much when

Dinah jerked her finger into the air at the steep side road and yelled, "The truck."

As a last measure, the guy had apparently released the parking brake and the truck was rolling backward fast, a speedball of steel streaking toward them.

Segal screamed and Dinah jumped. The truck ran up over the cruiser, completely flattening the roof, wheels spinning, fender busted, smoke curdling the carriage as it ended up at rest on top of the borrowed police car.

Sirens and lights announced the arrival of the backup Dinah had called for.

Segal approached the van, Dinah and the backup officers by his side, pistols aimed. He was not hopeful. The van was empty.

"You think they prearranged changing vehicles?" Dinah asked.

"That would be my guess," Segal said, rubbing dust from his eyes. "Or at least it was arranged as a contingency. They could have planted a car in the garage here. Or else met someone up the hill on Haywood Street."

Segal peered into the empty shell of the van. He would have the forensic techs go over it but had little hope of finding anything useful.

"There's no blood that I can see," Segal said. He was checking out the side door which was where the man had fallen when Dinah shot him. "I know you hit him."

"Must have had a vest on," Dinah said.

"He's gonna be pretty sore and pissed off," one of the backup officers said.

"Yeah, well I'm a little sore and pissed off myself," Dinah answered.

The scene was beginning to draw a crowd, more police cars, civilians, and a reporter. Segal's boss rounded the corner, trudging up the hill toward them. Segal groaned. Meanwhile, the two patrolmen were dropped off by their crashed and flattened cruiser. Segal saw one of them reach in and pull something out. It was a lunch box flattened almost as much as the car.

Segal gave Dinah a one-sided grin.

"You want to talk to the chief or those two patrolmen?" Dinah asked.

"Oh, I'll take the chief," Segal said. Dinah appeared to put on a game face and headed toward the men by the wrecked car.

CHAPTER 19

Nature Center

Segal drove across the bridge over the Swannanoa River, glancing at shallow ripples above a sandy bottom. It was soothing, and he could use a little soothing after what he and Dinah had just been through. He drove past the public swimming pool and up the hill to the entrance of the Western North Carolina Nature Center. It was a long time since he'd been there, well before the troubled time in his life, and he found himself wanting to see the animals again—normal creatures, not the ones trained by Francis Elah, and not ones wrapped up in the murder case and maybe more.

Inside the entrance, people waited in line to pay the fee, an operation that was apparently hugely complex. Segal flashed his badge at the person by the door. After considerable squinting on the door guard's part and an assurance by Segal that he was there on official business, he was motioned through.

After a step, he pivoted toward the guard. "Did you happen to see a lady with a girl in a wheelchair?"

"You mean Mrs. Elah and Suzie? They should be down by the barnyard area by now, or close to it. They volunteer with some of the farm animals."

Segal passed the reptile house. Following the path down the hill, he passed the river otters. Two were in the water and a third lounged on a rock in the sun, licking its webbed paw. Segal watched the otter glance at him, then resume licking its paw. Segal sighed. He realized he could well be reading too much into the facial expressions of animals now. He walked on and came to a sign. The cats and wolves were on the trails that forked up the hill. The deer, bears, and farm animals were on the lower path.

He followed the path that led down the hill. This soon took him onto a wooden boardwalk high above the fenced area below. In the first of the enclosures, he saw half a dozen white-tailed deer grazing in a sunny area. He remembered Lucile Devroe's pictures and noted that the ears really were much smaller than the mule deer's. He moved to the second enclosure and searched high and wide before he saw a massive black bear pacing a worn path in the grass under a sparse grove of poplar trees. Generally, pacing seemed like a pathological response to confinement. In this case, Segal had the sense that the bear expected something to happen.

He wasn't sure where his intuition stopped and magical thinking took over.

A group of people came up on his right. One of them asked if it was feeding time, and Segal heard a voice from his left. "Yes, the attendant will be here in a minute."

He turned to see Emily Elah pushing her daughter up in her wheelchair. They both wore dark blue wide-brimmed hats and tilted their heads to see him. The little girl seemed radiantly happy. Emily smiled toward the bear. "You should watch this, lieutenant. I think you'll like it, and I think it will give you a better idea of what kind of work my husband does."

Below, the bear paced. He was also swinging his big head side to side, sometimes at the platform where Segal stood and other times at the steep wall of the enclosure against the side of the hill. After a minute or so, one of the park attendants appeared at the top of the back wall carrying a five-gallon bucket, which she set down beside her. As soon as she appeared, the bear stood on his hind legs and pointed at his wrist.

"What's he doing?" Segal asked.

"It's a wristwatch," Emily Elah said.

It was a perfect pantomime of a cranky man pointing to his watch to complain about his companion being late for a lunch date. The park ranger made a big production of apologizing, then lowered the food. Surprisingly, the bear waited for the bucket to reach the ground before he sat, pulled the bucket between his outstretched legs, and began to eat out of it. He put the food in his mouth with enjoyment and interest but without any savage hurry. The scene reminded Segal of a fat boy at a family picnic. After the bear ate most of the food, he grasped the bucket between his two paws and tipped it to his mouth, presumably to get the last morsels.

"And your husband, Francis, he taught the bear to do that?" Segal asked.

"It only took him a few days," she said, still watching the animal.

"Amazing."

"That's what I said, but Francis just shrugged it off and said the bear was highly motivated by food."

"Still . . ."

Emily nodded. "That's the last time they let him work with any of the animals here. Something about not respecting the dignity of the wildlife. Personally, I think he respects the animals more than anyone."

Segal returned his attention to the bear, who licked his lips and muzzle with a circular motion of his tongue before returning to all fours to check the surrounding terrain for any stray scraps. Emily had said this would help him understand her husband. Segal had trouble drawing any specific inferences from the bear with the wristwatch. It was difficult for him to imagine the man who did something this whimsical, suddenly transforming into the stone-cold killer ONI presented him to be. An image of Guilford with his snotty nose and tissues and perfect brown shoes flashed into his mind.

"Do you want to come with us? It's time for Suzie to feed the goats," Emily said.

Segal followed them down the ramp toward the barnyard area. Suzie turned her head to watch the bear as long as possible. Her face was a tiny moon beneath her hat. Segal followed suit. The bear was seated, his back propped against a tree, the picture of contentment. If there had been a couch and a TV with a football game on, the bear would have qualified for the American Male of the Year Award.

After a couple of minutes, the barnyard came into view. Emily got a bucket of feed from inside a shed. She hefted the feed over to the side of the fence, put the bucket on the ground and positioned Suzie's chair against the fence so she could feed the goats from the palm of her hand. Emily withdrew a few steps. Segal did the same. He watched the girl feed the goats, listened as she talked to them in a soothing voice.

"I don't suppose you came out here to feed goats and bears today, lieutenant," Emily said. Her dark blue hat tilted dramatically over one eye.

Segal cleared his throat. He told Emily the latest bad news from Creatures 2.0, about Gloria. Emily inhaled sharply, cupping her hands over her nose and mouth, and turned away. Segal realized the little girl had stopped talking. He saw she was watching them. He smiled at her and thought again, Suzie was not to be taken for granted. Suzie resumed feeding the goats.

Emily put her hand on Segal's arm. "What's going on?" she asked in a hushed voice.

"I was hoping maybe you could shed some light on that."

"What do you mean?" she asked, louder.

Suzie let the food fall from her hand. The goats nudged her wrist.

Segal walked a few steps with Emily.

"You can see the implications here," he said. "Charles Atley is killed. We don't know if it was some random event or what. Now, someone else from Creatures 2.0 is dead, murdered, and in the lab on top of that. I have to rule out the random element and focus on the connections with Francis, or at least with his work." Segal kept his voice low and calm, and when he checked on Suzie in his peripheral vision, she was giggling, feeding the goats. He chose not to elaborate on the truck and van adventures of the morning.

Emily shook her head. "I don't know," she said. "I really don't get involved with Francis's work. I can't think why anyone would kill Gloria. Especially Gloria. She was a receptionist and secretary. I don't think she was involved with the projects, other than working on notes and reports."

"Well, it's possible she was simply in the wrong place at the wrong time. We think someone broke in, possibly to steal something valuable, something they knew was inside—not a random theft—and she walked into the middle of it."

Emily clutched his arm. "Are we in danger? Is Suzie in danger?"

"If what you say is right, I doubt it. If this has something to do with Creatures 2.0, and if you don't know anything, then I would say you're probably in the clear. On the other hand, I would be careful if I were you. Please call me if you see anything strange. In any case, we're putting more protection for you at the Grove Arcade."

Emily took a deep breath.

"The other issue is Francis. You haven't heard from him since we talked last, have you?" Segal asked.

"I haven't seen or heard from him. I can't seem to convince your friend from ONI of that."

Segal started to ask her about Jerome Guilford but paused when Suzie spoke up. "I did. Daddy visited me," she said. She never took her eyes off the goats. "He hugged me and kissed my head."

Segal crossed his arms in front of him, gently shrugging off Emily's vice grip. "When did he visit you?"

"Last night. When Mommy was at the roller derby." The tone of her voice was matter-of-fact. Segal couldn't tell if she was describing something that happened in real-time or a dream of what she wanted to happen. Emily shrugged. Without his arm to lean on, she seemed to readjust and push her hat until both of her eyes were shaded.

CHAPTER 20

Vampire Movie

"Tell me again, what this film is about?" Dinah asked.

The young man leaned across the table in the chocolate lounge on Pack Square. He darted his head side to side, swung in his chair toward the rear of the lounge, twisted with a grimace, and brushed a dark shock of hair from his left eye. Taking in a troubled breath, he paused and spread his hands and bowed his head.

"Okay, there's this vampire loose in Asheville," he said.

"Yup."

"I mean scary."

"Yup." Dinah let him talk. She sipped her coffee during the preamble. *Let it be his show.* After three minutes she set her empty cup down and mouthed to the waitress for more coffee. She raised a forefinger to interrupt. "I read someplace vampires are out of vogue."

"Some people say that. But vampires are always in. There are just different parts of the vampire cycle. See, we had traditional vampires going back to Bela Lugosi. Then came Anne Rice. That was a reinterpretation of the vampire—*The Vampire Lestat*, for instance—where the vampire is the protagonist. That opened the door to the whole teenage vampire craze that turned on the coming-of-age/sexual development themes."

"You mean like the vampire versus werewolf stuff?" Dinah asked.

The young director nodded.

"You're doing something like *I Was a Teenage Vampire*?"

"No. Definitely not."

"Okay. Explain."

"We're going into the next phase. That phase explores historical figures as vampires." He pushed the dark shock of hair from his eyebrows.

"You mean like *Abraham Lincoln: Vampire Hunter*?"

"Yeah, and *Pride and Prejudice and Zombies*," he said. "Only those two were kind of tongue-in-cheek, making fun of the genre. This film is more serious and brings the sexual element back—which, in my opinion, why do vampire without the sexual element? For that matter, why do any movie without a sexual element?"

"And who is the historical figure?"

"Thomas Wolfe." The director smiled and took a drink of his coffee and a bite of chocolate biscotti. He crunched loudly.

"Thomas Wolfe? Our Thomas Wolfe, the writer?"

"Yeah. The working title is *Look Homeward, Vampire*."

More biscotti. More crunching.

Dinah let it soak in. It never ceased to amaze her what people could get funding for. The director told her he had investors—six million, which apparently was peanuts for movie making. She summarized. "Dracula comes to Asheville, huh?"

"Sooner or later, everyone comes to Asheville," the director said. "Starts with a mysterious visitor coming to his mother's boarding house."

Dinah let the conversation drift among the details of the making of the film—camera angles, lighting, shooting schedules. Directors loved that kind of shop talk. One of Dinah's teammates on the Blue Ridge Roller Girls was a friend of the director's, which was how Dinah made contact with him. The teammate was also in the movie, one of the many girls to fall victim to the vampire Thomas Wolfe.

"Tell me about the shoot you're doing this evening," Dinah said, steering the conversation.

"It's set in Riverside Cemetery—you know, the one off Montford Avenue." He was talking about a place a mile or so from where they sat. "In this scene, Thomas Wolfe kills a publisher who's figured out that he, Wolfe, is a vampire. Wolfe lures him there and sucks his blood, and I mean all his blood. He doesn't leave enough for the guy to become one of the undead. He's totally dead."

"I've heard the publishing business can be tough," Dinah said. "Is that where the crows come in?"

"Yeah, after Thomas Wolfe drains all the blood out of the publisher, he drops him on the ground, and a bunch of crows come to eat up what's left, to make sure the guy is totally gone."

"That would take a lot of crows."

"There are only going to be a few. I get a shot of the publisher lying on the ground. He's white because all his blood is gone. Then I get a shot of Thomas Wolfe looking up at the sky, probably yelling and holding up his hands like this." The director demonstrated.

"Like he's calling the crows?"

"Exactly. Like he's calling his friends, the crows, from the underworld or wherever. Then we get multiple shots of crows flying and landing among the gravestones. When I edit all those together, it looks like a hundred crows rocketed toward the earth and ate the guy."

"How does the scene end?"

The director made a dismissive gesture. "Easy. I replace the publisher with a fake skeleton sprawled on the ground, and by the time I piece it all together, you think you saw a guy get eaten by crows. Cue dramatic music. Wolfe exits stage left, drunk on the blood of a publisher."

"So, that's how the director knows Lucile Devroe," Segal said. He was riding in Dinah's car through downtown toward Riverside Cemetery later that afternoon. Dinah had filled him in on her conversation with the kid director.

"Right," Dinah said. "Originally, the director contracted Francis to work animals for the movie. Apparently, Francis did a lot of that. Movie people love him because he can get good performances out of almost any animal. Francis called him at some point and said Lucile would be standing in for him, but the director didn't know why, nor does he have any idea how to get in touch with Francis now."

Segal nodded.

"He didn't seem upset about it. He said Lucile was really good," Dinah said. "In fact, he's trying to talk her into taking a part in the movie herself."

Segal pictured the lines of Lucile's neck with her head bent in a vulnerable position. "Is she going to do it?"

"She's thinking about it. In the meantime, she's bringing some crows for the shoot today."

Dinah pulled up to the entrance of the cemetery, where a guard let them through after seeing their IDs. She wove through the park-like setting of huge oaks and maples, past markers and mausoleums of classical design. It didn't take long to find the film crew. A man with an expensive-looking camera was getting shots of the inscription on the Wolfe grave marker: *Tom, son of W. O. and Julia E. Wolfe: A Beloved American Author.*

A large man, presumably the actor playing the vampire Wolfe, sat in a folding chair while a girl worked on his makeup. Several other people milled around; some occupied, most not so much. One guy sat on the tailgate of a pickup pretending to share a cigarette with the fake skeleton. In the back of the pickup were four cages with dark bird shapes inside. On the other side of the truck was Lucile. She was feeding the crows little pieces of bread, which she tore off a baguette. When Segal came on the scene, she winked at him.

Dinah cleared her throat. "Nice," she said.

The director spoke up. "Lucile, we're ready for the birds."

Lucile opened the latches on the cages, and one by one the birds hopped out and perched on the side of the pickup's bed. "What are we doing first?" she asked.

"Let's do the high stuff first," he said. "I like the way the branches are contrasted against the sky."

Lucile put a whistle in her mouth, gave a short tweet, made a quick gesture with her hand and wrist, then pointed. The birds took off and flew into the branches of an oak tree nearby. One of the highest branches was dead, and that was where they chose to alight.

"That's beautiful," the director said.

Segal went to her side.

The camera crew filmed. Segal assumed it was hard to tell what shots might be useful in the final editing. Lucile called the birds back with whistle and gesture, and they repeated the assent to the tree several times. On one of the descents, the director moved the cameraman close to the truck, so it would look to viewers like the birds were diving right at them. Lucile spread some treats on the ground behind a grave marker and got several sequences of birds descending to that place.

"That's to set up the skeleton scene," Dinah said.

Segal grinned. Sometimes, he wondered what was going on inside his partner's head. Sure enough, the director yelled out, "Skeleton!"

The guy smoking on the tailgate of the pickup tossed his cigarette butt to the side and wheeled the skeleton, still hanging from its rack, across the grass. Aided by a couple of others, the guy gently removed the skeleton from the rack and arranged it on the ground. The makeup lady came over with a wig that matched the hair of the publisher.

"Looks like they want to give the skeleton the personal touch," Dinah said.

"This is supposed to be one of the big scenes, one of the turning points of the movie. They want it to be shocking, so they have to get it right," Lucile said.

Segal felt his heart speed up. Lucile petted and calmed the birds, particularly the leader. This was the most important bird. If she could make the leader feel calm and follow directions, the rest of the flock would follow its example.

The director and the cinematographer spent a lot of time arranging and rearranging the skeleton on the ground. When they finally got it positioned to their satisfaction, they took several shots from different angles.

"Okay, Lucile," the director called, "time to drop the birds on the skeleton."

Lucile gave the birds a hand signal telling them to stay while she walked over and stood near the skeleton. "Very lifelike," she said. "Or should I say, very deathlike."

The cinematographer smiled. "I like the white bones against the dark green grass."

Lucile sprinkled some feed pellets among the bones, concentrating on the rib cage and the eye sockets.

"Excellent," the director said. "We'll get the crows coming in, then we'll need footage of them pecking the hell out of the skeleton. Then I need them to take off all at once. Can we do that?"

"Let me know when you're ready," Lucile said.

They quickly got two cameras set up, and the director yelled, "Action!"

Lucile blew the whistle, and the birds rose back to the tree branch. She blew it again and pointed to the skeleton. They flew down in a flurry and fed voraciously among the bones.

"We can speed this up and make it look even better," the cinematographer said, not taking his eyes off the camera viewer.

After a minute, Lucile spoke up. "I think the food is running low. Are you ready for them to take off?"

The cinematographer adjusted one of the cameras for a wider shot. "Put the spurs to them, Lucile," he said.

She raised the whistle to her mouth and made a rising and falling tweet, followed by a short blast. The lead crow rose, followed a split second later by the others. The camera crew closed in. When the crows alighted on the dead branch, the lead crow raised its beak and let out a squawk. Immediately, a gunshot exploded.

Segal ducked out of instinct. "Dinah," he shouted.

She already had her pistol out. After a second, three more shots followed in rapid succession.

"Everyone down!" Segal yelled. He drew his sidearm. The command was hardly necessary, as everyone had flattened into the grass—everyone but Lucile, who was looking up toward the tree branches for her crows. Segal put a hand on her shoulder and guided her lower.

"Segal, the shots came from downhill. I'm going down," Dinah said.

"Right behind you," Segal said. "Stay down and call 911," he whispered to Lucile, then turned to follow his partner, running in a crouch.

Ahead, he saw her moving with the same grace she displayed on the skating track—probably the same tactics she had used in Afghanistan leading a rifle company. She sprinted from cover to cover, from tree to gravestone, always alert, always with her weapon ready.

Segal tried to do the same with as much speed as his leg would allow. He could tell she was right. From down the hill, the smell of burnt gunpowder rose in the slight breeze that issued from the west. As he moved, he strained to remember what was below them on this hill.

Near the bottom of the cemetery grounds was a mausoleum, and thirty yards beyond it a dense line of trees with a thick undergrowth of rhododendrons. Dinah waited for him behind the stone structure, peeping around the corner.

"Did you get a look at the shooter?" he asked.

"Just a glimpse, going into the woods there. Tall, running. Not enough for any kind of ID."

"And he went into the trees?"

Dinah nodded. Segal peeked around the stone structure. The dilemma was clear. The shooter was either beating a quick escape or waiting in the trees and undergrowth, ready to pick them off as they crossed the thirty-yard gap.

"Cover me," Segal said, and before she could protest and before he could analyze the situation himself, he took off.

The second he was in the open a burst of rapid gunfire came from the trees in front of them. Segal dived behind another monument a few feet to the left. A bullet hit the polished granite and sent chips flying. He swung in Dinah's direction, then around again.

She had leaned out from the other side of the mausoleum and returned fire, placing three carefully aimed shots toward the muzzle flash in the darkness of the trees.

It was over in a couple of seconds. Segal saw that Dinah was OK. She had pulled around to the back of the mausoleum and was leaning against the cool marble taking a couple of deep breaths. She gave him the thumbs up. He motioned that he was moving forward.

Instead of running straight toward the place where the shooter had disappeared, he angled left and made it to the tree row in a few seconds. He knew Dinah was covering him, her pistol aimed. He waited a couple of breaths and then moved toward the place where he'd last seen the shooter.

The poplars and white pines were thick and the rhododendrons made a tangled mess, but in between he found the slightest of trails and pushed ahead. He heard the sounds of the highway well before they emerged on the other side. Down a bank and across a ditch were the northbound lanes of I-26. He stood with Dinah, out of breath, looking across the busy road, their fingers entwined in the chain-link fence. There wasn't much to see, other than the place where the fence had been pried up enough to let a man squeeze underneath.

"Perfect set up," Dinah said.

"Yeah," Segal said. "Pull a car off to the side of the road, probably leave a driver with it. Send your shooter in. He exits on foot. Can't give chase. Our cars are too far away."

"We could call Highway Patrol, but what would we tell them to look for?" Dinah added.

She started tracking the ground. Segal turned away from the highway and started slowly back through the trees, studying the ground as he went.

"Hey," Dinah said. "Shell casings."

He went over to her. Near the margin by the clearing Dinah was circling the brass shell casings, careful where she stepped. She pointed them out to Segal.

"This is a classic cover and retreat operation. They had two guys, three counting the driver. The main shooter goes in, does his thing and beats it back through here. The cover guy is waiting here with an assault rifle and gives a couple blasts to deal with anyone like us following."

"And by 'deal with' you mean...deal with," Segal said.

"Right. I say he used an assault rifle. This is military issue ammunition," Dinah explained.

He bent over to see the brass casings lying among the leaves. Dinah held the palm of her hand close to them as if feeling the low embers of a campfire. "Still warm, in case there was any doubt," she said.

She watched a drop of fresh blood hit the forest floor and looked up. "You have a gash near your left eye." She stood up and touched his head to see better.

"I think I was hit by a piece of granite from that gravestone."

"We'll see if they have a first aid kit up there. You OK, Segal?

He knew she meant the cut from the marble, but she also meant it in a broader context as well. Counting the crow assault on the rooftop, this was the fourth time they had been attacked, and so far, anyway, his nerves were intact. He nodded to her. "Fine."

They pushed through the brush in silence and up the hill until they passed the mausoleum where they had taken cover. "Seems like a professional sniper situation again," Segal said, perhaps stating the obvious.

Dinah made a slight sound of agreement. She walked slowly, keeping her eyes to the ground.

Segal continued to think out loud as they walked. "Professional except for one critical detail, of course." He paused. Dinah continued to walk and study the ground. "They didn't hit their target. As far as I can tell, everyone is okay."

"Yeah, well, I felt very much like a target and they got plenty close to me and to you too," she said.

"I don't know that we were the primary targets, though." Segal touched his gash and winced from the pain.

"I don't think the primary target was a person," Dinah said. She stopped and kneeled. "They were after the crows."

She used a pen to pick up an empty shotgun shell. Segal understood immediately. No one would bring a shotgun to pick off a person at long range, but it was the perfect weapon for bird hunting. He glanced up the hill toward the site of the filming. "Come on," he said and he hurried up the hill with Dinah following.

When he arrived, he found Lucile kneeling beside a dead crow on the ground near the skeleton. Dinah blew out a breath behind him. The rest of the movie crew was in a circle around Lucile, giving her the distance the situation seemed to require.

The cinematographer approached quietly with his hand-held camera. "We got footage of the bird getting hit, but we had nothing at ground level that would help you see who did this."

"And none of the crew was hurt?" Dinah asked.

"Everyone's pretty upset, but no one was hit or physically hurt," he said.

One of the film techs found a first aid kit and administered to the gash by Segal's eye.

Segal walked up behind Lucile and put a hand on her shoulder. "Was that the leader of the flock?"

Lucile nodded, clearly in shock. "Why would someone do this?"

Segal took in the whole scene. "Because they thought this crow was Richard."

Later, as Dinah drove away, the adrenaline rush wore off and she began to examine the situation in a critical light. "On the plus side, we didn't lose anyone today," she said. From her military experience, she knew this was a blessing not to be taken for granted. The light on Oak Street was green and she kept her foot steady at forty miles an hour. They were in a residential neighborhood, parks, neat little homes, an elementary school.

"On the other hand, we got nothing getting us closer to an ID," Segal said. He fingered the butterfly bandage across his temple.

"Once again we confirm we're not dealing with a lone guy. Like I said, that was classic strike/retreat/cover."

"That doesn't make me feel too much better," Segal said.

"There's one other thing I think we can be sure of. The way that cover man with the assault rifle was set up, we couldn't get a look at him but he sure as hell got a good look at us. We may not know who they are, but between this and the morning at the lab, they know exactly who we are and what we look like."

CHAPTER 21

Just Like the Night

Francis Elah was asleep in a chair in a darkened room, his breathing slow and deep. His mind began to drift toward consciousness, as though his body floated upward from some depth of warm ocean water toward a surface that was only a little brighter.

He became aware of a humming, buzzing vibration, first on, then off, then on again. It fit into a dream he was having, imagining himself alone in a foreign country, but the intermittent sound became more insistent and would not allow itself to be molded into the dreamscape. He became more aware, degree by degree. His eyes opened. He recognized the darkened room and remembered where he was and how he got there. Not Kabul, not Fort Meade—he was in West Asheville, but probably in more danger here than he had been in the other places. He identified the sound as the vibration of a cell phone lying on a wooden table, which acted like a sounding board, amplifying the buzz like the body of a guitar amplified the vibration of the strings.

The buzzing was answered by a rustling sound. A black shape hopped from the top of a chair to land on the table-top beside the phone. There was a tapping sound on the cell phone, which activated the screen, sending forth a cool white light. In the glow of this light, a large crow was visible, its beak and eyes in direct light, its wings and tail feathers catching a few slanting rays. A bizarre shadow was cast against the wall and ceiling. The bird lowered its beak to the phone screen and made a left-to-right sweeping motion.

Francis moved off the couch, and the crow looked up when he approached the table. He touched the bird's head with his open palm and stroked down its neck and onto the space between its wings. "What the hell are you doing here, Richard?" he whispered, but there was no element of scolding in his voice. "You're going to wake up our host, then there'll be hell to pay."

He switched off the phone, glanced into the adjacent room, and saw that the big girl on the bed had not been disturbed. He knew she came home tired and needed her rest. She lay in a tangle of sheets, one long leg exposed above the bedclothes. Near the foot of the bed, an antique dresser with chipped veneer was cluttered with makeup, clothes, and musical instruments, including a small squeezebox and a well-worn Gibson without a case.

As Francis continued to stroke the crow, his fingers encountered the small plastic bridle and the camera mounted on it. "Where did you get this, Richard?" Clearly surprised, he glanced to where the girl slept and slowly closed the door so as not to wake her. He switched on the light. "At ease,

Richard," he said. The bird stopped his shuffling and rubbed its head on Francis' yellow shirt.

Francis gently lifted him and studied the camera. It was one that he and Lewis had redesigned. Only a couple of people knew about the camera. Why had they put it on? Did they want Richard to film something, or were they sending Francis a message, or possibly both?

Francis checked the camera apparatus as much by feel as by sight. He pressed the catch on a tiny door and felt a memory chip eject partway. He pulled it out and looked at it and then at a laptop on the table. The computer belonged to his host. He had left his own phone and computer behind. He knew the phone had a GPS function, which would allow its location to be tracked, and he had to assume the same was true of the computer. He placed Richard on the table, sat, opened the laptop, and took a few minutes to locate the video processing program. He inserted the memory chip. After a few clicks, he pulled up an image.

As usual with the bird cam, the image was disorienting at first. It took a moment for Francis to figure out that Richard had been perched atop the Creatures 2.0 lab building when the video started. It was dim, and the night vision function of the camera had self-selected, as it was programmed to. The figure of a man approached the backside of the lab. Richard and the camera were focused almost straight down on him when he opened the door and entered. Francis could not make out the man's face, but the mass of his shoulders and the way he moved seemed familiar. The door closed slowly, as though the man was a burglar, trying to be quiet.

Richard panned around after the man disappeared. Then the image was jumbled as he glided down to the lawn. Several moments passed. Then Francis could see dim light coming from the windows and the French doors leading to one of the rooms. This room, Francis knew, was the main lab he himself had used and the one Lewis would now be using. Two quick flashes followed, flashes that showed through other windows as well. A moment later, the back door opened and the man came out. He moved quickly but with no suggestion of panic. He turned to close the door, but before he could do so his head jerked up as if he had heard something. After that, he moved into the shadows and the trees behind the building, where his dark clothes made him disappear from sight. But in that instant when he turned to close the door, his face had been visible.

The image bounced again. Richard must have been hopping to the open door. There was a blinding light while the camera made its transition from night vision to normal light. Francis watched as Richard hopped through the lab. It was an odd perspective of a familiar room, the vantage being about eight inches off the floor. The camera panned up to an open drawer in the lab bench, then switched quickly to the open door leading to the reception area. Beside the desk, he could just make out something on the floor. The scene advanced toward the door as Richard hopped up to a lab bench. From this vantage, the reception area was clearly visible. Francis recoiled. It was Gloria lying in a pool of blood, and there was absolutely no doubt she was dead. His jaw dropped in shock. The video came to an end. The bird by some instinct or circumstance had chosen to advance no closer to the body of the beautiful young woman.

For more than a minute, Francis sat there. He shut his eyes, but that did not prevent the tears from flowing. At length, he drew a sleeve across his eyes. He studied the computer, then studied Richard, still standing on the table. He placed his fingers on the keyboard, typed in some commands, and then, leaning in toward the screen, used the mouse to back up the video to when the mystery man left through the back door. Frame by frame, he zeroed in on the exact moment he turned his face into the light. He squinted at the image, then used the editing controls at the bottom of the screen. He pulled up the cropping tool, put a frame around the man's face, and enlarged it.

A gasp escaped his throat. He knew the man, although not by his real name. The last time he had seen him was in Afghanistan. He had not liked him in Afghanistan, and the thought of him—this killer—being here in Asheville made Francis's blood run cold. He sat there thinking about what the man had done, thinking about what he himself was going to do.

He jumped when he felt a hand on his shoulder. It was Mattie, who had awakened in the next room and silently joined him and Richard. She leaned in to see the screen, too.

"The last time I saw a face like that, I was reading a Dick Tracy comic book," she said.

"Believe me, there is nothing comical about this guy," Francis said. "If you ever see him, let me know right away. And never under any circumstances talk to him or let him know you noticed him."

"So, he's as bad as he looks?"

"Worse. You have no idea." He struggled to find words. "Most of the guys I met overseas were the salt of the earth. They were regular guys with the best of intentions, there to do a difficult job to protect the rest of us. I loved them. But this guy and a few others like him were different. Fortunately, only a few. They thrived on the worst of the stuff going on over there." Francis stopped. "There are lots of people, maybe even a majority of people, who think we need guys like this. They think this is the kind of guy we need to unleash on our enemies to protect ourselves. Well, I've met these guys, and I can tell you they're not protecting anyone. This is not the good guy with a gun people like to talk about."

"This guy is in the military?" Mattie asked.

Francis shook his head. "Private contractor."

Mattie gave him a hug.

He figured partly in sympathy for his plight, and partly because his speech was beginning to convey the enormity of the evil he was talking about. He shivered.

"And you think this guy is in Asheville now?" she asked.

Francis nodded.

"Then I know what you need to do with this picture," she said.

CHAPTER 22

Montford Avenue

Dinah was deep in dreamland. She felt herself flying, overlooking where she lived on Montford Avenue in a house built in 1921 and most recently renovated in the neighborhood's 1990s renaissance. She lived there with two other women. Montford was a mixture of large estate houses, modest cottages, and a few stately apartment buildings, all put together by the same artisans who had created the Biltmore Estate. The predominant aesthetic was Arts and Crafts.

The house Dinah lived in was no exception to this. She had the attic floor, where, as she swooped down in her dream, she caught a glimpse through the dormer window, observing a pleasant room under the slanting planes of the roof.

The room had, to be generous, a lived-in look. The shades on the other windows were drawn most of the way, creating a subdued light. On the small stand beside the bed, Dinah's iPhone was inserted into a speaker/charger. On the floor beside the bed were the crumpled clothes she had peeled off and dropped the night before—or, more accurately, when she had arrived earlier that morning. She had been exhausted and needed her sleep and needed more of it now. Flying was fun. She spread her arms and the air hit her face and she felt refreshed and not as exhausted as she'd been the day before.

That morning, Richard the crow was, in fact, standing on the roof and looking in through the dormer window. The crow saw the girl lying on the bed, covered by a light flannel sheet pulled up to her neck. Her bare arms were exposed, one beside her body, one running under the pillow, where the wild abundance of hair spread out.

After checking the roof, Richard tapped on the window. He tapped three times, paused, and then tapped three more.

She raised her head with apparent difficulty after the second triad of taps. The crow cocked his head at the window, then tapped three more times. This time, she came awake with a start, looking around for the source of the tapping. She flipped around under the covers, opened the drawer of her bedside stand, and took out her gun, all in one smooth motion. She scanned the room with eyes and gun in a methodical sweep. The crow watched her with one cocked eye, then tapped twice more on the pane.

Dinah heard the taps and saw movement at the window and sprang out of bed, holding the sheet against her body. As her head cleared, she approached with caution. The crow tapped again, and she looked at him before putting the gun on the bookcase beneath the window, undoing the lock, and opening the sash. The crow did a little hopping dance for her, opening and closing his beak.

"Richard?" she said.

The crow bobbed his head in an exaggerated motion and gave out caws that certainly sounded like a positive response, even to Dinah's untrained ear. Unsure what to do next, she took another step forward and slowly extended her hands, palms up toward him, simply because it felt like the least threatening move she could make.

Richard responded by leaning in and rubbing the side of his head against her palms. Dinah smiled and petted the bird, stroking gently along his head and down his back. She noticed he no longer wore his camera, but he did have something attached to his right leg.

She bent to get a better look. Richard stood still, allowing her to examine it, first with her eyes, then with her fingers. It was a small black plastic capsule attached with a couple of elastic straps. When she gently unclipped the straps and removed the object, Richard hopped around as if happy to be relieved of it.

She studied the capsule a second and removed the lid. She shook the contents out into her palm. It was a tiny computer memory chip. She started toward her computer but realized this card was much smaller than any she had seen, so she had no idea how to read what was on it. She thought for a moment and realized she would need help. She would have to go out. She looked at Richard, still waiting outside her window. She went to the bedside table and took a notebook and pen from the drawer. She ripped out a small piece of a page and wrote, "Message received." This she folded, rolled, and inserted into the capsule before fitting its cap on. She turned toward the crow, unsure how he would feel about her putting the capsule on his leg.

"Here, Richard," she said in a cooing voice.

He tilted his head, giving her that quizzical expression. She tried the move with the open palms again, and it worked. Richard hopped toward her and allowed himself to be petted. When she gently grasped his leg, he made no move to escape. She got the capsule rig attached with a minimum of fuss and stood upright, pleased with herself and with the bird. Now, she wondered how to tell him to take the message back to the sender.

"Fly home," she said.

Head tilted; Richard stared.

His eyes are so clear and brown. "Fly home now, Richard."

This time, he did a sideways hop, raised his wing, and made a motion with his beak, rubbing it against the wing. He did this twice, then looked at her as if expecting something.

It looked familiar. Dinah remembered her first meeting with Richard and Lewis at Creatures 2.0. "You want something to eat!" she said.

The bird bobbed his beak.

Dinah did a one-eighty scan around the room. On the table was a plate with the crust of a day-old sandwich. "You like peanut butter and jelly?" she asked as she retrieved the plate and broke off a small piece.

Richard did. He ate that piece and another and another until the crust was gone.

"Now, fly home, Richard," she said, and the bird gave one caw and took to the air.

Dinah propped her elbows on the wooden table in the doughnut shop.

"You got this how?" Segal asked.

She believed it a fate of cops that she was in a doughnut shop again. This time, it was the one called Hole, across the French Broad River from the River Arts District. Vortex Doughnuts was too close to the station, too likely to be populated by other cops. Dinah wanted to be alone with Segal, without distractions. *He's appearing a little worse for wear,* she thought, *still sporting a bandage over the cut by his eye.* "Richard delivered it," she said again.

"Richard?" Segal had taken a bite of a cardamom-honey doughnut and spoke the question awkwardly, his mouth mostly full.

"Richard the crow," she said. "At least I think it was Richard. He answered to the name Richard, anyway." She shoved a chocolate glaze into her mouth.

"So, he came knocking at your window like the ghost of Edgar Allan Poe? Tapping at your chamber door?"

"Exactly." Dinah nodded and smiled, her cheeks full.

"So now, in the age of cell phones and the internet, we're back to using carrier pigeons."

She swallowed. "I'm pretty sure Richard would take a beak to your head for comparing him to a pigeon, but I get what you mean. That's why I think it might be a communication from Francis Elah. Think about it. The guy has disappeared from a secret government project. We know from our friend with the brown shoes that they're looking for him. With their technology, if he picks up a cell phone or signs on to the internet or uses a credit card, they'll be all over him. That's what they do best, track communications."

That made sense to Segal, and it also meant the little girl, Suzie, might not have made up that story about seeing her father. Segal always did have trouble dismissing what the girl said, yet he was not easily swayed or gullible. Dinah as usual, remained neutral.

"If that's right, he's still taking a big chance sending something to us. It would have to be something important. Let's see what we've got," Segal said.

He looked at the memory card Dinah handed him. It seemed to be a standard camera card until Dinah pointed out that embedded in this card was a much smaller one, less than a quarter of an inch square. "That's what the crow actually brought to me," she said.

"How did you know what to do with this?" he asked. "I always feel like I'm one step behind on technology."

"I didn't," she said. "I took it over to Charlotte Street. Guy over there owed me a favor. I thought it would be better that way." Ordinarily, Dinah would have taken this to one of the technical guys at the station, but she was less and less confident about who had access to their information and what was being done with it.

She whispered this to Segal and he nodded.

Dinah took a laptop out of her bag and put it on the wooden table in front of them. When she brought up the image from the card, the first thing they saw was a still photo of a man's face and upper body lit from the side. The bottom of the frame bore a time and date stamp.

"That's about the time we have for the murder at Creatures 2.0," Dinah said.

"Yeah, we have a good fix on the time 'cause the cops saw the flashes when they were patrolling the neighborhood."

"That could be the back door of the lab, but who is the guy?"

Segal shook his head. "No clue. Advance it to see if there's more."

There was: a video. It showed the back of the lab building, the man emerging and fading into the shadows, the camera moving into the lab and farther into the building until it discovered the body of Gloria, the receptionist. The video stopped. Dinah pressed a key to advance the file. What followed were a few more pictures of the man's face turned at slightly different angles to the light. That was it.

They sat in silence until Segal held up three fingers to the cook behind the counter.

"You're hitting the pastries pretty hard," Dinah said.

"One for me, one for you, and one for Andrew Roche. We're going back to the VA to see if he knows who this is."

CHAPTER 23

Redeployed

Segal and Dinah walked slowly into Andrew Roche's room in the VA hospital. Segal sensed the change immediately. Everything from the bare walls to the dust floating in the shafts of light in Andrew's space proclaimed he was no longer there.

Outside in the hall, a male nurse pushed a cart, the top of which was dominated by a computer and a multi-compartment box for medications. He stopped at the door and asked if he could help them.

Segal flashed his badge and said, "We're looking for a man who was in this room, Andrew Roche."

"Sorry, I'm new on this ward," he said, turning his attention to the computer. He punched the keyboard with rapid strokes and squinted at the screen. "Redeployed," he said.

"Redeployed?" Dinah asked.

Segal moved forward to see the screen. Indeed, this was the one-word description under the status column. "Redeployed when? To where?" he asked.

The nurse hit a few keys. "All I can tell you is the record was updated early this morning."

"Does it tell who gave the order, who updated the record?" Dinah asked.

The nurse frowned. "Those fields are blank. Not blank, exactly. I mean blacked out, redacted."

The nurse indicated he had to go on with his rounds, and Segal nodded.

The pictures were gone. Segal checked the drawers of the desk, knowing they would be empty. He rummaged around, pushed his hand flat and felt along the inner drawer for anything solid. *Empty.* He wished they'd come sooner. He felt a reluctance to leave, felt there must be something more for them here. His mind searched for answers.

"I guess we could check at the administration office, see if there's any forwarding information," Dinah said.

Segal didn't answer right away. He was catching on to the way all things federal were working out for them lately.

Dinah grabbed his arm. "Hey, it's just about raccoon time," she said, nodding toward the wall clock.

The rec room was down the hallway.

Fewer people were there today; an older black man in a wheelchair whom Andrew had introduced as a Vietnam vet and the younger man pushing him were the only familiar faces. The raccoon entered as Segal came up. No one spoke as they watched the animal go through her paces, making a perfect hand-rolled cigarette. Again, as she raised it to her mouth to lick the glue on the paper, Segal thought he perceived a sense of pride. Or maybe he was falling into the trap of reading too much of his own ideas into the animal, as so many pet owners did. He watched with fascination as the raccoon twisted the ends, carefully placing the cigarette in the box, before pulling the lever for the bite-sized Snickers. It made much the same sound as a conventional vending machine.

A kid with red hair and freckles wheeled up in a chair. Segal remembered him from their previous visit; he couldn't have been more than twenty.

"Damn, that looks good about now," the kid said.

Segal smiled at him, not sure if he meant the candy or the cigarette.

"My turn today." The kid wheeled up and removed the cigarette from the apparatus. "I'm heading outside," he said, more to Dinah than Segal, then wheeled toward the door to the patio area. Dinah raised an eyebrow.

Outside, the kid took the cigarette and a Bic lighter from the pocket of his robe. He fired up.

"You're a friend of Andrew Roche?" Dinah asked, sitting beside him in a lawn chair.

He took a shallow drag on the cigarette and slowly exhaled. "Yeah, I guess so. You get to know people pretty good, hanging around this place. I mean, you got nothing but time." He paused. "That's what I thought, anyway."

"You talking about his redeployment?"

The young man answered with something between a snort and a laugh.

"Did he talk to you about it? Say anything about where they were sending him?" Dinah asked.

She's good at this, Segal thought, getting people to tell her things. He remained standing in front of Dinah and the kid, his bad hip acting up.

The young man took another hit. "Didn't have time. He came to my room last night and woke me up, said he was shipping out. Said it was a security assignment. Meaning he couldn't say anything else."

"How did he seem?" Segal asked.

The kid looked at him and exhaled some smoke. "How did he seem? He seemed scared as shit is how he seemed. He seemed shaken up. You saw him a couple of days ago. Did he seem like someone that needed to be heading back overseas? Besides, it was weird, them coming for him so late and helping him pack."

"And this morning he was gone?" Segal asked.

"Like a turkey in the corn," the kid said.

"I guess we can go through channels, find out what outfit he's with. Do you remember his division?" Dinah asked.

The kid looked at them, surprised. "I thought you knew," he said. "Andrew started out army, but then he signed with Cormorant after he came here. It was Cormorant that came for him."

"The private contracting company?" Dinah asked.

The kid nodded.

"It didn't seem like Andrew thought much of those guys," Segal said. He was thinking of Andrew's first conversation with him and Dinah.

"None of the guys do," the kid said, "but there are certain realities to deal with when you get messed up over there." He made the universal sign for money, rubbing his thumb over his fingertips.

"When you saw him last night, did he talk about anything else?" Dinah asked, leaning in.

"Not much, really. We talked about the raccoons. He said he stocked up the paper and tobacco and candy bars, but I should be the one to check it after he was gone. He said that a couple of times. I should be *the one*."

Segal watched his face and waited for him to continue.

The kid smiled. "Tell you the truth, I was surprised. I mean, that he would ask me to do it. There're guys been here longer than me who love those raccoons."

Dinah stood immediately. In this kind of interview, this kind of situation, they were looking for anything that seemed out of place, and this qualified.

"You think we could check the apparatus now?" she asked. "If it's not too much trouble." She smiled at him, "I would really like to see it."

That's all it took. The kid said "Sure" and started to wheel inside.

Segal and Dinah followed as he swung by his room and picked up a small key, then proceeded to the lounge area. It was after breakfast, when most of the guys were off doing physical therapy or other tasks.

The kid strained to reach up and unlock a panel, then had to push the chair away to allow the panel to fold down. With this, the inner workings of the raccoon vending machine were exposed. They included drawers that could be released with a simple latch.

The kid unlatched the first drawer and pulled it out. Segal leaned over to see. It was nearly full of the little Snickers bars. The kid must have read something on Segal's face because he said, "Go ahead, lieutenant, take a couple. There's plenty here."

Segal shrugged, took a couple, and tossed one to Dinah. "I guess I'll owe the raccoons," he said.

The second drawer held tobacco—four small, string-tie bags, to be exact. The third held several small packets of cigarette papers. Immediately though, Segal saw something else in there as well. A thick manila envelope was wedged against the rear wall of the drawer. "What's that?" he asked.

The kid reached in and pulled it out. Written on the envelope was the name Andrew Roche. The kid looked at the envelope, uncertain what to do with it. Dinah reached for it. Segal helped the kid shut and lock the apparatus while Dinah took the envelope to where a couch and some easy chairs surrounded a coffee table. She spilled the contents—a number of camera prints—onto the coffee table and sat on the couch to sort through them. Segal sat beside her, and the kid wheeled his chair opposite them.

Dinah picked up the pictures one by one, examining each closely and passing it to the others, the way people did, Segal thought. Like going through a family album. "I recognize some of these," Segal said. "They're the ones from Afghanistan, the ones he showed us before." He was looking at the face of the woman they had dubbed "the mystery lady."

"Not all of them, though," Dinah said. She held another picture that included Francis.

"Why do you think he left them like that in the box?" the kid asked.

"Good question," Segal said. "Especially since he made it a point to wake you in the middle of the night and tell you to take care of the raccoons. That tells me a couple of things. One, he wanted it to be you who found the pictures."

"And two, he especially wanted to make sure the guys picking him up did not see them," Dinah threw in.

"It seems odd that they would help him pack up. Is that normal for transport guys to help like that?" Segal asked.

The kid shrugged. He started to say something, but Dinah interrupted before he could speak. "Check this out, Segal." She pointed at the photo of Francis beside a group of four tough-looking guys in camouflage uniforms. "You recognize this guy right here?" she asked, tapping her finger on the one closest to Francis.

Segal nodded. He didn't want to say it out loud. It was the same guy in the photos Richard had delivered to Dinah. No doubt. He took the photo from her, and the kid leaned in to see, too.

Segal pointed to the patch above the guy's shirt pocket. It showed the silhouette of a bird with its wings spread and its head turned to one side. "Is that what I think it is?"

"That's what I was telling you about. That's a Cormorant patch," the kid said.

CHAPTER 24

Again with Dr. Gold

Segal was inclined to skip his appointment with Dr. Gold, being so deep into their investigation, but Dinah insisted on dropping him off downtown.

"Do you really want to explain to the captain why you skipped?" she asked. "Especially with people shooting and lobbing hand grenades at you?"

Segal agreed.

The door at the top of the stairs was open, and as he walked past the Colebrook painting, he had no problem noticing the robots or Jackie Kennedy. His eyes were open. He could not believe he hadn't seen them before. What else had he missed these last months?

Dr. Gold's hair was done in two long braids hanging down her shoulders today. Segal liked how she wore her hair like a young woman sometimes in spite of the gray in it. Likewise, the rich red and gold of her sweater seemed soft and relaxing.

She didn't get up from her desk when he entered, just motioned him to the green couch under the window. He knew what this meant: a session of what Dr. Gold called "guided meditation." He glanced at her before sitting down. She seemed different today, and there was a folder on the desk in front of her which he recognized. He lay down and began a pattern of three deep breaths with slow exhalations, followed by conscious relaxation of his limbs, one by one.

Dr. Gold waited a few minutes. "Good," she said. "I want you to trace your steps to the back of your mind. It is two years ago today."

Segal had not realized it until she said this. It was the anniversary of his shooting. This nearly jolted him out of his relaxed state. He took another deep, slow breath and remained calm.

He heard the sound of the folder opening. He knew it was the official police report of the incident. Although they had spoken about some aspects of that day before, Dr. Gold had never asked him to recount it in detail.

"You were called to a disturbance on Church Street," she said.

Segal understood from the way she read that sentence that she wanted him to continue the story from there. "Not exactly called. We heard it on the scanner and my partner and I were pretty sure we knew who it was so we went to help."

"And it says here the man causing the disturbance was your cousin?"

"Tommy was a distant cousin, like second cousin. A troubled soul. The rest of the family had pretty well written him off." The memory was clearly difficult for Segal, and he had to take a couple deeper breaths.

"Yes, and you tried to take care of him?"

"Not as well as I should have, not really. I didn't know how to help him and neither did anyone else. He got picked up a couple of times for public disturbance and his mom asked me to step in and keep him from getting locked up. Which I did. Talked him down, took him home, got him back on his meds, and he was OK for a while."

"It says here this time, the last time, he was hanging out at the front entrance to one of the churches yelling out the same phrase over and over again," Dr. Gold prompted.

Segal nodded. He declined to pick up on her cue to continue.

"It says the phrase he kept shouting was 'On pain of death, all men depart.'"

"It's from Shakespeare. *Romeo and Juliet.* It's what the Prince says when he's breaking up a street brawl between the Capulets and the Montagues. He's tired of them disturbing the peace and he reads them the riot act, and that's what he says at the end of the speech. 'On pain of death all men depart.'"

There was a moment's silence. Segal was clearly out of his meditative state.

"Segal, why would your cousin be quoting from *Romeo and Juliet*? There's nothing about that in the report."

Her question seemed to come more from a place of pure curiosity than from part of a guided meditation. He opened his eyes and sat up. He looked at her, then sighed deeply. "It was my fault. One of the times I tried to help Tommy I promised him I would always do my best to answer any question he had and that I would always tell him the truth, unlike the other people in his life. A few days later I saw him downtown and he asked me the million-dollar question every guy wants the answer to."

"Which is?"

"How do I get a girl to like me? He was madly in love with a girl and that's what he asked. How do I get a girl to like me? I hemmed and hawed and fumbled around and I finally told him guys have been trying to figure that one out since the time of the cavemen and no one really seemed to have the answer. Then I thought of *Romeo and Juliet*."

"A copy of which you just happened to have on your person," Dr. Gold filled in.

"In the back seat of my car. Next time I saw him he had it down, the whole plot, scene by scene, characters, everything. Amazing. And this was a guy who supposedly had learning problems. He worked in a quote about every other sentence he spoke. Who knew it would take over his mind like that? That's the power of the written word."

"And what exactly was the outcome you were hoping for?"

Segal seemed surprised by the question. "I guess I hadn't really thought that one through in any detail. He asked about love so I gave him one of the most famous love stories of all time and hoped for the best. I figured he just needed to work it out the way everyone does. Only Tommy wasn't so good at working things out."

Dr. Gold's face relaxed. She seemed to let that sink in for a moment, then said, "OK, Segal, I want you to lie back down and relax, and once you are relaxed just simply tell me what happened after you arrived on Church Street. Tell it in the present tense as if it's happening right now. I won't interrupt."

Segal did as he was told. This time it took a few minutes to calm his breathing. Then he began. "It's early evening. We roll up on Church Street. There are a couple of cruisers blocking off part of the street, no tape or anything. It's not a very busy street anyway. I see one of the officers I know well and he seems relieved to see me. I ask him if it's Tommy and he nods and says he thinks so. At first, I don't see anyone at the church, then Tommy sticks his head out from behind one of the pillars between the arches and yells, 'On pain of death all men depart.'

"It's Tommy alright. One of the officers tells me that's all he's been saying since they got there. I call to him and he just says it again, 'On pain of death all men depart.' Then I tell him I'm coming up to talk to him. He doesn't say anything, and I start walking up slowly. I'm talking to him as I come and when I'm about halfway there he peeks out a little and yells, 'No Segal! On pain of death, all men depart. I mean it Segal. On pain of death, all men depart.' He sounded upset, even more than usual. More desperate.

"I take a couple more steps toward him and he peeks out again. Then he steps out in full view and he's got a gun. I stop. I can't believe it. How could Tommy get a gun? Who would give it to him? That's what I thought in that instant."

Segal stopped.

"That instant?" the doctor asked.

"That instant before he shot me."

"And the instant after?"

"All kinds of things all at once. I went down. I knew I had been hit, but it's like I knew it on an intellectual level. I knew it but I didn't feel it. And I kept looking at Tommy standing there with the gun in his hand, and I knew if he didn't drop it immediately . . . I knew what would happen next. And you know what comes into my mind next? Another line from the same play: 'Stand not amazed.' It's what Benvolio says to Romeo after Romeo kills Tybalt. Stand not amazed. And I think I tried to say it to him but I don't know if any sound came out."

And then Segal paused.

"And after that, you passed out," Dr. Gold said.

Segal nodded. The meditative state was gone. He sat up and looked at the doctor. She looked down at the open file.

"It says here two of the officers shot him and he died on the scene."

"That's what I heard. They had no choice. A man with a gun just shot a fellow officer. That much makes sense. I just can't make sense of the rest of it."

"And you are the person who makes sense of things other people can't figure out."

Segal stared at the doctor. "You think I need to make sense of this before I can move forward?"

"No, *you* think you need to make sense of it before you can move forward."

"And what do *you* think I need...to move forward?" he asked.

Dr. Gold gave him her best shrug and smile. "Sometimes, you don't need anything. Sometimes, you need to leave behind everything you don't need."

CHAPTER 25

Foreign Correspondent

S omeone once asked Segal what his favorite brewery was. There were many to choose from in Asheville. He said he was spreading himself around.

That evening, he was spreading himself around Wicked Weed. More precisely, he sat with Dinah at the bar, and more precisely still, the upstairs bar, sipping on a glass of their Rick's Pilsner. Dinah was considering the possibility of squeezing lime juice into her Sweet Talker Ale. Between them, it was a split decision on whether or not this was advisable.

Earlier Dinah had asked him what he talked about with Dr. Gold. He just said "Romeo and Juliet." Now he tried with her, to sort out what they had learned since that morning. Segal felt there was yet something more they could do before they gave the captain an update in the morning. The police station did not feel like the place to be.

The TV above the bar was on, the sound turned down so low he couldn't hear much above the background noise of people coming and going and talking. It was a news talk show, and he looked up when a new guest came on. The guest was charismatic on camera, the kind of guy who got people's attention. He was middle-aged with a full head of long, dark, wavy hair. His face was smooth. His eyes seemed heavy, and Segal thought that perhaps they were eyes that had seen too much.

Segal sipped his drink. He thought, *It's the eyes that make people listen to him.*

"I've seen this guy before," Dinah said.

Segal had reached the same conclusion a second or so earlier. He motioned for the bartender to turn up the sound.

The host of the program introduced the guest: "He's the only journalist allowed into the compound where Osama bin Laden was killed a few days ago in a nighttime raid by navy SEALs. Please welcome Peter Olson."

"Yeah, he's a foreign correspondent. One of those guys they bring out every time there's some kind of terrorist act," Segal said.

The foreign correspondent joined three other people on the set; two men and a woman.

On the TV screen, the commentator asked Peter Olson about what he had seen in Pakistan, and Olson answered in short, clipped sentences, painting a graphic picture with words, a picture of violence and surprise and much else.

"Peter, what do you make of the fact that the body, supposedly bin Laden's, was buried at sea? Isn't that bound to raise questions about whether it was, in fact, bin Laden?"

The question came from one of the other men, a well-known commentator, Andrew Evans. He was affiliated with right-wing media and gave the camera a frozen smile. Segal watched Olson's face closely. He saw a brief expression of anger and suspected the anger was less in reaction to the question and more about the weaseling way it was put, slipping in that little word *supposedly*.

"There is no *supposedly* to it," Olson said. "It was bin Laden, as confirmed by the photos of the body. Shared with appropriate people in the intelligence community all over the world, and as confirmed by DNA tests as well. The identity has not been challenged by any source. Credible or otherwise. Not anyone in the Al-Qaeda organization, not anyone in any other Muslim group, not by members of the extended family in Saudi Arabia. Not anyone."

Peter Olson's answer made the right-wing commentator slither back in his seat like a snake hit by a garden rake. Segal smiled. *I've seen Peter Olson before. Recently? Where?*

The host resumed. "One aspect of this incident that I find interesting is the report that we—the U.S. government, that is—did not have 100 percent confirmation before the raid that bin Laden was really living there. Is that your understanding, Peter?"

Peter Olson drummed a finger on the armrest of his chair.

"I know I've seen this guy's face somewhere," Dinah said. "Not just on shows like this. I feel like I've seen him more recently."

Segal said, "Me too." He glanced at her as she took another swig of beer.

Olson spoke. "I don't want to say too much until I've had a chance to interview more sources. But yes, that is my understanding. From what I've heard so far, the team, headed by the CIA, tracked the movements of a man known to have been in personal service to bin Laden. They had been watching him for some time. Traced him to this compound in Abbottabad, Pakistan. The compound had all the characteristics that would be needed to accommodate bin Laden and his family. They watched the compound for months. They had satellite pictures of a tall individual walking in one of the rooftop courtyards. However, the resolution from a satellite photo is only so good. And they could not get photos from the ground because the walls were too high."

"Why not fly a plane over. Or maybe a helicopter or drone?" the other man asked. The woman commentator nodded.

"Too risky. The last thing they wanted was to spook bin Laden, to have him get away and hide. Then it could be another ten-year search before we found him again. Or maybe we never would."

"And I suppose for the same reason we could not enlist the help of the Pakistani government or intelligence network?"

"Right," Peter answered. "Given that he was living in Pakistan, there was simply no way we could know in advance whom we could trust and not trust with that kind of information."

At this point, the video feed of the commentators was replaced by a series of photographs. "Could you describe what we're seeing here, Peter?" the host prompted.

Peter filled in details. He described the compound as displayed in the photos. First, the walls surrounding it, then the interior, describing the rather squalid-looking rooms within the buildings themselves. Various people in military garb could be seen poking around. In one picture of the inner courtyard, where one of the helicopters had landed and subsequently been destroyed, Segal caught sight of a woman dressed in field garb; vaguely military in appearance. She had straight, dark hair sticking out from a cap. Segal studied the lines of her face.

"Did you see that woman?" he asked Dinah.

"Yeah, I saw her."

"Is she the same woman as in that picture with Francis? The one Andrew Roche showed us at the VA hospital?"

"Exactly what I was thinking, boss," Dinah said, setting her beer down on the bar.

Another picture flashed on the screen. It was the courtyard from a different angle, giving Segal another view of the woman. This one was closer and more head-on. The woman removed her glasses. Bingo, Segal thought.

"Yeah, that's our girl," Dinah said.

The host began to wrap up that segment of his program. "And thank you, Peter. Thanks once again for joining us this evening. I understand you are off on a tour to promote your latest book about the war in Afghanistan."

Before Peter Olson could answer, Dinah's face lit up. "That's where I've seen this guy before. The window of Malaprop's Bookstore! You know, where they line up the books and pictures of the authors coming to give talks. He was on a poster."

"You mean he's coming to Asheville?" Segal asked.

Dinah smirked, "Sooner or later, everyone comes to Asheville." She already had her phone out, looking up the Malaprop's website. After a couple of minutes, she said, "In this case, sooner. Like tomorrow. He's giving a talk there about his book."

"Good. We'll corner him and question him about Francis. If he knows that lady, maybe he knows our man, too," Segal said.

"Maybe he's already in town tonight," Dinah said. "This program is rebroadcast from yesterday."

He downed his beer and then headed out with Dinah in the lead.

From the manager at Malaprop's, Dinah found out that Peter Olson was staying at the Hotel Indigo. Then, she found out that the desk clerk at the hotel had made a dinner reservation for Olson at a tapas place called Zambra on Walnut Street.

Another address conveniently close to the nexus of all things, Segal thought. In fact, Zambra was around the corner from Malaprop's. It was an upscale restaurant, clean, a perfect place to meet a foreign correspondent. The lighting was subdued and the furnishings dark and exotic. Segal followed Dinah, case files under his arm. He passed the bar, entering a larger room filling with patrons. Peter Olson was at a table near the window. He was turned away from the table with his legs crossed, wearing a dark suit with a white shirt open at the collar, no tie. On the table was a small glass of red wine. In his lap, he held a folded magazine. Segal was pleased to see that no one else was at the table with him. When Dinah approached and introduced them, Olson rose and shook their hands. He didn't seem at all upset to be interrupted.

"We're hoping you might be able to help us solve a mystery," Segal said.

"Sounds more interesting than the magazine I was reading." Olson smiled and motioned that they should join him. Dinah took the window and Segal slid into his chair. The waitress came, and before Segal could decline Dinah ordered several tapas dishes for them.

Segal leaned forward and placed a manila folder on the table. From it, he withdrew a pair of pictures from their visit to the VA hospital; the two that showed Francis Elah and Andrew Roche in Afghanistan with the mystery woman in the background.

When Olson studied the pictures, his face changed from the welcoming smile to something else, something more serious. Segal thought it looked like a combination of fear and surprise and interest—definitely interest. "Do you recognize anyone in these photos?" Segal asked.

Peter Olson stared first at Segal and then Dinah. "I don't know either of the two men in the foreground. I am acquainted with the woman. You don't see many pictures of her." He picked up the photos and studied them. "Clearly taken in Afghanistan."

"Yes, we saw footage of you on the news. Shots of you in Pakistan checking out the compound where bin Laden was killed. We thought we saw this woman there, too."

Olson nodded. "I can't wait to hear what this has to do with Asheville, North Carolina," he said sitting back. He folded his hands on the table as if ready for a good story.

Segal glanced at Dinah. They had talked about how much to tell this guy and had decided to let him know basically everything, possibly excluding some of the more graphic details. They hoped he could bring some perspective to help them make sense of what they were seeing. Besides that, this guy was a professional reporter. He would expect some degree of information trading and would know how to keep his mouth shut where and when it was appropriate.

Segal told him about the murder of Chickey Atley, and how Atley was associated with Creatures 2.0, trainers of special animals. He told him about looking for Francis Elah, who had gone missing while on a special government project with a specially trained crow, Richard, who was back home in Asheville, even though Francis had not yet surfaced. He told him about their interview with Andrew Roche at the VA hospital, which was where they came across the picture of the woman who apparently knew Francis in Afghanistan.

When Segal paused, Peter Olson took a sip of his wine. "Is there more?" he asked.

Segal turned to Dinah. She gave a slight shrug.

Segal leaned in closer. "Look, what I've shared so far is information we turned up as a result of a fairly routine local investigation. At least it started out that way. This next part I'm less comfortable with. We may be getting into national security information, which I'm pretty sure we're not supposed to have in the first place. Whatever we share with you has to remain confidential."

"You told me you saw the news footage of me with U.S. and Pakistani intelligence personnel in Abbottabad. I am the only member of the news media—any news media anywhere in the world—to be given access to that site. That should tell you everything you need to know. Do you know how many contacts and sources I've had to cultivate over the years to earn that level of trust? If I had not proven over and over that I can be trusted with information, do you think I would have earned that position?"

At that point, the waiter brought out the first of their tapas dishes. Without taking his eyes off Segal, Olson reached down and picked up a piece of crostini bearing a generous application of olive oil and some sort of pâté. He took a bite with an audible crunch.

After a few beats, Segal said, "Good point, Mr. Olson."

"Call me Peter."

Segal opened the folder again and took out a picture of the camera Richard had removed from the other crow, the one he killed on the roof of the Grove Arcade.

"What exactly am I looking at?" Olson asked. He took a drink of wine and picked up another piece of crostini.

"It's a camera that can be attached to the head of a crow, making it possible to see what the bird is looking at," Dinah said. She said this in a casual manner between bites.

Olson put the crostini down. He stared straight ahead and finally blinked. "And you say this man, Francis Elah, is or was an animal trainer?"

Segal nodded.

"Do you think he could have trained the crow to do something like fly from one building to another? I mean, a specific building?"

"I'm pretty sure from what we've seen that Francis Elah could easily get Richard to do that."

Dinah snorted. "Tell him about the raccoon and the cigarettes."

"We can talk about raccoons another time. Right now, I would like to know what you're thinking."

Olson grimaced. "Now, it's my turn to wonder how much to disclose." He touched a napkin to his lips. "You told me you've been watching the news about the raid that got bin Laden? You may not realize this was the culmination of ten years of work by a group in the U.S. intelligence community. That's ten years of gathering information. Ten years of logging information. Ten years of following every possible lead, even every rumor they heard. They were desperate to find bin Laden. Here's the guy that masterminded 9/11. We wage a war in Afghanistan, mostly just to find him and bring him to justice. And he vanishes without a trace."

"I remember reading they had him cornered sometime in the early part of the war," Segal said. Like most Americans, he was woefully fuzzy on exactly what had happened in that conflict.

"Maybe, maybe not," Olson said. "There were a few junctures where some people thought we were close. It was confusing. I was there, on the ground. I had excellent sources in the government and elsewhere, but I could not swear how close we were. In any case, about the time we pushed the

Taliban fighters and Al-Qaeda back into the mountains, the war in Iraq started—or rather, we started it."

"And then all bets were off?" Segal asked.

"No, not all. We definitely entered a time when the focus of the military operation was off finding bin Laden. Some people would say we didn't really have a military focus in Afghanistan after that."

"Speaking as one who was there," Dinah said, "I would be one of those people."

Olson gave her an appraising look. "As far as the military effort, I would have to agree with you. However, let's talk about the intelligence community. All those years, and all the time leading up to the raid on the compound in Abbottabad, a task force was working on locating bin Laden. For that group, there was no lack of focus—not ever, not for a day, nor for an hour. Their job was to find Osama bin Laden, and they finally did. As you know."

Segal picked up his napkin and played with it. "And this group was part of the Office of Naval Intelligence?"

"No, the group was run out of the CIA, although they had close ties with ONI and all the other intel groups. And close ties in that community are a rare thing, I assure you."

"And that woman in the pictures? She had something to do with this group?" Dinah asked.

"That woman *was* the group. Nancy Lund. She was the one in charge from day one. She was the one that put all the pieces of the puzzle together." Olson's eyes lit up.

"What are the chances we could call her and find out if she knows anything about Francis Elah. Or anything that could help us?" Segal asked.

Olson grinned. "I would say your chances are very slim. There are just too many secrets, and those secrets include an interconnected web of sources. If you start pulling at one thread in the story, you don't know what else is going to unravel. It's much easier for people like Nancy Lund to say nothing at all. Hard to get in trouble keeping your mouth shut."

"But you know her pretty well, right?" Dinah said.

"If it wasn't for Nancy, I would never have gotten into the compound to get those pictures you saw on the news. I had other contacts, but it was Nancy who convinced them it was important to have a journalist there. And that the journalist should be me."

"So, you could ask her about this?" Dinah cocked her head.

Olson put his palms together. "I'll have to think about it." He looked at Segal and must have seen the disappointment on his face. "Look, it's not that I don't want to help you. And it's not that I don't feel this is important. Nancy and her team have been generous with their information. If your man Francis was involved with the operation in some capacity, they have not shared it with me. If they have not shared it with me, I have to assume there is a reason. A lot of people think that reporters push everyone for information all the time. That's not how you gain people's confidence in a lasting relationship."

Segal let that soak in. It was pretty clear he was giving them advice, as well as explaining his own situation. "Suppose we leave contacts and information aside for the time being," Segal said. "Knowing what you know, and knowing what we've told you about what's going on here in Asheville, what do you think Francis could have been doing over there?" Segal raised his hand, already knowing Peter Olson would shake his head. "And before you tell me you don't like to speculate without all the facts, let me say, we can use all the ideas we can get."

"All right, then." Olson pushed the tapas dish away. "You might have caught the discussion on that news program about what happened after they suspected bin Laden was in the compound in Abbottabad. They struggled to find a way to confirm it *really* was bin Laden. They certainly didn't want to do anything to spook him because then they would have to start the whole search over again. That meant they couldn't fly planes or drones at low altitude over the compound. They definitely couldn't ask the people in the neighborhood. They didn't want to involve the Pakistani government because, regardless of what the official position was, there were factions that had more sympathy for bin Laden than for the U.S. So, the official story is that the raid by the SEALs was ordered without definite confirmation. That part has always bothered me. It's a big step to take without confirmation."

"I see where you're going with this. The CIA gets Francis over there. Francis sends Richard to take pictures with his special camera. The CIA gets their confirmation, and no one thinks anything about a bird flying around."

Olson nodded. "Makes sense to me."

Dinah chowed down her tapas.

Finally, Segal said, "It does, although it's hard to imagine someone from Asheville getting caught up in international affairs on the other side of the world."

"Unless you count soldiers as people," Dinah said.

"Good point," Segal said. Like many ex-military people, Dinah said so little about that part of her life that it was easy to forget she had been over there. "But in your case, what happened in Afghanistan stayed in Afghanistan. Assuming we're right about Francis and what he did, it still doesn't tell us what's going on here at home." He addressed the first part of this to Dinah, the second part to Olson.

Olson squinted and polished off his wine. "That I don't know. I think you can assume something went wrong, either between Francis and the enemy or between Francis and the government. Any way you look at it, Francis has made some powerful enemies, and if you're getting involved with this, you may be getting in the way of the same people." Olson enumerated, ticking them off on his fingers: "The Taliban, Al-Qaeda, Muslim Brotherhood, CIA, U.S. military, military intelligence. Take your pick. I wouldn't want any of those guys looking for me."

"What about Cormorant?" Dinah asked. "Were they involved in this operation?"

Olson's face took on a new mask of seriousness. He leaned forward and lowered his voice. "I don't know for certain. Some of their personnel were around the base at the time. I heard a rumor they did some of the advance work in Pakistan. That is done sometimes because if they're caught or killed, it's a private company, not U.S. military. The U.S. could have denied any connection. Frankly, I have no desire to make inquiries because I'm not going to write anything about that group, not now and not anytime in the foreseeable future."

Peter Olson had transformed before Segal's eyes from a fearless man of the world into someone else, someone filled with fear and loathing.

Peter finished his wine. He motioned to the waiter for another glass. "Listen, I know this company is highly regarded by some here in the U.S., but I've seen the aftermath of their operations. Money goes into that organization and things get done and no one asks how." He fell silent, seemingly lost in some memory. "I've met some of their people. I'm not talking about the bosses who negotiate contracts and organize missions. I'm talking about their people on the ground." He shook his head. "Our regular military commanders, army and marines, they won't let our troops around these guys. Fortunately, the company keeps them on the other side of the world, well away from us. The thought of these guys loose among the population here in the States? I don't even want to think about it."

Segal said nothing. He opened another folder. "What about this guy?" He showed Olson the picture of their suspect from Richard's camera. "Do you recognize him?"

"Yeah, that's one of them," he whispered. Olson took out a business card and wrote a number on the back. "Call me if I can be of any help," he said. He folded his napkin on the table, pushed his glass away. The waiter brought a full glass of wine. Olson stood as if he didn't care about it.

"And Nancy Lund?" Dinah asked.

"I'll see what I can do."

Segal took the card and thanked him. "Where are you off to next? After your book signing tomorrow?"

"Somewhere safer than Asheville," he said. "Like Damascus or Baghdad." He walked away from them.

Dinah reached for the full glass of wine and pulled it towards her. "We never did get to tell him about the raccoon."

CHAPTER 26

Court Order

Stuff built up. Segal felt it the next morning—the red Spanish wine and all they had learned at the VA and from Peter Olson, not to mention the gash above his eye and the cut where the dive-bombing crow had hit him. He had been up half the night, first with work, then too keyed up to sleep. He was up and down, reading an Elmore Leonard book, twisting in bed like a strand of DNA.

A sloppy rain fell now at eight-thirty, and all the good parking places were taken, making him get wet before he was inside. He stepped into a puddle, soaked his shoe. All this for a meeting where he'd get to tell his boss what a mess this whole case had become.

In the entrance hall, he passed two uniformed officers heading out, apparently in a mood that matched his own. "Man, I had tickets," one was saying to his partner.

The partner shook his head. "You know better than to make plans."

Segal was curious. "What's up?" he asked.

"I hope you weren't planning anything next week, lieutenant," the first one said.

"All hands-on deck starting Monday. All leaves and vacations postponed," said the other. "They're not saying why. Something's up."

"I had tickets," the first one said again as they walked on.

When Segal tracked dripping water through the hallway leading to the office and conference room, he was soaked and in need of coffee, and his bag kept slipping off the shoulder of his damp raincoat. He knew he would be walking into a bitchy squad room. For comfort, he reached under his coat and checked the paperback in his pocket. *For Whom the Bell Tolls*, at least, was dry. He knew Dinah would not be pleased he was reading Hemingway. Sometimes he had to.

He dumped his stuff at his desk and started for the coffee machine when Dinah rounded the corner so fast she could have been wearing skates. Her face was a mask of stone. He was about to ask what was wrong when she grabbed his arm and led him to the back of the office complex, to a room where a video monitor was set up. The monitor allowed the officers to watch the proceedings inside the closed interrogation room next door. She planted Segal in front of the monitor and pointed.

On the screen, he saw a woman, her elbows planted on the table, face collapsed in her hands. She wept, almost silently. He could tell by her Egyptian haircut and the line of her shoulders it was Emily Elah.

Two men and a woman sat across the table from her. One of the men was the ONI guy, Jerome Guilford. He was sitting back, legs crossed, the better to display one of his perfect brown shoes. Beside him was a proper-looking woman with her hands in her lap, a manila folder in front of her on the table. Beside her was a man in a gray business suit. He pushed a paper across the table in Emily's direction.

"This is the court order we referred to, Mrs. Elah," he said.

Emily Elah made no move to look at the document.

Segal moved toward the door, but his boss, who had come up behind him, caught his arm. "We can't go in there," his boss said. His face left no room for argument.

On the screen, Emily Elah composed herself enough to look the man in the eye.

"I'm afraid your husband's disappearance and your refusal to be of any assistance in helping us find him leave us no choice. This is an order allowing us to freeze your bank account until a full audit can be made to determine how much of the money in it comes from his unfulfilled contract with the federal government." The man in the gray suit had a raspy voice.

"We don't have to exercise this order if you're willing to cooperate," Jerome Guilford said.

Emily Elah shifted her gaze and said nothing. Guilford cleared his throat. The woman with her hands in her lap moved those hands to the folder on the table.

"Mrs. Elah, I am from the Department of Social Services, Child Welfare Division. At the request of Mr. Guilford, we have conducted a preliminary review of the status of your daughter, Susan Elah. Our information reveals that your daughter is confronted with several severe physical challenges, possibly ranging beyond the ability of a single parent."

Emily stared at her, mouth slightly open and eyes wide. The woman leafed through several pages that appeared to be medical reports.

Outside, watching the monitor, Dinah said under her breath, "What are they doing? They can't do this."

The woman held up a piece of paper. "We have also been given access to all police reports related to your family. This is a report filed by Lieutenant Ira Segal."

Segal flinched.

"It describes an incident dated two nights ago in which your daughter claims she was visited by your husband."

Emily voiced the same thought Segal had. "I can't believe you're using that. She was probably describing a dream."

The woman raised her hand. "It does cast doubt on your story about not knowing where your husband is. Also, there is the point that your daughter was left alone."

Emily slumped in her seat.

"Do you dispute that your daughter was left alone?" the woman asked.

Emily's head gave the slightest of shakes. "Suzie is perfectly okay by herself. Especially with neighbors so close."

"Mrs. Elah, we are taking no formal action at this point. However, we are putting you on notice that your daughter's case is under review with the consideration that she be removed from your home for her own welfare and protection." The woman shut the folder and returned her hands to her lap.

Emily swept the three of them with her eyes. "Is there anything else?" Judging from her face, fear was turning into anger.

"You tell us. Is there anything else, Mrs. Elah?" Guilford asked. He looked and sounded quite pleased with himself, like a chess player who had just put his opponent in check.

Emily blew out a long breath, regained her composure. "May I go now?"

Guilford made a gesture with an open palm. "You can go, Mrs. Elah. Be fair warned, I'm not going away. Neither are these problems. Not until we find Francis. I would advise you to start cooperating."

Emily Elah stood, turned, and walked through the door. She started down the hall and quickly came up beside Segal as he departed the monitor room. She stopped, blinked at him with tears in her eyes, and glanced at the monitor beyond him. He twisted to see it showing the three government bureaucrats still at the table. He twisted toward her again. Her gaze bore down on him.

"Enjoy the show, lieutenant?" she asked after a beat. "I'll be sure to tell Suzie hello from you."

Segal stuttered on some kind of lame excuse, but the self-monitoring part of his brain stopped him before he said something idiotic. Emily swung around and walked down the hall and out of the police department.

Segal felt glued to his spot. He felt Dinah and his boss looking at him. He turned toward the interrogation room, but before he could take a step the others started to file out, first the child-services woman with her eyes down, then the man in the gray suit, who met Segal's eyes without speaking, and finally Jerome Guilford with a smug grin. He stopped and nodded to Segal, Dinah, their boss.

To the boss, he said, "Thanks for the use of the room, captain."

Then Segal felt Guilford's eyes boring into him. "What the hell, Guilford?" Segal said. "Was that some of the enhanced interrogation you were telling us about?"

Guilford widened his condescending smile. He started to speak and to reach out toward Segal's shoulder. Before he could connect, Dinah made a lightning move. In one motion, she stepped between them, knocked Guilford's arm high into the air, and brought her full momentum, shoulder first, straight into Guilford's chest. The result was like a defender slamming into a wide receiver on a football field, only in this case the wide receiver didn't just fly out of bounds. He flew into a bank of filing cabinets with a rattling bang and sprawled on the floor. Dinah remained perfectly balanced, standing over him. The captain gently put hands on her arm and waist and guided her down the hall before the situation could get more out of hand.

CHAPTER 27

Comfort Food

It was late afternoon when Segal pulled to the curb in front of the big house on Montford Avenue, the one Dinah lived in. When he got out, he saw Dinah's two housemates on the wide front porch, one in a swing, the other sitting on the steps trying to tune a mandolin.

"If this isn't an Asheville picture, I don't know what is," he said, taking it in. The girl on the steps was wearing a flannel shirt with the top two buttons alluringly left undone. It was tied at the waist, revealing a little skin above her cutoff jeans.

"Heyyyyy, Segal," they said in unison, drawing it out with as much innuendo as they could possibly pack in, carrying forth their tradition of shameless, over-the-top mock flirtation when he drove up. (At least Segal thought it was mock, though he wondered sometimes in his weaker moments.)

He stood there smiling while the girl with the mandolin did a competent rendition of "Weaver's Pond" on the little instrument. He allowed his gaze to drift up the side of the house to the top floor and the slanted roof and the dormer windows. He half-expected to see Richard up there, rapping on Dinah's chamber door again.

The song ended and the girl got up from the steps. "I'll go and let her know you're here," she said. The other girl rose from the swing and said she had to be going as well. It occurred to Segal that he had never actually been inside the house. People had different ways of keeping their work persona separate from their personal life. Dinah had never said anything about it, but on the other hand, she had never actually invited him in either.

She came out on the porch wearing blue jeans and a flowered cotton top, a little on the soft side compared to her normal choice of dress, but then she was off-duty. She had half a grin to go with her toned-down look. "How much trouble am I in?" she asked.

Segal sat on the swing, closing his eyes after the first kick, enjoying the motion and the creak of the chains against the eyehooks in the ceiling. After searching for something reassuring, he said, "I don't know. For now, you're not suspended or anything. I assured the captain that cooling down this afternoon and getting some rest would restore your professional demeanor. I promised I would read you your rights, like in the future, any federal assholes you slam against a filing cabinet may be used as evidence against you." He could not help smiling when these words brought back the mental image of Jerome Guilford sprawled on the floor.

"You filled him in on the case, too?" she asked.

They had talked about that meeting, things being such an unresolved mess. Segal knew Dinah felt bad for making him face that alone. "I gave him a quick recap. He seemed distracted, didn't ask his usual questions. Seems like something else big is coming down the pike. He just said to get it wrapped up."

"Did you talk to Guilford?"

"I did," Segal said. "He's not going to do anything about the little body check you laid on him, which may or may not be all good news. Could be he intends to hold it over our heads as a bargaining chip for future play."

"Pissant," Dinah said.

Segal smiled. *Pissant* was a term rarely heard these days. When he was growing up, people called each other pissants all the time. It was a handy insult that could be spit out from pursed lips, dismissive and insulting at the same time. It certainly fit in this case.

"Well, he said he was going to turn up the pressure, and I guess this was what he meant," Segal said. "He also told me he would be conducting his own surveillance with his own people, so we better not hold back information."

"Trouble is, how far can we trust him?"

"No clue. I don't like this state of limbo. Are we on their team or are we not on their team? Especially after Guilford's latest efforts to win friends and influence people."

"His idea of advanced interrogation," Dinah said. "In my book, you find ways to lean on a dangerous criminal. That's high-pressure interrogation. On the other hand, you pick on a woman with a missing husband and a troubled little girl, you're a bully."

Segal continued to swing. He knew that, for Dinah, a bully was about the worst thing a person could be. She could overlook faults in people, but seeing a bully in action was not a situation she was prepared to tolerate.

"Well, if he wants to bully them anymore, he's going to have to find them first," Segal said.

Dinah got an odd look on her face. "Guilford is looking for them already?"

"Yeah, he called just before I pulled up. I guess he had a follow-up in mind, but he can't find them. Wants us to call if we have any ideas."

Dinah did not meet his eye.

Segal picked up on that stoic concentration of hers and stopped swinging. "Do we have any ideas?"

Dinah opened the door and said, "You better follow me."

Segal walked through an entranceway into a large living room and then a bright kitchen that spanned most of the back of the house. Suzie Elah was pulled up to the kitchen table, eating a toasted cheese sandwich, and her mother, Emily, was at the stove making another. They both looked up when Segal came in.

Dinah whispered into his ear. "A mutual friend brought them over about an hour ago. They don't feel safe anymore. Not from the government. And not from whoever is responsible for, you know, what happened to Chickey and Gloria. They asked me to help them find a place to hide."

For a long moment, Segal said nothing. He was thinking he was not exactly in a position to lecture Dinah on the wisdom of offering people sanctuary in her home.

Finally, Emily held up a toasted cheese sandwich with her spatula and said, "You want some comfort food, lieutenant?"

After another pause, he sat at the table next to Suzie. "We're going to need all the comfort food we can get before this thing is over," he said.

CHAPTER 28

The Eleventh Rule

"Do you ever get the feeling we're being followed?"

"You're not getting paranoid on me, are you, Segal?" Dinah asked, shifting on her bar stool.

She sat next to Segal at the bar at Barley's Taproom, a good, loud place to have a private conversation. She could lean in close to him and no one, including the bartender, could hear a word she said. She could see the door to their left, in case someone walked in, and she could even see the rest of the room in the mirror without turning around for surveillance. It was the lunch hour. Waiters and waitresses moved around the dining landscape with pizzas and beers held aloft in a seamless, flowing dance. The background music was bluegrass with an Asheville edge. It was a place where she should have felt at home, but with the accumulation of recent events, nothing seemed exactly right anymore.

"In this case, I'm talking about the guy sitting over at that table eating garlic knots and swilling beer." Segal had his coat on, a book in the pocket as usual. He reached up and scratched his head.

Dinah glanced up at the mirror and down at her salad. "You're going to have to be more specific."

"The one checking out your butt."

Dinah's gaze flicked to the mirror. "Again, you're going to have to be more specific."

Segal frowned. "You really can't tell who I'm talking about? Like, which one of these objects doesn't belong with the others?"

"Blue shirt."

"Got it."

The blue-shirted guy polished off another garlic knot and wiped his fingers on his khaki pants. He pretended to watch the baseball game on the TV above the bar, and from time to time checked in on the two detectives, with a special pause at her butt.

She shrugged. Could be someone following them. Could be just some guy who liked the way she looked. Could even be a roller derby fan. On the other hand, she and Segal were in this case deep enough to warrant the attention of various agencies of various governments, foreign and domestic.

"Okay, point taken," she said.

"So, where are we?" Segal asked. "First of all, did you get your houseguests stashed somewhere out of the way?"

"Yeah, they're out of the way, all right." She sighed, played with her salad. "Look, Segal, I'm sorry about that."

Segal held up a hand.

"No, I mean it. I should have talked to you first. They showed up. We went from there."

"Sometimes, you have to make a call on the spot." He made a dismissive wave as if it were no big deal. "Rule number 1 of police work," he said. "Back up your partner."

Dinah stuck a forkful of chicken in her mouth.

"What are your thoughts on a next move?" Segal asked.

She swallowed, then said, without much enthusiasm, "We've got forensics and autopsy reports to follow up on. Both Chickey and Gloria." They had talked about this before, and neither one of them expected much in the way of breakthrough information.

"How about witnesses? Are we overlooking anyone? Anyone who might have seen something? Anyone else on background?" Segal reached for a dish of olives.

"We've got two guys canvassing the neighborhood around Creatures 2.0. Asking the neighbors if they saw or heard anything."

"Rule number 8 of police work," Segal said. "When you don't have any exciting stuff, follow up on the boring stuff till something gets exciting."

"This is the boring stuff, all right." Dinah had heard Segal's rules before. Although they tended to change in both number and content, they were pretty good.

Segal glanced toward the mirror. "Blue-shirt is making me hungry for garlic knots," he said.

"What about the picture Richard brought us?"

"I still don't know what to do with it," Segal said. "I mean, who do we trust? Even if I trusted Guilford personally, we don't know where it would end up. Could be tipping off the very people we're looking for. Then there's the problem of explaining how we got the picture using a crow and a crow camera we aren't supposed to know about."

"Suppose we show it to some of our most reliable eyes on the List," Dinah said. "We don't tell them who the guy is. We don't tell them why we're looking for him, only that they should call us if they spot him."

Segal popped an olive into his mouth and chewed.

"The List," as Dinah and Segal called it, was a group of people they consulted from time to time: street singers, guys who got the drum circles going, a couple of guys who played chess in Prichard Park, and a host of mobile food vendors. This was a network they had used in the past, their own private lookout team; people on the streets all day, present and unnoticed. Over time, they had cultivated relationships, figured out who they could trust and who could keep their mouth shut when that was called for.

"I keep thinking about Peter Olson's reaction. If he's right, this is a dangerous guy. Very dangerous, which we know from our own experience. If we pass out that picture and it somehow comes to the attention of the wrong people, we could be putting them in danger," Segal said.

"A lot of people seem to be in danger already."

"You have a point. It would have to be a very short list."

Dinah nodded as she discussed possible team members with Segal, arguing over some and quickly coming to an agreement.

"I'll start making the rounds," she said.

"You haven't had any more messages from Richard, have you?"

"Nope."

Segal swirled his drink.

Dinah had a swallow left; he had more.

"Why don't you take off first," he said. "I want to see if the guy follows you or sticks with me."

Dinah drank up and stood to leave.

"I guess that's it, then," Segal said. "You do your thing. I'll follow up on forensics, and in the meantime, we invoke rule number 11 of police work."

"Remind me what rule number 11 is."

"Rule 11 is work the case and wait for the bad guys to do something stupid. And sub-rule number 11.1 is sooner or later they always do something stupid."

"They better do something stupid pretty soon. We're running out of time."

Segal watched her push open the door and disappear into the bright sunlight. Then he checked out the length of the mirror as the garlic knot guy followed. *Hope he got a good look at her butt 'cause he'll never find her now*, he thought. That girl knew every alley and backroom in Asheville. He turned away and was surprised to find a woman on the barstool where Dinah had been. Her elbow was on the bar, and she leaned forward, resting her cheek on her hand. His grin faded as he suddenly felt much less smug about stealth operations.

"Interesting book," the woman said.

Segal was not sure if she was talking about the Hemingway or his notebook, open on the bar. He turned toward her and recognized who she was. She slid a business card to him, and he looked at it and read the name he expected to see. "Nancy Lund," he said.

"Peter Olson told me you have some questions about Francis Elah. He seemed to think something big might be happening here in Asheville. I feel like I owe it to Francis to help out if I can, considering the chances he took for us." She had a low, alto voice that reminded Segal of movies involving women conspirators. Secrets told in whispery shadows.

"Do you know where Francis is?" Segal asked softly.

"No," she said without hesitation. "Francis went off the radar a couple of weeks ago and took Richard with him."

"He was working with you?"

She frowned. "It's complicated. He worked a project for us. It involved going into another country, officially an ally of ours. We put him with a private contractor, so if things blew up, we could have some plausible distance from it."

"Cormorant?" he asked.

Nancy Lund blanched. "That's not a name you want to say out loud in the wrong place."

"We think some of them might be here in Asheville."

She leaned into the bar and pushed Dinah's empty glass out of the way. "That's not good news. Not for you or for Francis."

"If they work for you, why don't you call them off?" he asked.

"We used them for this job. That doesn't mean we control them. They have what people call 'a high level of autonomy.' At least this particular unit. It's led by a guy who really gives me the creeps, Colonel Arlon Peters. He calls himself 'the good guy with the gun,' as in, 'The only thing that can stop a bad guy with a gun is a good guy with a gun.' Believe it or not, there are people high up in our government that eat that stuff up."

"He's still a colonel even though he's with a private company?" Segal asked.

"Well, his history is very hush-hush, however word around the drinking fountain is that he was drummed out of the army over some incident in East Africa. Some incident that no one especially wants to talk about. Let's say only that the supposed good guy with a gun stopped a lot of bad guys that didn't turn out to be so bad after all. Anyway, he hooked up with Cormorant so the colonel is gone but not forgotten. To my mind, it's debatable who he hates more, our enemies or the current administration. Between you and me there is an investigation into Cormorant going on right now. It's slow going though so you can't expect much help out of Washington any time soon."

"You think he's looking for Francis, this colonel?" Segal asked.

"Probably Francis and Richard both," Nancy Lund answered. "Look, I can't tell you what they were doing. I can tell you Francis, along with Richard and a group from Cormorant, were tasked with a very specific, critical, and dangerous operation. They pulled it off perfectly. Ironically their part of it required no guns. Everything should have been fine."

"And it wasn't."

"Soon after they got back to the States, I got a frantic call from Francis. He told me he had to go underground. He said

Cormorant wanted him for another project. He refused, and Cormorant didn't like it. He was told he didn't get to choose."

"Did he say what this other project was?"

"No. They hadn't let him in on the details. Only gave him a rough idea. Enough that he knew he wanted nothing to do with it. He told me he would try to get some specifics. So, we could stop them. Then he was gone."

"Cormorant is looking for him because he knows too much about something they're planning?"

"That would be my guess," she said.

"And why is ONI looking for him? Are they working with Cormorant?"

She shook her head. "This ability for Francis to use Richard to observe certain things without drawing attention, that's a capability we would rather keep under wraps. ONI was tasked with getting Francis and Richard back, one way or another."

"What should we do?" Segal asked.

"You should be careful is what you should do. Cormorant are not your ordinary guys."

"If you figure out what this mysterious project is that Francis didn't want to do, will you let me know?" Segal asked.

Nancy Lund reached over and took a drink of Segal's beer. She wiped her mouth and said, "Ask not for whom the bell tolls, lieutenant."

And Segal watched as she, too, disappeared through the door and into the sunshine.

CHAPTER 29

Nasty Fox

"I am not falling for this animal crap again," said the man with the muscular build. In spite of the fact that he was wearing civilian clothes, he came off as military in appearance and bearing. His companion, a much thinner man, did not.

He stood beside a stone wall bordering an open field, watching a fox approach on a well-worn footpath. The fox took a few stumbling steps, paused, looked around, and seemed to consider its lot in life. Then it staggered sideways and continued its advance toward them.

"That fox is not right," the thinner man said. "I've seen plenty of foxes in the wild. They move real smooth and graceful. This fox has rabies or something."

The muscular man put his hand flat against the wall. "That's what they want you to think. That fox was trained by Francis Elah. Or someone who works for him, and I'm tired of them making fools of us. Think about where we are.

We're on the Biltmore Estate, where we know he trained lots of animals. That fox was supposed to act like it has rabies just to scare us off. If it even is a fox. Maybe it's some kind of dog made up to look like a fox."

"Either way," said the thin man, "I say we shoot it." He withdrew a pistol from a pocket in his cargo pants.

"I'm not falling for this crap again. I almost got killed falling off that Grove Arcade building when that crow tried to peck my head off. Then I had to explain it to command. I'm not going through that again. Fool me once, shame on you. Fool me twice, shame on . . . whatever," he said, forgetting the line. Then he, too, checked his pockets, but instead of bringing out a gun he produced a box of Milk Duds. "Watch this," he said.

By this time, the fox was less than twenty feet away. The man shook out a Milk Dud, held it on an open palm, extended his hand, and advanced slowly toward the fox.

The thin man said, "Chocolate's not supposed to be good for dogs."

"Really?" the muscular man said. "You're ready to put a nine-millimeter round in it, but you're worried a Milk Dud might upset its stomach?"

"How do you know it even likes Milk Duds?" the thin man said. He backed away while his companion advanced.

"Who the hell doesn't like Milk Duds?" All this time, he had not taken his eyes off the fox. He crept slowly forward with his hand extended. "You like Milk Duds, don't you, little fella?" he said in a sweet, coaxing voice. He got within a couple of feet and knelt. The fox leaned to one side and opened his mouth, allowing a blob of foamy saliva to drop to the ground.

"You still think he's faking rabies?" the thin man asked.

"He's just salivating 'cause he sees food," the muscle man persisted. "Yeah, it looks good, doesn't it, little fella? Here." With that, he extended his hand with the Milk Dud right under the nose of the fox. The fox bit into man's hand with savage speed and force. His diseased teeth sunk deep into the web of flesh between the thumb and forefinger and the fox rapidly shook his head in a motion designed to make the teeth sink in even deeper and to rend the skin and muscle and sinew.

The Milk Dud dropped to the ground.

The man screamed as he stood and stumbled. When the fox held on to his hand like a pit bull, the man spun around, as if maybe the fox might fly off by centrifugal force. It did not. "Do something!" he yelled to his companion.

The thin man was panicked for his companion but also terrified of the fox. He had a vision of the fox coming loose from the guy's hand and flying toward him with snarling teeth. He didn't know the best course of action, so, having a pistol conveniently in his hand, he shot the fox the next time his friend's bizarre spinning motion brought the animal back around to a favorable position. It was a good shot, even if it was at close range.

Although the animal hung limp, the jaws did not release and had to be pried open with a stick they found by the wall.

Segal returned to the station to check the forensic reports. He heard raucous laughter well before he reached the break room. When he entered, he saw four uniformed officers around one of the tables. They hunched over an iPad. "Play it again," one of them said.

Segal assumed they'd found a new YouTube video, not an uncommon occurrence in a police break room. Probably, it was a drunk driver video. Cops loved drunk driver videos, especially videos of young women pulled over for traffic violations and undergoing sobriety tests. The drunker they were, the worse they did on the tests and the funnier the videos.

Segal walked over to the coffeepot. The owner of the iPad had started the video over, as suggested. "Oh, man. There he goes," one of the guys said. The others were making sounds of anticipation, even though Segal realized they knew exactly how this thing was going to end.

"What is that he puts in his hand?" another cop asked.

"I told you, I think it's a Milk Dud," the first cop said. "Yeah, there. You can see the box in his other hand."

"Why would you give a Milk Dud to a fox?" the other cop asked. "Would a fox even like a Milk Dud?"

"Who the hell doesn't like a Milk Dud?" said the owner of the iPad.

Segal's attention peaked considerably. "What are you guys watching?" he said, leaning in.

"You gotta see this, lieutenant," the first cop said.

The man on the iPad advanced, hand extended, toward a fox.

"That animal doesn't look right," Segal mumbled.

"No shit, lieutenant. That fox is rabid as hell."

Segal watched in horrified amazement as the scene unfolded, perhaps one of the worst judgment calls ever captured on camera. When the man's advance stopped and he knelt in front of the fox, one of the cops said, "Wait for it, wait for it." When the fox struck the hand, everyone in the room yelled, "Damn!" And when the fox shook his head to sink the teeth in deeper, everyone said, "Oh, shit!" It was so perfectly bad Segal could not look away.

"Where did you get this?" he asked. "Is it on YouTube?"

"Not yet it isn't," the one with the iPad said. "This is from one of the security cameras at the Biltmore Estate."

For Segal, this stopped being a funny home video. "When did you get this?"

"Yesterday. I mean, it happened yesterday. Animal Control got the call from Biltmore security. Film footage shows the outside of the wall around the flower garden."

"People there heard the shot?" Segal asked.

"No, that was the weird thing. I mean, one of the weird things. People in the flower garden, just on the other side of the wall, heard the guy screaming and saw the two men running away. No one heard a gunshot. It was only when they pulled up film that they saw the gun. Then they went around and found the dead fox."

"I need a copy of this right away," Segal said to the cop with the iPad.

The cop nodded and raised his eyebrows. "Sure."

Before leaving the room, Segal turned and said, "And no posting to YouTube. Not yet."

"What do you think?" Segal asked.

Now, he had his own iPad. He was showing it to Dinah. She was trying to cool down from running all over town. A drop of sweat fell onto the screen. He was showing her a still picture of the guy bitten by the fox.

"I can't tell if it's him." She dried the drops on the screen with a napkin, then flicked back to the file that held the other photos. Segal let her take the iPad. She was better at this stuff than he was. She dragged the photo so the images were side by side. She also held up the copy she had been passing out to selected lookouts. "The lighting is different. They're built kind of the same. I can't tell if it's the same guy."

"Yeah, me neither," Segal said, feeling disappointed. "It's similar, but somehow you don't get the same impression. I mean, these guys seem like knuckleheads, like, 'Hey, y'all, watch this.' The guys who attacked us were nothing if not professional."

"I know what you mean," Dinah said. "Especially if the killer trained as a sniper. The ones I knew were professional. Army Rangers. The best of the best."

"Either way, we need to track these guys down."

"We should put out a notice to the emergency rooms to inform us if someone comes in with a bite like that," Dinah said.

"Already done. It's standard procedure with rabies. The Animal Control people were already on it."

"So, the fox did have rabies?"

"Oh, they'll confirm it with tests. The vet said there there's no doubt it was rabid as hell," Segal said. "The knuckleheads actually did a good deed putting it down."

Dinah took a sip of soda. They were at an outdoor table. The afternoon was waning, but it was still hot. "You're pretty sure they were there at the Biltmore Estate checking out Lucile's crows?"

"She showed me the crow habitat she set up over there," Segal said. "I don't know what else would bring them there. My guess is they're still looking for Richard."

"What else can we do with this?" She was watching the video again.

"I'll tell you what the guys at the station want to do. They want to put it up on the internet."

"Like, YouTube?"

"Yeah, YouTube." Segal gave a little laugh, and so did Dinah.

"The thing would probably go viral," Dinah said. "You did invoke rule number 11, and sure enough someone did something stupid."

Segal's phone rang. He listened to dispatch. "Really? Tell them to stall the guys. Keep them there till we can get over." He smiled at Dinah. "That was dispatch. Two guys just showed up at the ER at Park Ridge. One has his hand bandaged up. The other is asking if rabies can fly through the air. Looks like we finally caught a break."

Park Ridge Hospital was not the closest emergency room to the Biltmore Estate. It was a few miles south. Apparently, the two men had tried to put off the inevitable for a day, then decided they might be able to conceal their mishap by traveling that distance. The plan greatly underestimated the efficiency of modern communications, especially where out-breaks of rabies were concerned.

Dinah drove. It took them about twenty minutes to reach the ER. Segal leaned into the receptionist's office and dis-creetly showed his badge, and the two of them were ushered into the treatment area. The nurse and doctor were paged away to make sure the men were alone in the room when they entered. Dinah unclipped the strap on her holster.

They stood in the hallway. The door to the room was open. The muscular man from the video sat on the bed, reclined against a pile of pillows. His right hand was mas-sively wrapped with white gauze. In his left hand, he held a brochure.

He's going to suffer good, Segal thought.

The brochure said, "Animal Bites and Rabies." Segal could picture it describing the long and painful series of shots the patient would experience over the next few weeks. A thin man was sitting on a chair by the bed, absorbed in the screen of a large smartphone.

Dinah entered and Segal followed.

The thin man made a reflexive move with his hand inside his jacket. Dinah flicked her gun out and said, simply, "No." The thin man brought his hand back out, and Segal reached into the man's jacket pocket and removed a nine-millimeter automatic. The gun had an attachment on the muzzle end.

He held up the gun for a better look. "This is an interesting little addition you have," he said. He ejected the clip and checked to make sure no bullet was in the chamber. He turned the gun around and inspected it from different angles. "Is this a silencer?" He could not imagine what else it could be, although it was much smaller than any silencer he had seen.

"Suppressor," the man on the bed said.

Dinah shrugged at Segal.

"We call them suppressors," the man said, as if that clarified the situation.

"And who exactly is 'we'?" Segal crossed his arms over his chest.

"Huh?" the guy asked.

"I'm Ira Segal, Asheville Police Department." Segal took out his badge. "I'm asking who you are and who you work for."

The guy in the bed turned to his friend.

"They already know who we are," Dinah said. "You could see it on their faces the minute we walked in." She took out a pair of handcuffs and stepped toward the thin man. "You're both under arrest. Put your hands behind your back."

"What are you arresting us for?" the thin man asked.

"Hunting foxes out of season and anything else I can think up," she said. "We've got a lot to talk about." She clamped the cuffs on.

Segal pulled out another set of cuffs. He looked at the guy with the bandaged hand, which made it much too big for the cuff.

Then he heard a commotion in the hall, one of the nurses telling someone the area was off-limits. Mr. ONI, Jerome Guilford, perfect brown shoes and all, walked through the door. He stopped and gave the room a quick appraisal. "You can take off the handcuffs, sergeant," he said. "These men are agents in the employ of ONI."

Segal glared at him.

Dinah unlocked the cuffs and pushed the guy's hands away.

Segal looked at Guilford for further explanation.

"They were staking out a location known to be visited by Francis Elah. By chance they came across a rabid animal which had to be put down," Guilford said.

"Is that how you're going to report this?" Dinah asked.

"There won't be any report. We need to keep this incident under wraps. These men are working undercover."

Segal realized that their big break had just collapsed into nothing. The man on the bed was not the man in the picture that Richard brought to Dinah. He was not their suspect.

Dinah punched the screen of the cell phone she had taken from the thin man and pushed it into Guilford's hands. "Hope you're a fan of YouTube," she said.

Segal followed her out the door, not waiting to see Guilford's reaction.

CHAPTER 30

Call of the Dog

Dinah knew that the hot dog vendor, Conover by name, liked to set up on Pack Square, especially by the little plaza in front of the Diana Wortham Theatre and the art museum. He explained to her once that if he didn't get too close to the entrance, no one hassled him. Business was good from tourists as well as from people who worked in the office buildings on the other side of the square, across from the Vance Memorial. He was even close to the courthouse and the police station, which was how Dinah met him.

"But the real reason I like it here, I like the action of people coming and going, and I like to think about the history," he told her.

Dinah understood what he meant. South from the hot dog stand, the replica of Thomas Wolfe's angel was just to his left, less than a hundred feet away. It marked the place where W. O. Wolfe, Tom's father, had his stone-carving business.

It was around ten in the morning, and Conover was already serving dogs. Many vendors didn't set up that early. Conover found that a surprising number of people heard the call of the dog at this hour, perhaps making up for a missed breakfast or simply as a midmorning snack.

He had just finished preparing a dog with ketchup, mustard, and onions for a girl who may or may not have had any sleep the night before when a man walking near Pack Square caught his eye. He hurried to complete the money part of the transaction before the man passed by. He handed the girl her change and thanked her while the man was still several paces to the east. Conover was pretty sure he recognized him as the guy in Dinah's pictures. When the guy pulled closer, Conover said, "Breakfast dog?" As he hoped, the guy angled toward him so he got a good head-on look. The guy actually seemed to give the suggestion thoughtful consideration before shaking his head and proceeding on his way.

As soon as the guy was a safe distance away, Conover took his cell phone from the pocket in his apron and pulled up the pictures for confirmation. He pressed Dinah's number.

"Dinah here," she said.

He didn't slow her down with small talk. "Just spotted your bogey at Pack Square. He's headed west on Patton Avenue, on foot."

"What's he wearing?"

"Khakis and a dark green golf shirt, some kind of emblem on the front of it," Conover said. The guy rounded the corner where Patton took a little jog and disappeared from Conover's sight.

Dinah changed her path. She'd been headed toward her car in her gym shorts and tank top after a morning workout, but walking would be quicker from where she was. Even so, she hesitated, realizing she did not have her gun or badge. She didn't expect to need them, nevertheless, it didn't feel right without them. Force of habit and conditioning: if you did police work, you had your gun and badge. Well, she didn't have them and she needed to see where this guy was going. She imagined herself headed down College Street, possibly catching sight of the guy by the time she got to Prichard Park. Then she realized she would probably be a couple of streets behind. She continued walking quickly as she pulled up a number on her phone.

"Hey, Di-nah," said the voice on the other end.

He always drew out the first syllable to sweeten it up. "Lester, are you at the boards?" she asked. "This is serious. I have a live one."

"Yeah, we here. Got no game going yet, but we here." Her friend was a small black man of indeterminate age, sitting next to a nerdy, overweight white guy. The unlikely pair often claimed their places at the chessboards at Prichard Park.

"Our man is headed your way, west on Patton. Khakis and dark green shirt. I need you to see which way he heads when he gets to the park."

"Got it," Lester said.

"And Lester, keep your head down."

"Even you won't know I'm here."

Dinah turned onto College Street and walked quickly up the hill toward the park. She saw Lester as soon as she came to the traffic light. He gave her a little motion with his hand, indicating the guy had turned right. She scanned that direction in time to see the guy turn left at the next corner. The guy hesitated for the briefest moment and glanced in front and behind him. She pulled back behind the building at the corner, hoping he had not seen her. She was not sure if she would be recognized, especially out of her normal work clothes. She didn't want to take any chances. She held a second, then turned right on Haywood and followed. After a short distance, she peeked left on Battery Park and turned the corner with caution, hoping to catch sight of the guy but having no wish to be spotted herself.

Only a few feet farther there was an odd intersection where Wall Street came in at an angle to join Battery Park. On the other side of this intersection was a wedge-shaped structure known as the Flat Iron Building. Nearby was a little plaza with a sculpture; a big flatiron. At this plaza by the sculpture, musicians liked to set up to play, and it was there that Dinah saw Mattie, with a mandolin in her hands and blowing into a harmonica fixed to a metal bracket that rested on her shoulders, Bob Dylan style. She was accompanying a couple of guys playing guitars and singing. Mattie nodded her head down Wall Street, giving Dinah a serious gaze with her eyes.

Dinah went left into the small street. She walked quickly through the plaza but then stopped. After a slight turn,

Wall Street became a narrow path in a canyon formed by tall buildings. Dinah's instincts took over—instincts formed from police service, instincts formed by military experience, including deployment in Afghanistan, instincts formed from the fundamental forces of animal evolution. Without thinking, her hand went to her hip, where she normally carried her service pistol. *Damn. No gun.* It was not a good feeling. She considered waiting for backup of some kind, knew this was a unique chance.

Instead, her hand moved to the cell phone in her pocket. She pulled up Segal's number to let him know where she was. He didn't answer, and she left a brief message, all the while inching along the sidewalk, eyes on full alert.

She rounded the bend to the point where she could see straight down the street, almost to the end where it joined Otis Street across from the federal building. To her surprise, she saw no sign of the man. He had disappeared. Only a few people were on the street, not as many as she would have wanted, no crowd into which *she* could disappear. She walked ahead, trying to take in everything, trying not to draw attention to herself.

She passed by little shops on her left, pretending to window shop, searching the interiors for the man and also checking the other side of the narrow street by studying the reflection in the glass. She saw no sign of him. The deeper she got into the street, the more she felt the unease of being trapped in that canyon of brick and cement and glass.

Cautiously, she progressed about halfway down the street. To her right was a parking garage that opened onto Battery Park on the opposite side. On her left was one of the best-known vegetarian restaurants in town, the Laughing Seed Café. Still no sign of the guy in the green shirt. Farther on, there were fewer shops, and then only the narrow lane that ran between the elevated decks of the parking garage on one side and the backs of buildings on the other.

Dinah needed to think. She perused the window of the Laughing Seed as if to read the menu. She glanced to her right, looking for any sign of movement, then to her left, wondering if she had missed the man in one of the shops. She was confused and frustrated, but even more than that, her sense of danger was cranked so high she had to consciously slow her breathing.

The man waited on the top deck of the parking garage, checking to make sure he was alone. He caught his breath, wincing with pain every time he inhaled deeply. He checked the street. He was pretty sure no one had seen him do the quick ascent, almost three stories straight up, using the handholds of the climbing wall built into the side of the structure. His ribs hurt like hell where she—The Dinosaur—had shot him a few days before dead center of his body armor. He saw her come into view on Wall Street and crouched to make sure she didn't spot him. He smiled. The climb was part of his training. A quick, unexpected change in elevation almost always confused pursuers. Any doubt that she was following him vanished. This was trouble. He had wanted to take care of these "local complications," however, the colonel put a low priority on it. This changed everything. He knew the colonel approved of decisions in the field dealing with significant changes in status. Well, this was certainly significant. This was his call, and he had a good setup.

He glimpsed over the wall. The woman cop (he never called them by their names; made it too personal) stopped in front of a restaurant, pretending to read the menu way too much. He snapped a couple of pictures with his cell phone. Then he calmly put away the phone, withdrew the gun from his pocket, and pointed it at her, leaning against the wall for stability. He slowed his breathing as he lined up the sights.

Dinah's cell phone rang. It was Mattie. Dinah used her peripheral vision and saw her leaning against one of the buildings at the top of the street, trying to act nonchalant. But when Dinah answered, Mattie was anything but nonchalant. "You need to get off the street right now," Mattie whispered, cupping her hand over the phone and her mouth.

The urgency in her voice left no room for doubt. Dinah opened the door and stepped into the vestibule of the restaurant. She whispered into her phone, "What's going on?"

"Your guy. He's on the top floor. The parking garage. He's got a gun."

Dinah knelt and, staying within the shadows of the vestibule, peered through the plate glass to the top floor of the garage. Sure enough, she got an image of the guy leaning over the edge. She kneeled to make sure he didn't see her. Wondering how he had managed to get up there in such short order, she caught sight of the climbing wall at the end of the parking garage across the street. It explained how he got up there, however it did not make her feel better. Free-climbing as quickly as he must have done was no easy feat. She thought of the guys she had met in the military. Special Forces were the only ones she knew who would have tried something like that.

Still kneeling, she whispered into the phone, "Mattie, thanks. Walk away casually. Don't draw attention. And if you see this guy again, give me a call."

"Be careful, Dino," Mattie said.

Dinah had that certain feeling that the hunter had become the hunted, a slow-burning sensation in the pit of her stomach. She was alone and unarmed. She knew exactly what Segal would tell her. It was the same thing any of her mentors throughout her training and deployment would have told her: *Get out and live to fight another day.* She turned and walked into the restaurant.

The man on the parking garage waited for the woman cop to come out. It was odd. People left a restaurant to talk on a phone; they didn't go inside. He sized up the street, saw nothing unusual other than that hippy musician girl with the long legs. She was leaning against a wall talking on her cell phone, too. *That's all people do these days*, he thought, *talk on their cell phones.*

He scanned the street below, divided into sharp contrasts between dark shadows and bright sunlight. A few people walked up the ramp of the garage deck, talking loudly. He concealed the gun and walked toward them as if he had just left his car there. He ran down the steps onto Battery Park and then down the stairs that led to Wall Street across from the Laughing Seed; his turn to play the casual diner.

He stopped inside the door, allowing his eyes to adjust from the brightness outside. The main room of the restaurant was down a few steps, tables to his right, bar in the center, more tables straight ahead.

A girl approached with some menus, and he asked if he could sit at the bar for a quick drink. As he descended the steps, he scanned the room again, still not seeing the big-haired cop. He sat and ordered one of the blended drinks, acted casual as he kept tabs on the comings and goings, especially down the short hallway that led to the restrooms, where, he theorized, his target must be. He saw no other exits. He had her trapped.

Five minutes passed. He was getting a bad feeling about the situation when the girl brought him his drink, something called a Tropicalia. He squinted at the first taste—not that the drink was bad, although not what he was expecting.

A motion to his left caught his eye. A couple gathered their things at one of the smaller tables. The girl stood and unslung her purse from the chair where it had been hanging, a good-looking girl in a nice, loose dress. The guy signed the credit card slip and fumbled for his wallet to put the receipt away. Then they surprised him. They headed not for the front door but to the side of the room, where he watched their heads disappear as they descended a flight of stairs. He had not seen the stairway because it was concealed behind a low partition topped with a planter.

He felt a moment of panic. He took another hit on his drink, getting used to it. Trying not to show too much haste or attract attention. He pulled a bill out of his wallet, left it on the bar. He walked to the side of the room, where he found himself at the head of the stairway. He could not see where the stairs led. It was not until he reached the landing and turned the corner that he saw he was in a bar called Jack of the Wood. Even at this early hour, a small crowd filled the place and a band brought instruments and mikes up on a stage. Worse yet, the front door led out to a street. It was easy to forget, with all the buildings distorting the landscape, that Asheville was a mountain town with lots of elevation changes.

Where had the lady cop gone?

He swung around and confirmed what he already knew. She was not there. He saw the couple from the Laughing Seed winding their way through the crowd and walking out the door into the sunshine. He followed and found himself on the busy sidewalk of Patton Avenue. He scanned the street and started walking west, pulling out his cell phone to make a call he did not want to make.

CHAPTER 31

Protective Custody

"Am, I being held in protective custody?" Lucile Devroe asked. She lay beneath a set of tan sheets and had yet to open her eyes for daytime use. She wore one of his white T-shirts. That was all.

They were in Segal's apartment, where he stayed for the morning, ostensibly to update reports away from the distractions of the squad room. To be sure, he had reporting to do on the rapid developments in a case that had started simply enough with the body of one man floating in the river. Now, it was quite complex. Well, more than complex. It was a mess. The captain had barked at him to "tie up loose ends." That was a laugh. A huge snarl of loose threads was more like it. Not only that. With various federal agencies involved, he knew that anything he committed to writing would be scrutinized and possibly used as evidence against him. It made him nervous.

And yet, on a deeper level, from his decades of experience, he felt confident that it all somehow made sense and that he and Dinah had the ability to figure it out. That was the payoff for all of this. To be the ones to put all the pieces together and to be the first to see the truth of the picture. The more complex and difficult the pieces, the more beautiful and profound the moment when they clicked into place.

With Dr. Gold, he had explained this feeling of security in solving cases more than once.

The first time, she'd asked him, "Why do you think you carry those old books around with you all the time?"

He didn't hesitate. "I like to read in my spare time. It makes me feel good."

"But why those particular books?"

"I don't know. They're good books. Things make sense in these books."

"I think you're on to something there. I think your basic perception of the world is that things *need to* make sense. Things happen for a reason, if only you can figure it out. And you're the person who's supposed to figure those things out." Dr. Gold sighed.

"I guess that's my job."

"But you can't see the reason for getting shot," Dr. Gold said.

Segal said nothing.

Dr. Gold spoke gently. "Segal, your body is healing. You are making great progress on dealing with PTSD. This is your last hurdle. You had one of your core beliefs blown away on that day. You're not sure the world does make sense anymore, at least in the way you used to think. The remainder of your life will come anyway, and you'll figure out how it makes sense when it does."

For the first time in a long while, he felt and believed that himself. Based on what exactly, he wasn't sure. Having Lucile Devroe in his bed made him more certain than anything else. Life came together. Mostly for the "good."

He had risen early and resisted the temptation to check news or email, as he generally did to start his day. He had slipped out on the balcony with his laptop and phone and orange juice and begun to type away. On this morning, his apartment was not without distractions. Lucile had awakened and called to him, and the task of writing was no competition for what he saw when he looked toward the bed. And there he had returned. After some time, he was dressed and passing the bed again when Lucile asked the question about protective custody. He was trying to frame a reply that contained both lighthearted humor and sincere affection when his cell phone sounded from the table on the balcony.

He stepped through the sliding glass door. As he picked it up, he said "Crap" under his breath. He saw it was Dinah, and he saw he'd missed a call from her a few minutes earlier. How often had he stressed the importance of partners being available to each other?

Dinah said, "Segal, I need you to pick me up. I got a look at the shooter. We need to follow up, and I don't have wheels." She told him her location and asked how soon he could be there.

"Five minutes, tops," was his answer.

Four and a half minutes later, Segal pulled up in front of the restaurant where Dinah had taken refuge. She flew out and joined him, her bare legs doing a scissor kick when she jumped in.

"We need to turn around. Our guy was headed west on Patton," she said, all business.

Segal nodded at the way she was dressed, before shifting into gear and moving out.

She noticed and said, "I don't have my piece or my badge with me. This thing came on fast. I could either follow or lose the guy. I followed."

"Sort of a come-as-you-are kind of affair," Segal said as he swung around the block. He didn't feel like giving any lectures this morning. In the first place, she already knew she had taken a chance and almost found out the hard way what the consequences could be. Second, he did not feel on especially high moral ground, having missed her first call for assistance. Mostly though, he wanted to hear what had gone down. "When you saw the guy, did he see you?"

"Not at first. Later on, he did for sure. I'll give you details in a minute. Right now, let's see if we can get any clues where this guy was headed."

After he got them pointed the right way on Patton, they cruised down three or four blocks before Dinah said, "Turn left here. I got a call from one of the chess players at the park. He thought he saw the guy hang a left, definitely down one of these streets. Trouble is, you can barely see from where the boards are."

Segal did as she told him, taking them onto one of those odd, mixed streets that had probably been residential until a few years ago. Much of it still was. In the first block off Patton Avenue, businesses had displaced some of the homes, and other homes had been converted into offices for doctors and accountants.

They cruised down the block on high alert but saw no sign of their man. The second block was more solidly residential, mostly large houses, many broken into apartments.

"What do you think?" Segal asked.

"I think we're going too slow," Dinah said. "Let's not attract attention."

He saw she was right and sped up a little.

Then he pointed.

"You're kidding," she said.

In front of a nondescript house on the left was an old and majestic oak tree, and on the topmost branch, a large crow perched. Segal tried to keep his head forward as they drove by. Dinah, who was less visible from the house, ducked down. She read the house number out loud.

"Turn left at the corner," Dinah said. "I think an alley runs behind these houses."

"If you told me a week ago we'd be taking our cues from crows, I would have thought you were crazy," he said. He turned into the alley. He let the tires roll slowly, and when they approached the rear of the house in question, he saw something glinting up in a tree. In a small black walnut tree was a platform, much like the one Lucile had shown him on the Biltmore Estate.

They circled and made one more pass in front on the street. Segal explained about the platform. "Let's get to the station and look up some information on that house," he said.

"Get me a bagel on the way," Dinah said. "Sesame seed. Toasted. Cream cheese." She finally settled in the seat and blew out a long breath of decompression.

Segal didn't press her until he put a bagel and a bottle of juice in her hands and they were at the station. She wolfed the food, still in her shorts and tank top. He wanted a detailed account, and he planned to hash out how this helped shape the picture.

With her cheeks full, she recounted the call from the hot dog vendor and the first part of her pursuit. "Then I turned onto Battery Park, and thank God Mattie was there. That was the only way I knew to follow him into Wall Street." She described how going into Wall Street brought her back to the creepy feeling of street patrols in Afghanistan. "Then I never would have seen him on top of the parking garage if Mattie hadn't called."

"Yeah, thank God for Mattie," Segal echoed. His brain traced a shadow in his mind. There was something odd about that detail. After a moment, he said, "You know, I was thinking about that list of people we came up with the other day. The street people we asked to be on the lookout."

Dinah nodded; her mouth crammed with bagel.

"I don't remember putting Mattie's name there."

She swallowed. "Mattie wasn't on the original list. I assumed you thought of her later."

Segal's eyes narrowed. "Dinah, I didn't call her. Are you saying you didn't either?"

"Nope." She cleared her last bite of bagel and took a drag on the juice bottle. "Then, to ask the obvious question, how did she know what was going on? How did she know

I would be tracking this particular guy on this particular morning?"

Segal had the sense they had just been handed a major piece of the puzzle. It would take some care to use it correctly. He thought about Mattie, what he did know about her, what he didn't know, and how he felt about it all. What he did know was very little. She came and went, as many musicians do. Come to think of it, he didn't have a clue about her last name. What he felt about her, though, was much more than facts could bring to the table. He felt she followed a path of her own—her own style of dress, her own style of music. There was a solidness to it and a depth that always struck him as unique in an intelligent and self-assured way. It was as if Mattie was aware of things others didn't see or experience and she was letting them in on the secret one musical note at a time.

Then Segal thought of the night of the roller derby match. "How well does Mattie know Emily Elah?"

"They're friends," Dinah said. "It was Mattie who sent Emily and Suzie to me for protection."

"I saw Mattie talking to Emily Elah at your roller derby match. It didn't seem like a casual conversation either."

Dinah moved her jaw side to side as if it were aching. "This is Asheville," she said. "People know people."

Strange as it sounded, he understood what she meant. It was a characteristic of the city that locals cultivated acquaintances with a wide range of people with various backgrounds and interests, as if they were building and storing collections. It was one of the things that added strength and vigor and character to the place; a web of people interconnected in all sorts of ways. "Yeah. People know people. I wonder what people Miss Mattie knows?" Segal asked.

At that point, a uniformed officer came in and handed Dinah a piece of paper. It was the information on the house. It listed the deed holder and details about the last time the property had changed hands.

"I already called the owner like you asked," the officer said. "She told me she leased the place to a security company a few weeks ago. Here's the name." He slid a piece of notepaper across the table.

Dinah tapped it with her finger and slid it to Segal.

Segal sighed and put his hands over his ears. "I guess I'll go up and explain to the captain why we should raid a house in downtown Asheville because we saw a crow in a tree."

CHAPTER 32

Den of Thieves

The man pulled at his green shirt as he walked down Patton Avenue at a medium pace, a pace calculated to move him along without drawing attention. He passed the federal building, surveyed the roof, checking for any unusual surveillance, whether by human, animal, or electronic device. He saw no movement up there. He was aware the building was inhabited mainly by the NOAA and several other seemingly innocuous agencies. You never knew who might be on site.

He really wanted to know what that woman cop was up to, the one the roller derby fans called "the Dinosaur." In the interim, he'd learned a bit about her. She was no longer tailing him. Of that he was certain. Something had put the fear of God in her. He felt pleased with himself for picking up on her and then losing her in that narrow street, although he realized there was an element of luck, too. That move at the restaurant was weird. Before going in, she'd answered a call, and there was no mistaking the fear that crossed her face. He wondered what the call was and thought again about that girl with the long legs up the street, the street singer who dressed so weird. There was something off about how she was standing there and talking into a phone at the same time as the cop, even though they weren't in sight of each other. He had noticed her before, mostly because he liked girls with long legs. After that, he had lost her—the woman cop, that is; Dinah Rudisill. The colonel would not be pleased with that. He would not be pleased with any of this. Still, he wasn't psychic. How was he supposed to know she would recognize him and start following? How was he supposed to know she would be tipped off to his maneuver up the side of the parking garage? And above all, how the hell was he supposed to know that she could walk down the stairs from a vegetarian restaurant and end up in a Patton Avenue bar? What kind of freak show city was this, anyway? Tough. It was the colonel's own fault for not letting him eliminate the threats when he wanted to. That would surely change now.

He kept moving, feeling the need to get off the streets before the woman cop enlisted other resources. He darted left and picked up the pace, even though his ribs were killing him. He walked past the house, pretended to drop something in the mailbox at the next corner, then did a half circle and walked up onto the porch. He saw no sign of anyone watching.

At the door, he looked up at the security camera, expecting to hear the door unlock, but nothing happened, so he had to fumble for his key. They were getting slack and lazy in there, no one watching the security cameras on their own site. The military sucked in a lot of ways, but at least it was good for discipline—better than the private sector. The whole homeland was getting slack, and this town was a prime example. Good thing the countdown showed only a few days left. Then maybe he could get out of the country and into some real action someplace where they took things more seriously.

When he pushed through the door, the technician called to him from another room. The rest of the house was too silent, seemed deserted. The place was getting to be a mess, beer cans on the dining room table, boxes packed and unpacked, and the man was glad that, one way or another, they would be leaving soon.

He walked into the large room where the technician was working. When the house had been a private residence, it would have been the formal dining room. Now, instead of hosting guests or relatives, it was their main operational center. The technician had his monitoring equipment set up there. Taking up most of one wall was the big whiteboard where they posted pictures, wrote notes, and, in the upper right-hand corner, kept their daily countdown, lest anyone forget the timeline was tight. The technician, as usual, worked with a screen and a keyboard and barely acknowledged him when he came into the room.

The man pulled out his phone and called up the archive of photos. "I've got a couple of pictures for you to print out," he said. "One showing your girlfriend cop, and one of some hippy-chick. So far, the hippy-chick has not been on our radar."

This got the technician's interest.

As the man knew well, the technician had developed quite a thing for Dinah. The technician took the phone and downloaded the pictures of Dinah and Mattie to his computer. He exported them to the printer, then walked over to retrieve the first as it emerged. He held up the shot of Dinah and admired it, even sighing a little. "Shorts and a tank top," he said. "Daddy like."

The man frowned and went into the kitchen for a bottle of grapefruit juice.

The tech's voice followed him. "What were you doing? Waiting outside the gym to get me some good pics?"

The man returned. He took a drink and checked the monitor for the house security cameras. "No, I think she was hanging out waiting for me somewhere. Either that or someone put her on to me. One way or another, she was on my tail."

"On your tail? Jeez!" the technician said. Then he, too, checked the monitor. The technician panned out with one of the cameras and repositioned it to see more of the street.

"Why's that one off?" the man said, pointing to a blank square on the screen.

The technician muttered something under his breath and then tilted a box with several cable connections so he could see the back. He pushed on one of the cable connectors, and the square on the screen came to life.

It was the colonel's face looking into the lens; intense blue eyes and short neat hair. The technician jumped.

In the background of the video feed, the man could see a white van in the parking place off the alley. It was the camera at the rear of the house.

"Looks like the colonel is home," the tech said. He hit the button to unlock the back door.

A moment later, the colonel was in the room with them, followed by the fourth man of their crew. The colonel set his briefcase on the table and opened it. "You have pictures for me?"

"Yes," the tech said, handing them over.

"What do you have to report?" he asked when no one spoke up.

"She was on my tail this morning," the man said, holding his rib cage. He gave the colonel a quick and factual account of the chase and how he'd doubled the chase back on her, climbing high and watching Dinah from the parking garage.

The fourth man looked at the picture, too. "Same one who shot you the other night."

The colonel scowled. "What's your level of confidence that she didn't follow you here?" he said in a whispery voice, as if he might be heard outside the house.

"I was careful," the man said. "I don't think we need to worry."

"Well, we're going to worry anyway," the colonel said. He pointed to the tech. "Keep your eye on that monitor." Then, to the fourth man, he said, "We'll keep an eye out and see if they show up again. We're close to deadline." He pulled the picture of Mattie off the printer. "And what about this other woman?"

The man told the colonel about Dinah getting a phone call and ducking into the vegetarian restaurant. "I don't know," he said. "Maybe nothing. Maybe coincidence." The colonel gave him a skeptical look. Coincidence was bullshit.

"The hippy-chick does look familiar," the tech said.

"She's a street singer. You've probably seen her when you were walking around town," the man said, sliding his grip across his aching ribs.

"No, there's something else," the colonel said. "I've seen her someplace before. Not just singing on the street." He held the picture to his face. Then he snapped his fingers. "Can we pull up the video we took at the roller derby match?"

The tech clicked some keys and called out a file name and number. The colonel went to his laptop, brought up the file, and watched the jumpy video. The colonel hit fast-forward. When he got to the place where Emily Elah entered, he slowed down to normal speed, and when she walked to the railing and started talking to the tall girl with the long legs, he reduced it to slow motion. When the girl turned her face to the camera, he froze the frame and zoomed in.

"That's her," the man said. "Good eye, sir."

"It doesn't tell us who she is. She shouldn't be hard to find if she's a street musician," the colonel said. "It does tell us she's involved with the Elahs, especially after this morning. We definitely need to find her and see what she knows about Francis and everything else."

"That could change things," the man conceded.

"Speaking of changing things," the colonel said, "I haven't given you the headline news yet." With that, he went to the right-hand side of the whiteboard, crossed out the last date on the countdown and looped an arrow up to the preceding one.

The tech sat up straight, interrupted. "Hey, check this out."

The man came around and looked at the monitor in time to see an old Volvo pass by. The Colonel grunted. The picture was not good enough to see anyone or anything inside. The car was moving very slowly.

The man realized they were watching a crappy picture of something he could easily see with his own eyes. He bounded up the stairs to get to a window in one of the front bedrooms. He spied his mark and returned downstairs and paused in the doorway.

"You saw the car?" the colonel asked.

"It was them. The female cop and her boss," he said.

"There they are again," the technician offered, "coming down the alley."

The man dashed to the kitchen in the back of the house, moving the curtain slightly to peek out. He held his breath as the car glided past, and in the silence, he heard the call of a crow.

The colonel exhaled loudly. "Okay. Maybe we do something about these two. Just remember, we can't get carried away. And right now, we have more urgent business."

CHAPTER 33

We're Going In

When Segal met with the captain to talk about raiding the house, the captain didn't want to hear about the crow or the training platform. In fact, he seemed more than a little distracted and more than a little worried. Segal went through the part about Dinah following the guy based on a tip. He left out the part about asking the street people for help. He also left out the part about Dinah not having a badge or a gun. When he got to the part about the crow in the tree outside the house and the platform, his boss raised a hand.

"Just stop," his boss said.

"Look, I know how it sounds," Segal said. His boss wasn't buying it.

"No, I don't think you do. I think you've been working on crows and raccoons and mule deer so much in the past few days, you don't know how far you've departed from reality. Or how this stuff sounds to halfway normal people. Not that

I know that much about halfway normal people anymore," he added by way of stepping off the soapbox.

Segal opened his mouth.

His boss held up his hand again. "What I want you to say is that you think you have probable cause to go into that house. If you tell me you think you have probable cause, then I will meet with the judge myself and get a warrant."

This was not how Segal had expected the meeting to go. "I thought you would tell me I didn't have enough evidence for a warrant. Then I would have to convince you to give me more manpower to watch the house to get something more definite. We'd stake out the house."

"Well, Segal, I don't think you appreciate the time factor, brought on by events you have no clue about. I'm not telling you to sit on the house. I'm asking you to tell me you feel like you've got probable cause."

Segal knit his eyebrows together. The roles were reversed here. His boss was usually the meticulous one, telling him to take his time and document everything, one careful step after another. "Are we getting pressure from ONI?" he asked.

"We're getting pressure, all right. I'm not at liberty to talk about it other than to tell you we need to close this one with all dispatch."

The boss said it with an intensity Segal had seldom seen him reach. And when he was through, he continued to look Segal in the eye with the same intensity.

Segal absorbed this for a beat and then said with certainty, "Boss, I feel we have probable cause to go into that house for the purpose of apprehending suspects in the recent murders and also for collecting evidence concerning those crimes."

"Good," his boss said. "Start making your plans for later today."

Segal got up to leave.

"And Segal," his boss said, "you're taking ONI in with you."

Jerome Guilford was wearing a white shirt and blue tie and suit pants and over that a lightweight navy-blue windbreaker. On his feet were the perfect brown shoes.

"At least he looks good," Dinah said under her breath. "Kind of like a game show host dressed up to play FBI."

Segal winced. He sat in the passenger seat of his Volvo in the alley behind the house. A minute ago, they had cruised by, noting that the white van was gone. Earlier, it had been photographed sitting in a little gravel pull-off underneath a black walnut tree, and Segal had wondered how many vans these guys had. He also thought what a bad idea it was to have a walnut tree beside a parking place. Now, they were positioned where a small garage shielded them from prying eyes in the house. They were waiting for the signal from Jerome Guilford.

Between houses, they could see to the street. They saw Guilford and a couple of his men pull up in an unmarked car. At the same time, one of their own vans arrived across the street. This, Segal knew, contained several tactical people for backup.

The radio crackled. Guilford's hushed voice. "We're going in."

"I'll bet he's been waiting his whole life to say that," Dinah said.

Segal smiled. "The next sound you hear will be Jerome telling us the house is empty."

"Yeah, I feel it, too," Dinah said.

It was a thing they had discussed in the past, how a house had a certain look and feel to it when no one was there. He was reluctant to voice the words because he did not want them to be true.

He knew it was true.

The radio crackled: "The house is empty."

They got out and walked over, and Jerome Guilford opened the back door for them. Segal noticed the security camera as he came up the steps.

"Looks like they left in a hurry," Jerome said.

Segal could see why he said that. The place was a mess: empty boxes, cans, furniture askew. They walked through the kitchen and into the dining room.

Guilford pointed. "Looks like this might have been their command center." He stroked his gloved fingertips over the empty tables and the few chairs scattered around. At one of the tables near the wall was the junction box where the cables from the various security cameras came together. The monitor was in place, blank. The computer gone.

Dinah's main attention was on the whiteboard mounted on the other wall. It had been wiped clean, but the job had been hastily and not quite completely done. Here and there small black marks were visible. Segal joined her. Dinah put her nose close to the surface and gave a sideways glance toward Segal.

"Looks like they taped some things on the board, along with the writing," she said.

He made out the little rectangular places where the tape had been.

One of the ONI guys walked in with a small toolbox. He set the toolbox down and removed what looked like a work light from it. He closed the blinds in the room and switched on the special light and held it close to the whiteboard. The purple glow brought forth the recently erased letters. "Better get some pictures and notes," the guy said. "The traces of ink don't last forever."

Another ONI guy brought up a camera and took photos. Dinah secured one with her phone while Segal studied the scene, trying to reconstruct what the room and its occupants must have been like a couple of hours ago.

The special light confirmed what Dinah had said about tape on the board. They could see the little rectangles immediately above an open space where a picture must have been. Below, they saw names written in a precise and geometric hand: Francis Elah, Emily Elah, Suzanne Elah. In another column were the names Ira Segal and Dinah Rudisill. The column was entitled "Local Complications."

"Something I can add to my résumé," Dinah said.

"Looks like they had more pictures of you than me," Segal said, pointing to the numerous spaces and arrows.

"I'll try to take that as a compliment," she said.

Segal read the headings across the top of the board. "Seems they were doing at least some of the same things we've been doing. Tracking people, trying to figure out how they relate to each other." He pointed to the dotted lines and arrows connecting the picture spaces. He also saw that the names Gloria and Chickey had been roughly crossed out.

Dinah pointed to Lucile Devroe's semi-erased name.

Segal nodded. "Yeah, I saw it." He'd been trying to convince himself Lucile might not be in peril. Unfortunately, the board took away any illusion about that. Segal wondered what picture of her had been taped up there.

They moved on to the right side of the board and the column of dates. Each date was crossed out up to the current day. Three more were on the list. The last one had been crossed out and an arrow drawn looping up to the penultimate date, which had been circled.

"Looks like a countdown," Dinah said.

"Countdown to what?" Segal asked. "That's the question."

"Whatever it is, odds are it takes place the day after tomorrow," Jerome Guilford said behind them.

"It was moved up one day," Dinah said.

Segal thought hard as he studied the dates. "Is something of significance scheduled in town for the day after tomorrow?"

"Or better yet, was something that was scheduled for three days from now moved up a day?" Jerome Guilford said.

"I'll call Shirley Dawn at the paper," Dinah said, pulling out her phone. "I'll have her check with whoever puts together the community calendar section."

"Hey, we've got garbage here," a voice called. It was the same ONI guy with the special light.

Segal followed Dinah and Guilford and joined the other ONI man in the kitchen, where he was checking the cabinets. He held a small plastic garbage can in his hand. "I found it there," he said, nodding to the open door of the cabinet under the sink.

Segal took the can from him and carefully poured the contents onto the kitchen table. The cuisine at Chez Bad Guy seemed to have centered on coffee, Slim Jims, and takeout food in nondescript containers. Not much to go on. Segal poked around in the other cabinets, which the ONI guy had left open. He saw nothing there except some unused plates.

Jerome Guilford bent and stuck his head in the cabinet under the sink. Segal could see in there too. There was a twenty-five-pound bag of cat food that was about half full.

"Looks like they're cat lovers," Guilford said.

Dinah came over. "I don't think a cat has been here recently," she said. "I'm really allergic to cats. I'm getting nothing."

Segal examined the floor. "You're right," he said. "No bowls for water or food. No visible litter box or traces of litter or sand." He took the bag and unfurled the rolled-up part. "I know where I've seen this before. It's the same stuff Lucile feeds her crows out at Biltmore."

The ONI guy had been diligently opening the Styrofoam food containers from the pile of garage. Along with the remains of Kung Pao chicken, he'd found a miraculously clean paper napkin folded into the shape of a bird. He interrupted them, held the bird napkin in the air. "Someone was into origami."

Segal took it from him and slipped it into a plastic evidence bag. He held it up toward the ceiling light and showed it to Dinah.

"Looks like a swan," Jerome said.

Segal said it at the same time as Dinah did: "Cormorant."

Segal's phone sounded, and he saw it was the captain calling. It was unusual to get a direct call from him, rather than one routed through dispatch. He stepped out to take the call.

When he returned, he motioned toward Dinah and said, "We have to go."

"But Segal…"

He raised a hand to stop her. "The evidence-guys can process whatever else might be here." Then he looked at the ONI men and said, "You guys, too, of course."

Jerome Guilford held up his phone. "I need to go, too. How do I find the Grove Park Inn?"

Segal felt his lungs deflate. "You might as well ride with us."

CHAPTER 34

Grove Park Inn

Segal took the wheel. The drive to the Grove Park Inn brought them through the heart of the city, then through the old residential district to the northeast and almost past the building that housed Creatures 2.0. They rode in silence, Segal mentally processing. Dinah was in the shotgun seat, flipping through her notebook. Jerome Guilford reclined in the backseat of the old Volvo beside a pile of paperback books, about which he showed no interest. He looked out the window, and Segal watched him take in the sights of the city, its buildings, its people.

"What do you think this is about?" Jerome asked as they left the commercial district. "What's so important they call us out of a crime scene?"

Segal glanced at him in the rearview mirror.

"Not sure. But for the last few days, something's been going on." Segal believed it must be something classified for his boss to pull him out of the raid.

"I heard the Grove Park Inn is an upscale place," Jerome said.

"Hotel of the rich and famous," Dinah said. "Always has been since it was built. You'll see for yourself in a minute."

After Segal wound the car up through a neighborhood of large old homes, past an elegant building of condos, and around a bend, the hotel came into view against the mountains. He noticed Jerome straining to see the enormous structure of gray stone. *Impossible to take in. Too huge this close up.*

Segal swung into the driveway and showed his badge to a bellman. "They're expecting you," the bellman said, and waved him to a small parking area straight ahead, already partly occupied by several black SUVs. Segal wondered who exactly was expecting them.

When they got out, Guilford let out a low "Wow!"

Segal watched him gawk at the rear expanse of the inn. The walls were made of enormous blocks of gray, rough-hewn granite. The roof, which curved down slightly over the top of the walls, was red tile. Rows of multi-paned windows marked each story. The effect was weight, strength, luxury. Even Segal felt the atmosphere washing over him; this was the kind of place you didn't want to walk into looking like a slob. He straightened his tie as Dinah checked her hair in the mirror.

Segal entered the lobby with Guilford and Dinah following. He showed his badge to the girl at the main desk and asked for security. While she made a phone call, he took in the vast room. One of Segal's favorite places in Asheville, the Grove Park Inn had changed little since the inn's construction in the early 1900s. To his right was a huge sitting area with vintage Mission-style easy chairs and couches with wide armrests and generous, solid proportions. Segal thought about bringing a book there some rainy afternoon and sitting and reading for hours. Something by Fitzgerald or Hemingway—or better yet, Thomas Wolfe—would be excellent. Of course, this was one of those perfectly feasible plans that never seemed to materialize.

On either side of the room were two enormous stone fireplaces. There was no fire this time of year. Later there would be. As soon as the weather changed, guests could count on nice, warming blazes in both. On the other side of the fireplace to the left was a bar where, in his reading-day fantasy, Segal would have a drink after finishing his book. He could imagine Lucile Devroe joining him there, wearing a chic dress and that movie star hair of hers.

"Are you Segal?" A voice surprised him out of his trance. The man had a Grove Park security badge. He indicated they should follow him down a hallway to their left. As he walked, he saw photographs, mostly black-and-white, of various famous people who had stayed at the inn over the years. Movie stars, authors, Nobel laureates by the dozen. Politicians, too, were represented, including almost every president since the inn was built. It was photographic evidence that sooner or later, everyone comes to Asheville. Guilford grunted here and there. Dinah kept her notepad in front of her.

He turned a corner and entered a more modern addition to the inn which included various meeting and banquet rooms. He paused outside one of these, where another man in a suit stood guard. This one was not wearing Grove Park security credentials. Segal noticed he had an earpiece, and the way his jacket hung—a slight outward pucker of fabric—left no doubt that he was armed. The security man who had escorted them leaned forward and whispered something to the guard, and the guard nodded. He turned toward them, smiled, and asked to see their IDs. "Good to go," he said. He opened the door for them.

Segal entered a banquet room of medium size. It had been converted into an operations headquarters of some sort. Down the middle of the room was a large table scattered with papers, briefcases, and laptop computers. Several men in shirtsleeves worked at the table. More men and women were at other tables or pacing back and forth talking on cell phones.

Two large whiteboards were positioned beyond the table. Standing in front of these were Segal's boss and a man with an unmistakable air of authority. The man pointed to different notations on the board and spoke to their boss in a hushed tone. His gestures moved from left to right, as though he was narrating a sequence of events. The boss spotted them and motioned them over while still engaged with the other man. When Segal got there, the man stopped talking and gave him his full attention. Dinah walked to the side of Segal. Guilford lagged a little behind.

"Agent Straus," said the boss. "These are the officers I told you about, Ira Segal and Dinah Rudisill. And I believe you may already know Jerome Guilford with ONI. This is Agent Straus with the Secret Service."

They shook hands.

Straus struck Segal as a competent, smart, no-nonsense sort of guy.

"If you haven't put it together yet," Straus said, "we're here doing advance work. Asheville is getting a visit from the president of the United States."

Segal felt the tumblers click into place. No, he had not put it together. And yes, it explained why everyone at the station was talking about canceled vacation leaves and why their boss was so edgy about solving the case. The president was coming to town, and they had at least one murderer and his support group running around, to say nothing of Francis Elah, fugitive from the U.S. government.

Segal wanted to speak to Dinah.

With her fist, she gave a light tap on his thigh instead.

Wait, he thought.

"I understand we have some loose ends we may need to worry about," Straus said, "especially with regard to Francis Elah."

Segal noticed something in the man's voice. It was not just that the Secret Service officer had said the name, it was how he said it. He said it as if he knew the name well and understood everything connected with it, probably more than Segal knew.

"Francis Elah came to our attention while investigating a murder here in Asheville," Segal explained. He ran through the facts of the case. When he got to the meeting designed by Jerome Guilford to put pressure on Emily Elah, Guilford interrupted by literally stepping in front of Segal.

"And when we last checked in, Emily Elah and her daughter, Suzanne, have dropped off the grid," Guilford said.

The Secret Service man, Straus, gave him full attention. The dickishness of Guilford's interruption seemed to irritate him. "I heard there was an incident with a couple of your men at the Biltmore House," he said.

Jerome Guilford blanched. "Not in the Biltmore House exactly, but there was an interruption of our surveillance of a site of interest on the grounds. It had to be dealt with."

Straus didn't blink. "I heard a rabid fox bit the shit out of your guy, is what I heard. Is that what you mean by an interruption to your surveillance?"

Jerome stuttered.

Straus held up a hand. "Listen, Mr. Guilford, you are not in a meeting room in Washington. We are here, on site, preparing for a visit from the president of the United States. We need to deal with reality here in a straightforward way. Can we do that?" With this remark, Straus gave them all a quick scan.

Segal nodded.

"Good. We will note the unknown whereabouts of these people and assume they represent some sort of potential threat and act accordingly. In other words, please find them before the president gets here, and let me know if help is required. Now, let me fill you in on the plan for the visit as it currently stands."

With that, he moved them over to the whiteboards. Segal wanted to say there was more to the story, but Straus spoke with such authority that he went along. Besides, Segal really didn't know what else they had, and he did not especially relish the idea of discussing crows and raccoons and mule deer with the top advance man for the Secret Service.

Straus walked them step by step though the itinerary, beginning with Air Force One landing at the Asheville airport south of town, the motorcade to the Grove Park Inn, and some recreational things after that. "Fortunately," he said, "this is supposed to be a low-key vacation visit, only the president and his wife. No speeches, no black-tie dinners, should be no big crowds. That's why there has been no announcement as yet. Everything easy-going and casual—for example, he wants to go to 12 Bones barbecue. That will be Wednesday lunchtime."

"Sir, I think you mean Tuesday. Tuesday lunchtime." It was one of the men at the table working on a laptop.

Straus stepped from the boards. "You're quite right," he said. Then, to the others, "Just this morning, the whole visit was moved up a day. Looks like we changed the dates on the board but not the days of the week." He stepped forward to make the corrections. "That's why we interrupted what you were doing and called you in. Otherwise, we would have been having this conversation tomorrow morning, and we would have been better organized."

Segal stepped forward and spoke up. "This may be a coincidence—"

"—I don't believe in coincidence," Straus said. "Only facts."

He told Straus about the raid on the house across town and in particular about the countdown dates listed on the board. While he ran through this, the other people in the room stopped what they were doing and gathered to listen. When he got to the part about the dates, Dinah held up her phone to show them the picture she had taken of the board. After that, there was silence.

"Nothing else there?" Straus asked.

Segal shook his head. "We still have a crime-scene crew at the house. If you want to send some guys over, we can show you where it is."

Straus motioned to two of his men.

"I'll get a cruiser to take them. You and Dinah stay here," their boss said.

Straus motioned them to the map taped to a whiteboard. Dinah took out a pen and marked the map with small circles. "This is 12 Bones," she said, "and this is where the first body was found." Straus nodded. They were joined by a couple other Secret Service guys and, of course, the ever-present Guilford. "And over here," Dinah said, "is the building where we found the suspected sniper's nest." She drew a circle there and a dotted line connecting that with the site of the body—a straight, unobstructed shot.

Segal counted for a couple of beats. *Let it sink in.*

Straus motioned them to the table. "Let's figure out if we can spring a trap," he said.

CHAPTER 35

Spring the Trap

Dinah studied Segal in action. They'd driven back down in the River Arts district. A long expanse of gravel lot extended from the Wedge Building over to the railroad tracks and all the way to the gated entrance in the chain-link fence bordering Lyman Street. Anyone parking near that gate would have a long walk to the brewery, the studios, or anything else housed in the Wedge Building. In spite of this, a few cars were always parked at that end of the lot, which made it possible for Segal's old Volvo to blend in there. Dinah waited with him in the car, watched, and observed. It was as close to the action as the federal people wanted them to get, even though it had been their work, their intuition, their insight that had led the Secret Service to this location.

"No offense," Straus said, "but we're used to working as a team, and we have no history with you two."

"None taken," Segal assured him.

Segal was amazing, as was often the case. He negotiated at least this part of the assignment. Dinah knew he was worried about innocent local people getting caught up in the operation somehow. This way, they could give the feds a heads-up when they recognized locals, people with solid history coming and going. That, and they would be on hand to shut down the means of egress if things got out of hand. Jerome Guilford also had his team there by the Wedge Building, minus the guy the rabid fox had bitten the shit out of. The Secret Service made up the bulk of the expedition.

It gave Dinah a chance to talk to Segal. They were running and refining scenarios to see what held up and what did not. It was easy for them to sit in the Volvo or get some air and talk strategy.

Segal adjusted his position in the driver's seat. "So, let's assume your earliest read on this place was right," he said. "In other words, let's say it is or was a sniper's nest."

Dinah nodded. She had already been over her reasons for thinking this was the case.

She waited as Segal pulled a Sherlock Holmes compilation from the backseat and ruffled the pages. The feel of the paper on his fingertips seemed to have a calming effect on him. "At first, we assumed it was someone who was after Francis Elah. Chickey was in the wrong place at the wrong time. And he looked enough like Elah that the sniper shot the wrong guy."

"Either that or killing Chickey wasn't a mistake," Dinah said. "Think about it. We know they're after Francis. We know they're after Richard. We think they were after something at Creatures 2.0 the night Gloria got killed. For that matter, maybe killing Gloria was intentional, too. Maybe she and Chickey both knew something they weren't supposed to know."

Segal continued to ruffle the book pages. "Makes sense, as far as it goes. What doesn't make sense is what ONI wants us to believe. Which is that Francis is the killer. He has somehow gone out of his head, deserted from this big, secret military project he was working on. And now he's returned home to settle things on this end."

Dinah stuck her head out the open passenger window and sucked in some cool air. "That still doesn't feel right to me. What we've learned about the guy, what everyone says. Especially Nancy Lund. For reasons I don't understand yet, Francis seems like a stand-up guy rather than a defector or a terrorist. On the other hand, let's assume Francis got wind of an assassination plan. Why didn't he tell someone?"

"Who?" Segal asked. "He was already working for the government. They put him into Cormorant. How would he know who to trust? He had to come here and work things out? Even with proof, he might not have had enough details to be believable."

"Well, he sure knows how to win friends and influence people," Dinah said. "ONI, Secret Service, Cormorant. They all want him."

Segal started to say something, but Dinah looked to the side and whispered, "There's the red van again."

She slumped in her seat as an old, beat-up Ford utility van pulled into the parking lot for the third time that morning. If she knew nothing else, she knew this crew liked vans. Each time, a stocky man in coveralls had unloaded boxes out of the back and carried them toward the studio room they were trying to watch, although once he was inside the jig was up. They didn't have surveillance inside. For a split moment, Dinah actually wished for Richard the crow.

Segal held up a radio mic and said in a low voice, "The red van just pulled in again."

Jerome Guilford came back in a static-laden voice. "Copy that."

Dinah raised a pair of binoculars as the van pulled up near the building. The stocky guy got out and moved to the back doors. This time, instead of removing boxes, he took out a long canvas bag, which he hung from his shoulder by a set of straps.

"That could be a gun," Dinah said. "That's long enough to be a sniper's rifle."

Segal relayed that information over the radio.

Dinah put the glasses on the window of the studio in question. After a few minutes, more than enough time for the man to reach the room, she saw the window go up. "There's movement," she said. "He just opened the window."

Segal relayed.

"More movement," she said. "Something's protruding from the window."

Soon after that, flashes appeared.

"Crap," Segal said.

Guilford's voice came over the radio. "We're going in."

Dinah rolled her eyes.

Jerome Guilford and two of his ONI men gathered outside one of the entrances to the building. The Secret Service men were at the outside bar of the Wedge Brewing Company. Jerome watched as they stood and left as inconspicuously as two men in business suits could. They walked up beside the loading dock and went in by the same entrance their suspect had used a few minutes earlier.

Jerome went inside and more of his ONI team were waiting in the dusty hallway two floors up. He filled them in with hushed tones. There was a short and animated discussion on tactics and positions, and then they proceeded through the winding corridors as quietly as possible, the Secret Service taking the lead.

Most of the studio doors were closed, and judging from the sound level many were unoccupied. One door was slightly ajar, and as Jerome it, he saw a nude model watching them, her expression showing no particular surprise or interest that people were inside the building.

He went up another flight of stairs even more quietly, men in tow since they were drawing close to their destination. This floor seemed to be abandoned except for the room in question. As they approached its door, the Secret Service guys drew their guns and Jerome and the others followed suit. No one spoke. As the Secret Service men came even with the door, Jerome heard movement inside the room. He crouched behind the Secret Service in a ready stance with his weapon. A nod from the Secret Service man and a noise and bluish-white light flashed inside the crack around the door. One of the Secret Service men reached for the doorknob, turned it, and shouldered the door open, throwing his body into the room with the same motion. He shouted at the top of his lungs, "Secret Service! Drop your weapon and put your hands in the air."

As Jerome flew into the room with heart pounding, wondering where to point his gun, something heavy hit the floor. He turned to his right to see a man with his hands up. The man was wearing a welding mask and was visibly shaking.

"What's your name?" one of the Secret Service men asked.

The man said something unintelligible beneath the mask.

The Secret Service man reached forward to tip the mask up, exposing the face of a young man with a heavy brown beard. Seeing the men pointing guns at him did nothing to calm the man down. He tried to speak, but nothing came out.

Segal was getting the feeling that he would rather be anywhere but this studio room. In the hallway outside the room, a small group of curious people had gathered. They were young, dressed mostly in the casual clothes of working artists. They were the people from the nearby studios, coming to see what the fuss was about. The model from the studio on the floor below came up the stairs dressed in a robe and slippers. From time to time, the people approached the door with feigned nonchalance and tried to peek past the men in suits.

Inside the room, Segal joined the federal agents. Dinah was busy with Jerome. The head of the group, Straus, was standing by the open window looking at the view to the river and upstream to 12 Bones. Two of the other men were carefully searching the room, not that there was much to search. Another was going through the man's wallet while the man himself sat on an old wooden chair and watched the surreal spectacle.

Segal watched it, too. It was all too clear that they had sprung the steel trap of federal justice on a poor artist in the act of welding pieces onto a metal sculpture. A section of pipe rested on the sill of the open window.

Segal listened as Dinah finished with Jerome and got on her phone, changing her tone from authoritative to quiet. "Hey, Rhonda, Dinah Rudisill here. How's your husband? Good, good. Listen, we might have a situation. You have the art gallery...?" After a minute or so, she put the phone down and announced to the room, "Okay, the gallery owner confirmed that she has some of the welder's stuff on display."

Segal understood this meant there was no reason to think the guy on the chair was not exactly what he said he was and what he appeared to be. Segal looked at the piece the man was working on. It was a black bear wearing pants and an apron. The artist had been adding a pair of wire-rimmed reading glasses when he was so rudely interrupted.

In the momentary silence of the room, a small, crackling voice was heard. Straus put a finger to his ear and said "Copy that" into a microphone mounted in the cuff of his jacket sleeve. "The motorcade is headed into 12 Bones now," he said to the room. "We might as well hang here and secure this place till they leave." The others nodded. He directed two of them down to the parking lot to keep up a lookout for anything unusual. The earpiece crackled again. Straus listened for a moment, then said, "Go with the Carolina Sweet Sauce. The hot sauce might be too hot, okay?" He looked at Segal and rolled his eyes, then resumed his view out the window. This tiny gesture made Segal feel close to Straus. *Everyone has stuff to put up with*, he thought.

Voices in the hall grew louder. Dinah told Segal that word had somehow reached the group of people in the hall that the president and first lady were headed to 12 Bones.

Segal considered where to go next when Dinah nudged his arm and held up her phone to show him a message. It was from Lewis Abraham at Creatures 2.0.

The message read: *Richard is back.*

Dinah said, "That crow might be smarter than all of us."

CHAPTER 36

Chicken Little

"There's no use beating ourselves up about this one," Segal said. He and Dinah were winding down the hallways and stairways of the Wedge, heading for the parking lot.

"I know that," she said. "Everybody knows that. You can't take chances with this kind of thing." But the tone of her voice said otherwise. It conveyed the disappointment of someone who had gone from being a hero to being Chicken Little after the sky declined to fall. In other words, she was beating herself up about it, just as Segal was, in spite of what he said.

He said nothing else until they emerged onto the loading dock. Segal was turning over and over in his mind how else they could have arranged the known facts into some other picture. The conclusion seemed inescapable—the evidence of the sniper, the president's visit, right down to the change in date. Especially the change in date. And when they laid out the evidence, the Secret Service had been convinced, too. Segal was experiencing an intense sense of foreboding, a sense that they were not out of the woods yet, and neither was the president. Nothing felt resolved.

At Creatures 2.0, they found Lewis Abraham in the main lab, the one with the windows facing the back. When they asked what was going on, Lewis pointed out the window. Richard hopped down from the branch of an oak tree and strutted to the window, bobbing his head.

"Is that a sign for something in particular?" Dinah asked Lewis.

"I would say it roughly translates into, 'Look at me, I am Mr. Big-ass Bird, too good to turn over the goods to a lowlife like Lewis.'"

"Really, you got all that from a couple of head bobs?" Dinah scratched her forehead.

"I got that from the fact that he's been showing up for the last hour. You see he's wearing his camera, but every time I get near him to try to take it off, he flies away. Then, a few minutes later, he's back again. It's like he wants something and doesn't want me in on it."

Segal followed the bird, and he did that head-bobbing thing again.

Dinah walked slowly toward the window, and to their surprise, the crow made no attempt to move away. She released the lock and pushed open the sash, and the crow took a hop toward her. Dinah stepped back, and the crow came into the room and flapped up onto the nearest workbench. He allowed Dinah to reach forward, stroke him, and remove the camera from his head.

Dinah handed the device to Lewis. "That's weird. It's like he didn't want to give it to you. Maybe he had instructions to deliver it to me. Is that possible?"

"Oh, it's possible, all right. That or, like I told you, he likes to impress the ladies. Better give him one of his favorite treats for good behavior. He'll be expecting it." Lewis took a small can from a desk drawer and handed it to Dinah.

"Vienna sausages?"

"Oh, hell yes," Lewis said. "He loves those things. Don't give him more than one, though."

While Dinah fed one of the little wieners to the bird, Lewis removed the tiny memory card from the crow cam and downloaded the images to his computer. After a couple of minutes, he indicated he was ready to run through the video the bird had captured.

"This is beautiful," Dinah said with an involuntary breath.

Indeed, it was. Richard had apparently been soaring above a ridgeline in the mountains and then out over a valley. It was one of those days of mesmerizing beauty in the southern Appalachians—blue sky with only a few white, fleecy clouds to add dimension, the mountainsides and ridgelines covered with their variety of green trees and showing the occasional outcropping of granite, sometimes gray, sometimes covered with lichen, the shadows of those clouds drifting over them.

"It is beautiful. Where exactly was it?" Segal asked.

"I don't know where it was, but I can tell you when it was," Lewis said. "See the time stamp?"

The stamp showed the clip had been taken a little over an hour ago.

They watched a few seconds more in silence, then Dinah said, "Look, there's a road coming into view."

They saw a two-lane road winding along the mountain a hundred feet or so below the ridgeline. Presently, the bird seemed to fly just above the road.

"Is that the Blue Ridge Parkway?" Segal asked.

"Could be," Dinah said. The road disappeared into a tunnel. "Yeah, I think it is. I'm thinking of the parkway south of town, before it goes by Mount Pisgah."

"I see what you mean," Segal said. "You've been up there more recently than me, though." He was going over the terrain in his mind, and the farther the image followed the road, the more convinced he became.

Then the road dropped away as the crow climbed quickly. "Wonder if he caught an updraft," Dinah said.

It made Segal think of watching a hawk soar in the air currents above the parkway. Judging from the video, the bird had continued to climb until he was over the ridgeline itself. Then, all at once, a distinct mountaintop came into view, complete with an elevated platform and a large radio mast.

"There we are," Dinah said. "Mount Pisgah."

Segal had no doubt. He knew exactly where they were, or rather where the crow had been. He spotted the trail leading like a winding stairway up the steep slope to the observation tower, appearing and disappearing in and out of the laurel and rhododendron bushes and the twisted branches of oak trees tortured by the winds and ice of the high exposure. Then, judging from the video, the bird had made a wide, banking 360-degree turn around the peak.

"I told you he was a show-off," Lewis said.

The scolding note is gone. Segal thought he even heard pride there.

The next sequence showed the crow descending and finding the road again. As Segal expected, the Pisgah Inn soon came into view. The video swooped down above the treetops around the parking lot. And then the movement stopped with a jerk.

"That's Richard landing on a tree branch," Lewis explained.

A moment later, Dinah gave a quick inhale and put her hand on Segal's arm. He watched as a white utility van pulled up in the far corner of the parking lot. Four men got out and went to the back, where they unloaded a large satchel and two backpacks, conferred with each other, and disappeared into the trees, one down a trailhead and the other three toward the inn.

"They're after Emily," Dinah said.

"That might not be all they're after," Segal said. He took out his cell phone. Two rings and Jerome Guilford answered. "Where's the motorcade?" Segal asked.

"You know we can't talk about that on an open line," Jerome said.

"Give me an indication somehow."

"Let's just say certain people may or may not be going for seconds on the banana pudding."

"Where are they scheduled to go next?" Segal asked.

"I definitely can't say that on an open line."

"Don't let them leave until I get there," Segal said, his voice too raw for comfort. He remembered from the briefing that the presidential entourage was supposed to head out hiking, "supposed" being the operative word. Plans changed.

After a pause, Jerome said softly, "I don't think anyone is in a mood to take warnings right now from the local police. We've done two raids for you so far. Got nothing."

Segal hung up and looked at Dinah. "We've got to get over there right away."

Dinah took a step and stopped. "Wait. You go to the motorcade. Lewis can take me to my car. I'll head up to the parkway. Run interference. We can meet up there." She looked at Lewis, and he nodded.

Segal hesitated only a second and said, "Hurry."

"You hurry," she said. She held his eye for a moment before she moved out.

He knew what she wanted to say. She wanted to say, "Be careful." He wanted to say it to her too. Long ago they'd agreed never to tell each other to be careful.

CHAPTER 37

Ascent of Mount Pisgah

"Looks like it could be a plumber's van," Jerome Guilford said. He was staring at the picture on Segal's phone of the white van in the parking lot of the Pisgah Inn. Segal had rushed across town, and they were now in the parking lot of 12 Bones in the River Arts District.

"It also looks like the van we saw at the house on French Broad Avenue," Segal said.

"You mean the one you and Dinah say you saw. There was no van by the time we got there."

Segal exhaled loudly. Jerome knew perfectly well that if he and Dinah said there was a white van, there was a white van. "And you think it's a coincidence that they parked next to the trail the president and first lady are going to hike?"

Segal glared at Guilford's shocked face. His words had stopped the man from the Office of Naval Intelligence.

"Good point," Guilford conceded. He looked at the top Secret Service man. Segal could read his mind. Guilford dreaded bringing this up after the failed raid at the Wedge.

"What if I told you there's a good chance, you'll find Francis Elah up there, too," Segal said.

By this time, Segal realized that a considerable crowd had gathered around 12 Bones, partly for the barbecue and partly because news of the distinguished visitors had circulated, the way such news did. The numbers were a little short of a full-on flash mob. It appeared to him as if the president and first lady were shaking hands on their way to the black SUVs of the motorcade. No doubt, the organizers of this outing sensed pressure and were eager to move them out.

Jerome Guilford had his head down. After a moment, he said, "Give me the phone."

Segal slapped the phone into his open palm, and Jerome walked over to Agent Straus. The Secret Service and ONI men conferred as the president and first lady got into one of the SUVs. Segal did not hear the conversation. He could read the body language when the decision was made. Guilford returned.

"Okay," he said. "They had the Fine Arts League studio here in the River Arts District as a possible stop. Time permitting. They will go there before the hike, which will give us an hour or so to sort this out."

Segal turned and took a step toward his Volvo.

"Hold up," Guilford said. "Let's take something a little more muscular." He nodded toward a large SUV parked half in and half out of the road.

Segal sighed and followed him, climbing with difficulty into the passenger seat. He scanned the interior of the huge machine as he buckled in. "Hope this thing isn't top-heavy, considering where we're going," he said.

"What do you mean?" Jerome asked.

"You'll see soon enough," Segal said, as he directed Jerome across the river and out of the valley and south of town.

At Creatures 2.0, Dinah waited on Lewis as he brought up a video. Lewis transferred the video to a memory stick and gave it to Dinah. She started toward the door, turned back and faced Richard the crow. "We should take him."

Lewis stopped. "Take Richard? What for?"

"Where we're going, we might need an eye in the sky. You told me before you could pick up the feed in real-time, right?"

Lewis nodded.

"Well, let's put the camera back on Richard and take him along. He could help us find these guys on the mountain."

Lewis rubbed his chin. "Only one problem. I can put the camera on him. I've done that plenty of times. I can give you the receiver. It just hooks up to an iPad. But I don't know how to tell Richard what to do. I don't know the commands."

"Who does?" Dinah asked.

"Francis, of course," Lewis said, stating the obvious. "Francis and that woman out at the Biltmore House who was helping him. What was her name? Lucile."

"Lucile Devroe." Dinah took out her cell phone. She knew Segal would not be pleased about involving Lucile. *Desperate times call for desperate measures.* Besides, Lucile was already involved whether they liked it or not.

Lucile picked up.

Dinah talked quickly. "Lucile, I need your help. We need your help, Segal and me. Do you know how to give commands to Richard to get him to do what we want him to do?"

Silence. Then Lucile cleared her throat. "Yes, I helped Francis work with Richard. I can do the basics."

"Where can I pick you up?"

Silence.

Dinah read the pause. "Never mind. I know where to pick you up. I'll be there in five."

She walked over to Lewis and stood behind him. He already had the camera on the bird and was attaching a cable between a small black box and an iPad. He brought up a special application on the screen, and the next thing Dinah knew she was seeing a picture of Lewis on the screen. "Good," he said.

The bird nodded. Lewis nodded.

"Let's bounce," she said.

If Richard had any crow-hesitation about riding in a car, Dinah could not see it. He rode out of the building on Dinah's arm and hopped right into the backseat when she opened the door. Dinah thought she shouldn't be surprised at this by now. She was growing a bit fond of the bird.

Lewis drove her to her car, which was parked near the police station downtown. She bent down to the driver's open window and thanked him after transferring bird and equipment to her car. "You going to be around the lab the rest of the day?" she asked.

"I guess so," he said. "There aren't many of us left."

"Hang in there, Lewis," Dinah said. "If things go well today, maybe we can get your boss back." And she was off.

When she pulled up outside Segal's apartment, she saw no sign of Lucile Devroe. She was about to get out of the car when she caught movement on the second-floor walkway. Lucile emerged from the shadows and descended the stairway, putting Dinah in mind of a scene from an old Hollywood film. Lucile gave Dinah a quick, tight smile of greeting. Her stronger reaction came when she opened the car door and saw Richard sitting in the shotgun seat. Her eyes and her mouth opened wide. "Richard, is that really you?" she asked.

The bird opened his beak and bounced his head up and down.

Dinah got going. She called Segal. He gave her a timeline. Even with the detour and delay, they were on the parkway well ahead of her partner and Guilford.

A battered, valiant Honda Civic approached the Pisgah Inn. Mattie was at the wheel. Francis Elah was beside her. He'd wanted to make the trip alone, tried to convince her it was dangerous. She would have none of it, and he was in no position to insist. Besides, having her there might be incredibly important. If he could get to his family before anyone else did, maybe Mattie could get them out of there while he stayed behind and dealt with whatever forces of darkness were coming his way.

She pulled into the parking lot.

"Slow down," he said, spotting the white van. He was thinking of the Cormorant guys, but as their car crept by, he saw no sign of life around it.

Mattie parked.

Francis got out and surveyed the sky, daring to hope for any sign of Richard, not knowing if the bird had already done his job and delivered the evidence to Dinah, just as Francis had instructed. He'd come to rely on the crow, his beloved companion.

He was on alert as they eased up the steps and passed through the entryway that would take them through to the other side of the inn. On that side, an elevated walkway ran the length of the structure, providing access to the rooms as well as a perfect place to take in the magnificent view over Pisgah National Forest and points east. In the vastness of the sky, Francis saw a pair of hawks rising on thermals.

Francis heard a sound to their left. As they turned, a door opened and Suzie wheeled out onto the walkway. She did not see them at first, as her gaze was straight ahead, riveted onto the valley before her. Francis and Mattie took quick steps toward her. Hearing them, she turned and shook her head slowly, as if to say, *No*. They stopped, confused by the gesture and by the sorrowful shadow that darkened her face. Then a man Francis knew all too well stepped out of the room with an Uzi submachine gun slung from a strap over his shoulder.

"Hello, Francis," the colonel said.

Francis saw those cold Aryan blue eyes and short light hair and thought what a fine SS officer he would have made for Hitler.

Hearing footsteps behind them, Francis turned to see another man carrying an Uzi.

On the shoulder of a mountain overlooking the Pisgah Inn, the Cormorant sniper was finally doing something that made him feel comfortable, something that was dead in the center of his training, his experience, and his skill set. He was setting up a sniper's nest in the low bushes and the scrub pines overlooking a stretch of parkway that approached a tunnel. Specifically, he was digging in, sighting down the northeast slope of Mount Pisgah, where he had a beautiful, long view of the parkway as it led from Asheville up toward the inn. It felt so good it almost made up for his aching ribs.

CHAPTER 38

A World of Trouble Now

"This just gets better and better," the colonel said, "you both coming up here." Sweat was beginning to stain his thin khaki shirt, especially where the strap of the Uzi crossed his shoulder.

He marched Francis and Mattie across the parking lot. He held the gun on them, but his real leverage lay in the fact that one of his men was back at the room with Emily and Suzie.

"How come you still get to be called 'colonel' when you're in a private company now?" Mattie asked. "Is it like Colonel Sanders with the fried chicken?"

The colonel's smile widened as he marched them forward, her jibe enhancing his good mood.

"Colonel, I don't know how you think you'll get away with this. You know ONI is involved now. You know Secret

Service is here, to say nothing of the local police," Francis said.

"Don't forget the street singers. We've got them on our case, too," the colonel said, letting them know he knew about Mattie, letting them know how on top of the situation he was. Mattie glanced over her shoulder with a dirty look. The colonel laughed. "Yes, Francis, your friend here has been very helpful to us. Once we started following her, she led us right to your family."

"You won't be able to explain what you were doing here," Francis said. "Law officials will find it suspect from the get-go."

"No, they won't. We have a perfectly good explanation. In fact, we have a written directive which compels us to be here," the colonel said. He motioned Elah forward with the muzzle of the Uzi as he walked them past the white van at the end of the parking lot and on toward the trailhead.

He continued talking to them. "You forget, or maybe you never knew in the first place. The State Department, with the sign-off of the president himself, issued a directive which authorized us to cross international boundaries to follow Al-Qaeda and any other terrorist organization thought to be associated with them. I especially like that part: *thought to be associated with them.* Covers a lot of ground. No further authorization was necessary. Not after you and I set up our SEAL buddies for their little excursion into Pakistan. Getting prior authorization takes time, and as I explained to the powers that be, that could result in lost opportunities. That's all they needed to hear. They couldn't wait to sign those papers.

Personally, I don't think they wanted to know. What people really want is the necessary stuff taken care of and, following that, a nice, neat story that ties up all the loose ends."

"And how does that explain what a depraved outfit like Cormorant is doing in Asheville, North Carolina?" Mattie asked.

Francis sighed and fidgeted with his hands. "They followed a dangerous international terrorist here. Namely, me."

"Very good, Francis, very good," the colonel said. He shook his head and grinned. "I can't believe how well this is working out, like pieces of a puzzle fitting together without much work involved. You came up here to the parkway, to the very spot we needed you to be in. Saves us so much time and effort. So much less to go wrong. I could not have written the script any better." He shook his head again. "Yes, my team followed you, a dangerous international terrorist, here. Not only a terrorist, the worst kind of terrorist, a defector. One of our own people turned against us. People hate a traitor worse than they hate a snake. People are going to hate your guts when the whole story comes out. And, conversely, they're going to love us. That's how it works. The only thing that can stop a bad man with a gun is a good man with a gun. And a good story. Don't forget the story."

"Tragically," he continued, as if it were story-telling time in the library, "as it will be told around the campfire, we arrive moments too late. You assassinate the president. We take you out in your cowardly attempt to escape. All the pieces of the puzzle fit. I mean, jeez, with Kennedy they had to bribe the police. Get Jack Ruby in the next day to get rid of

Oswald. Very messy. So messy most people still don't buy the lone gunman bullshit. But this? This is a neat package, tied up with a bow, no loose ends.

"And you, Miss Mattie, this is icing on the cake, in case anyone has residual sympathy for Francis here. After Francis's desperate and depraved act of betrayal, after you are both killed in a deadly gun battle with our valiant team, the investigation will lead to your apartment, where evidence will be found that Francis, a married man and the father of a handicapped girl, was shacked up with you, the femme fatale. We won't even have to plant evidence. As a matter of fact, I think we'll stand back and let the other agencies investigate. That will make it look even better."

"You don't think other people will be around?" Mattie asked. "Witnesses?"

The colonel put a finger to his ear, where a small receiver was located. He grinned and looked up at the radio tower, where a tiny figure was just visible. "Yes, go ahead and cut the feed," he said.

"Not today. There won't be any spectators. Not when the president and first lady have decided to go hiking here. Our friends have made sure of that. No wonder they call them the Secret Service." The colonel laughed richly at his own joke. "Get it? *Service*?" He laughed some more. "And in case some busybody with a cell phone is around, we just lost cell coverage for this side of the mountain." He waved to the figure on the tower by the antenna, but they were too far away for the man to spot them. He was already climbing down. "It happens quite often up here, you know. With the winds and so on."

The colonel put a hand to his ear to touch the receiver. He listened for a moment, then said with his heart racing a tiny fraction, "Take the shot."

In the distance, two pops sounded. Then the screeching of tires. After that, dead silence. In his earpiece, another message came through. "Copy," he said. "These damned mountain roads up here. They are so unbelievably treacherous."

Segal regretted his decision to let Jerome Guilford drive the black SUV. He told himself he should have been warned by Jerome's choice of words when he said he wanted to take something "a little more muscular."

Jerome did all the things Segal associated with bad drivers. He accelerated at the maximum capability of the vehicle even where quick acceleration did no good—for instance, when he could see traffic stopped a block ahead. Such overwrought acceleration demanded more dramatic deceleration, which Jerome further mismanaged by waiting until the last possible instant before slamming on the brakes. Segal could stomach it only by looking away from the road. He found some comfort in watching Jerome's perfect brown right shoe do its frantic dance between the gas pedal and brake.

When they arrived at the entrance to the Blue Ridge Parkway, a line of cars was backed up. The Highway Patrol had a roadblock and was turning people around in preparation for the presidential motorcade. It was taking forever, as one by one the drivers approached the officers and leaned out the window to ask what was going on. Then they had to either turn around in the limited space available or turn left and take the parkway north.

As soon as there was space, Jerome jerked the SUV onto the shoulder and accelerated past the line of waiting cars, spitting gravel and mud and clumps of grass into the air. After he showed his badge to the patrolmen, Jerome accelerated through the turn onto the parkway south.

The driving only got worse from there. Jerome had an alarming lack of finesse in handling the big, top-heavy car on the sharp turns. Segal was glad to be on the uphill side, where he at least didn't have to stare down the steep drop-off on the other side.

After a couple of miles on the parkway, Segal said, "I'm going to touch base with Dinah." He pulled out his cell phone. Dinah answered.

"We're on our way, just passed mile marker..." her voice became faint and jumbled. "Just pulled . . . parking lot . . . Pisgah Inn . . . have Richard and . . ." After that, the call was dropped completely.

"I think she's up there," he said to Jerome. "Sometimes, the connections are dodgy on the ridge. I think she said she has Richard with her."

"Richard?" Jerome asked.

"The crow."

Jerome said, "Right," not taking his eyes off the road. Apparently, the over-steering, over-accelerating, and over-braking took his full attention. He made a total mess of the driving. And yet he must have been thinking about what Segal had told him before.

"You said you think there's a good chance we'll find Francis Elah up here," he said. "What makes you think so?"

"Richard the crow makes me think so," Segal said.

Jerome frowned.

"I showed you the video of the white van with the guys getting out," Segal said. "That was from Richard; from Richard's crow cam."

Jerome still looked blank.

Segal persisted. "Who put the camera on Richard? Who sent him to take video, and who sent him to Creatures 2.0 to deliver the goods?"

The ONI man inhaled and exhaled loudly and then said, "Elah? You think it was Francis Elah?"

"Who else could it be?"

"It could have been that woman at the Biltmore House, Lucile Devroe. She knows how to do that, too."

Segal's pulse jumped in his neck. He had not realized Jerome knew that. After a moment, he said, "No, it wasn't Miss Devroe, I'm pretty sure of that." *With any luck*, he thought, *the lovely Miss Devroe is still in Asheville, where I left her this morning.*

They rounded another bend, this one toward the mountain. The SUV slid slightly off the right-hand side of the road, making Segal think he might get dragged against the rough vertical rock face like a block of aged Gouda over a cheese grater. Just when contact was imminent, Jerome yanked the wheel left. He didn't straighten out before he was well left of the centerline, which turned Segal's mind toward plummeting off the cliff on the driver's side.

He pictured his cherished Elmore Leonard books and thought, I'm actually in one of his novels about to go over a cliff!

Before them was a gently curving stretch leading to a tunnel. Segal turned to Jerome and started to tell him they were too close to the edge when he heard a pop. The SUV pulled abruptly left, and in the next split-second Segal registered that their left front tire had been shot out. Before he or Jerome could react, a second shot shattered the windshield on Jerome's side, throwing Jerome's head against the headrest. Jerome had enough control to step on the brake, but it was too late, and he yelled "Shit!" as the car left the road and lurched over the side of the mountain.

Dinah guided her car into the parking lot of the Pisgah Inn, painfully aware that she had no clear plan of what to do next. *Crap.* She had spotted the white utility van near the trailhead, watching closely as she drove by. *No sign of life.* Richard seemed interested. He hopped off Lucile's lap and sat on the center console, looking right and left out the windows. She wondered if he sensed something, perhaps danger. She rolled slowly by the inn, past the part where the rooms were. *Nothing out of place.*

Her cell phone rang. It was Segal, thank God. Segal would know exactly what to do. The connection was all crackle and static and vacuum. They didn't have time to plan the next move before she lost him altogether. Dinah hung up. "It was Segal," she said to Lucile. "I think they're close. I think he said the mile marker, but the call broke up."

She continued her drive-by. She knew which room Emily Elah and her daughter were in since she and Mattie had stashed them there. Considering the presence of the white van, she had to assume they were in trouble now. She nixed the idea of walking up and knocking on the door. She had to do something with Lucile. If this building was going to be the scene of trouble in the next few minutes, it was not a good place for her to be.

"We'll drive on and find a place for you to deploy the bird," Dinah said.

Richard hopped on the console. He looked at her as if he were offended by being called "the bird."

She found a good spot a couple of hundred yards away, one of the scenic pull-offs, where they were alone with a magnificent panorama of Pisgah National Forest stretching before them.

"What do you want Richard to do?" Lucile asked, wringing her hands together.

"First thing we need to know is what's going on at the inn. If everyone is inside, I guess Richard can't help us much. But I want him to go around the back, to the side we couldn't see. Maybe we can learn something that will help. Can you get him to do that?"

Lucile nodded. Richard nodded, too, which made Dinah wonder if he understood every word she just said. At this juncture, she was prepared to believe just about anything concerning the bird. He appeared calm, his black feathers shiny even in the car.

"Okay, give us a minute," Lucile said.

Richard rode on Lucile's arm as they got out.

Dinah moved away, allowing Lucile to work with Richard without distraction. She walked nearer to the road and tried her cell phone again. No luck. She remained there, nervously pacing, trying to think what to do next, wondering how close Segal was. She glanced at Richard standing on top of the car. Lucile was gently holding his head between her fingertips as if she were massaging his temples. Then she took his beak between her fingers. She had her face close to Richard's and spoke to him softly but intensely. The scene reminded Dinah of a football coach talking to a quarterback on the sideline before a game. It was strangely intimate. Lucile made signs with her hands and pointed. After a couple minutes of this, she took a step back and picked up the iPad, presumably to check the picture from the crow camera. She nodded and made a final gesture with her free hand, which even Dinah could tell was the sign to take off.

Richard took off, wings magnificent in flight, gaining altitude.

Dinah came over and stood beside Lucile, craning her neck back and forth between the bird and the iPad.

"I've found it's better just to watch the screen," Lucile said.

Dinah tried this. Her heart sped up. She found she could not resist an occasional glance at Richard until he disappeared behind the peak of the hotel's roof. When the picture stopped moving, they could tell he had landed on the roof. He gave them a wonderful view of Pisgah National Forest. That was it.

Nothing else there. Darn it.

Lucile said under her breath, "Come on, Richard. You know what we want."

After a few seconds, the picture moved again and then stopped. This time, Dinah was seeing the inn from a higher vantage. Richard had landed on the branch of a red oak tree.

"That's my bird," Lucile said.

Dinah got a good picture, the one she wanted. It showed the walkway that provided access to the second-story rooms. This walkway also acted as a back porch for the rooms, complete with rocking chairs for taking in the view. In one of those chairs in front of the room in question was a thin man wearing camo-patterned fatigue pants and a black T-shirt. The chair was turned sideways and positioned in front of the door. The man was nervous, rocking too rapidly in the chair with an unnatural rhythm. Through the open door, Dinah occasionally saw a figure walk by. She watched for several minutes.

Lucile was silent.

"What do you think?" Dinah finally asked her. "I think it's just the one guy."

"And you're sure that's the room Emily and Suzie are in?" Lucile asked.

A figure came to the door. "That's Emily!" Dinah said.

Emily Elah stuck her head out, her short dark hair swinging. It looked like she asked the man something. He reached for his waistband and started to pull out a gun, but instead barked something at her and motioned her inside with his other hand. After she withdrew, he settled into his chair, rocking even more rapidly, taking frequent glances into the room.

Dinah studied the situation, trying to come up with a plan to get this guy out of the way. Judging from the earpiece he wore he had a radio. If she was going to take him out, it would have to be done before he could use his radio or get off a shot with his pistol.

"I need a distraction," Dinah said.

"What do you need me to do?" Lucile asked.

Dinah shook her head. "Oh, no. Segal's already going to kill me for getting you this close to the action. I'm not taking you anywhere near that guy."

"Maybe I don't have to get that close to him," Lucile said, batting her eyes.

On the other side of Mount Pisgah, the black SUV bearing Segal and Jerome Guilford sped on and went completely off the pavement. Segal put his arms in front of his face as he felt the nose of the vehicle rotate into a sickening downward orientation. The speed was diminished by Jerome's braking and by the crash through the guard rail, but as they reached eighty degrees to horizontal the speed picked up again as they continued down the grade. It felt like a vertical fall to Segal except when the wheels crashed into the ground, jolting the car. At first, there were no trees, only coarse grass and huckleberry bushes. Then he saw trees coming up and braced for impact. Solid impact didn't happen, only glancing contact with branches. The scraping of limbs across the hood and windows was frighteningly loud and added to the confusion but did little to slow the SUV.

When the big impact came, it came suddenly and without compromise. The airbag smacked Segal in the face as it exploded in front of him. After that, he was disoriented by the quiet and the lack of forward movement as the airbag deflated with the smell of burnt rocket fuel and engine coolant.

The reality of his situation came to him piece by piece. He felt his weight against the seatbelt and shoulder harness. He saw trees outside the window to his right. The car was still pointed downhill at something like eighty degrees. In other words, it was almost standing on its nose. He looked forward and down, trying to see what they had run into, what had stopped their descent. Then he saw it: a narrow footpath forming a terrace in the side of the mountain with trees on the downhill side. The SUV was wedged against a large poplar tree preventing it from falling farther.

He reached out for Jerome Guilford in the driver's seat. Guilford was slumped forward against the shoulder strap and seatbelt, the deflated airbag below. There was blood. Most of the windshield was shattered, and tiny, jewel-like fragments were everywhere. He remembered that the windshield had exploded violently inward on the parkway. It seemed long ago and far away from their current situation.

"Jerome, are you hit? Are you okay?" Segal asked.

Jerome groaned as if waking from a long sleep. Segal studied him carefully. Small cuts around face and neck. Segal also saw a larger red splotch on his right shoulder.

Jerome opened his eyes.

"Jerome, are you all right?"

He groaned and tried moving each of his limbs. When he got to his right arm, he let out a gasp.

"That's what I thought," Segal said.

Jerome closed his eyes again. "How are you?"

It was a good question. Segal checked himself out. "I'm okay. I think I'm okay."

Jerome kept his eyes shut. "I think I'm going to need you to drive."

Segal saw that the SUV, even though almost vertical, seemed to be held firmly in place, wedged between the bank and the huge poplar tree, and was in no danger of falling over or resuming its descent. "I don't think we're driving anywhere. Not anytime soon."

"Where are we?" Jerome asked.

Segal's eyes went to the trail and followed it into a grove of locust trees. There, he seized upon a horizontal board nailed to a post. It had some writing on it in yellow letters. "We're on the Mountains-to-Sea Trail," he said.

Just then, he saw three hikers emerge from the woods, young men bearing heavy packs. They stopped and took in the sight. After a moment of them looking at Segal and Segal looking at them, he motioned them forward. They dropped their packs and scrambled up to open Segal's door. Segal started fumbling with his seatbelt, and two of them supported him as best they could as he got loose and climbed out and then down the bank to the trail, where he experimented with standing up straight and putting weight on his feet.

Getting Jerome out was more difficult, as he didn't have the use of his right arm. The hikers persisted with minimum damage. They laid Jerome by the trail with a sleeping bag under his head. One administered first aid while Segal tried his cell phone, to no avail. The other two hikers stood with arms crossed, trying to figure out their next move.

"The parkway is up there somewhere," one of them said. "One of us could climb up and flag down someone for help."

Segal looked up. It would be a hell of a bushwhacking scramble, almost straight up. "You can't go up there," he said. "There's a man with a gun, a sniper." The hikers frowned. Segal showed them his badge. "I know what I'm talking about. That's how we ended up down here."

The third hiker stood after tending to Jerome with a first aid kit from his backpack. "I think he'll be okay," he said. "We've got to get him off this mountain." Jerome's shoulder was bandaged, and the small cuts were colored with iodine.

Segal nodded. He reexamined the mountainside. The climb seemed impossible, even without considering the sniper. He remembered telling his boss he did not expect to be climbing any mountains on this case. *Unfortunate choice of words*, he thought. He knew he would somehow have to do it anyway. He took a deep breath.

Accompanied by one of the hikers, he stumbled down the trail to the sign to see if it had any other information that might be of use. The sign read, "Mountains-to-Sea Trail. Motorized vehicles prohibited."

The hiker raised his eyebrows.

Segal looked at the hiker, then the ruined SUV. "Guess we're in a world of trouble now," he said, and tried to wink but winced instead.

CHAPTER 39

A Brace of Kinsmen

Dinah crept up the stairs to the second-story walkway. She dropped forward with her hands on the top step and lowered herself so she could peek around the corner with her head just above floor level. She clearly heard the creaking of the rocking chair and saw the man in it. The chair was angled so his back was to her. He continued to look between the view over the valley and the room with the two people he was guarding. The pace of his rocking had subsided, showing her he had less nervous energy than a short time ago.

Then, near the other end of the walkway, there was movement. The guard's hand tightened on the grip of the gun on his lap and he leaned forward. If there was going to be a problem with her plan, this was the time it would happen. Down the walkway, Lucile emerged from the other set of stairs. Dinah thought, *Go, girl.* Shorts, long legs, brown hair, checkered blouse with the top three buttons undone. She was better than nice looking. She looked like a movie star. *If that doesn't get his attention, I don't know what will.*

Dinah saw the man's hand relax on the gun. It was the sign she was watching for, and she knew in that moment her plan would work. She slid down a couple of steps and checked to make sure she had what she needed.

Lucile neared on the walkway, her footsteps slow and even. Dinah moved up the two steps and watched again. Lucile stopped around ten feet from the guard and turned toward one of the doors. She set down Dinah's gym bag. She had a key out and was fumbling with the door as if she were having trouble with the lock. Muttering under her breath.

The man remained still, chair rocked forward, fixated on the show she was putting on. Lucile raised her hands at the door, faking exasperation. She looked at the key, looked at the door, looked at the key again. She glanced at the man and gave him a quick and sheepish grin, as if to say, *Oops, wrong room.* Then she bent over, picked up the bag, and sashayed down the walkway.

By the time she turned the corner and disappeared down the stairs, Dinah had crept silently behind the rocking chair—not that complete silence was needed, considering the show Lucile put on. She had done her part, and now it was Dinah's turn.

A second after Lucile's exit, the man relaxed, as Dinah knew he would. The chair rocked back, just as she knew it would. When it did, she was ready. She grabbed the top of the chair at the apex of the rock and pulled it toward her with force, slamming the back of the chair and the back of the man's head to the floor. His reflex was to put out his hands to catch himself, including the right hand with the gun. Dinah knew this would happen, too, so her next move was to leap around and step on his wrist, releasing the weapon from his hand. She then swiped the communication rig off his head. He attempted a grab at her with his left hand, which she allowed him to do, as it gave her an opportunity to slap a handcuff on his wrist. Then, with her entire body weight, she lunged toward the outside of the walkway and clipped the other end of the handcuff to the wrought-iron railing. The whole thing took approximately four seconds.

She stepped away and picked up the guy's gun. The man lay in the chair with his legs up like a Mercury astronaut, left hand cuffed to the railing. He looked at her with anger, then let his head and his right arm go slack in complete submission.

"I don't envy you that climb," one of the hikers said. They were helping Segal get ready for his ordeal. He handed Segal a water bottle with a clip that would attach it to his belt.

"If I were you, I'd leave behind everything you don't need," another of the hikers said.

It stopped Segal in his tracks. This was exactly the advice Dr. Gold had given him, word for word. Then he realized this guy was talking about the climb, about lightening his load. He began to shrug off his coat when he felt the weight of the book in the pocket. For one irrational moment, he considered finding some other way to bring the book with him, even carrying it in one hand. But that would be ridiculous. He took off the coat, book and all, and handed it to the hiker.

Segal was soon breathing hard, sometimes leaning forward, stumbling at an extreme angle, more often crawling on hands and knees. He moved a few feet, stopped, pulled in a few ragged breaths, let his throbbing leg recover, then repeated. He thought of climbers ascending Mount Everest in halting fashion.

He had left Jerome Guilford in the care of the hikers, one of whom happened to be a male nurse, in one of those serendipities hikers liked to call "trail magic." They decided that one of them, the fastest, would go ahead for help while the other two stayed to care for Jerome.

It fell to Segal alone to deal with the sniper, though exactly how he was going to do that he did not know. The first step, he figured, was to get himself up there and see what the situation held. He hoped he could reconnoiter and call for help if the cell phone signal came back, but deep inside he knew that would not likely happen and he would have to face the man with the gun on his own. That is, if the climb didn't kill him.

Which it might.

It was difficult to make out the contour of the mountain, but he had been on that part of the parkway many times. As best he could remember, the tunnel they'd been heading for was cut into a hump in the northeastern flank of Mount Pisgah. He surmised that the sniper had established himself on that hump, which commanded an excellent view of the park-way as it approached the tunnel. Based on this, Segal reasoned that if he continued south on the trail, which paralleled the parkway, he could then climb the side of the mountain behind the sniper. Easier said than done—much easier. This was not the kind of climb anyone looked forward to.

He wheezed and coughed.

After a time, he could no longer see the trail and he felt profoundly alone. *No good thinking about it. Just do it, one step at a time.*

And so he entered into some altered state of mind, one in which there was only the side of the mountain leading endlessly up with its coarse grass and ragged scrub of weeds and briars. And of himself, there were only his limbs moving slowly, one at a time clawing upwards like the first primordial creature clawing its way out of the ocean up onto dry land.

After some unknowable passage of time, his limbs refused to move and he collapsed. The grass seemed to smother him and he could not get his breath. With the last of his strength, he rolled over in defeat.

His lungs heaved as he looked up at the perfection of the summer sky. Little by little oxygen and life reentered his body. After a few moments, a movement to his right caught his eye. It was a crow. He wondered if it was Richard. He couldn't tell. He turned and struggled to his feet. The crow was now off to his left, followed by several smaller crows. It was get-ting lower in the sky, closer to the hump of the mountain, under which the tunnel ran. He registered that the ground was not quite as steep here. He had climbed higher than he dared to hope, and he felt a wave of relief. Maybe he had not failed after all. Not yet. As he followed the flight of the bird lower, toward the curve of the land, he saw a man standing and pointing a rifle at him.

Unlike the time his cousin pointed a gun at him two years ago, this scene made perfect sense. Irrationally, the fact that he had actually made the climb was oddly freeing.

The sniper lay in his nest. He was used to long times of waiting. It was part of the training, part of the practice of his calling. On the crest of the hillside, he felt he was lying on the flank of the world. It was an excellent position and a beautiful day. He watched the road carefully, although he assumed, he would have a heads-up call on his radio headset well before the primary target approached. He was also prepared for anything. One never knew what might be coming along—perhaps some other target secondary to the mission.

He glanced to his right down the mountainside. His shots on the SUV had worked out even better than he hoped, and the recoil from the rifle hardly hurt at all. He'd taken out the drivers-side front tire, making the vehicle pull hard to that side, and had then taken out the windshield, just in case the driver had mad driving skills. The driver didn't, and the SUV smashed through the guard rail like it was cardboard and plunged out of sight. The sniper heard the crash when it hit something solid enough to make it stop. It was about what he expected—not too loud and certainly no big ball of fire like in the movies. That rarely happened in real life. Too bad. He didn't know how badly the two men in the vehicle were hurt, but given the terrain, he assumed they would be out of the action at least long enough for him to complete the mission. Nevertheless, he checked in that direction from time to time. If they came crawling up, then he would deal with that, too.

He also checked behind. On a normal mission, this would have been the job of his spotter, but he didn't have a spotter. It was the only thing not quite ideal about his present setup, and it made him uneasy. Every time he looked he, of course, saw nothing and then felt foolish for worrying.

Then he saw the crow come flying over the crest behind him. Its flight seemed to be meandering, as if perhaps it was scouting, rather than traveling directly to some destination. It was followed by a few other crows. The sniper wondered if it was that trained bird he had first seen in Afghanistan, the one called Richard, or maybe one of the birds their own guy had brought here to Asheville to help them with their hunt. Then he felt foolish again. He had no reason to think it was anything but a wild bird here in the great wilderness of Pisgah.

The sniper lowered his gaze to the ground, and there was a man, appearing out of nowhere. He looked ragged and unsteady. It was that Asheville cop. The sniper could not understand exactly how he got there, but he posed no special problem. The cop had nowhere to go, out here in the open. The sniper raised his weapon in a deliberate and businesslike manner. At the distance of fifty yards, he probably could have hit the guy shooting from the hip. Such was not his training.

This was professional stuff. He looked through the scope, saw the expression on the cop's face—surprisingly serene, even satisfied. He lined up the crosshairs on the middle of the cop's chest, the way he supposed that cop woman, Dinah had lined up on him.

Then he felt something touch the barrel of his rifle, a solid weight that should not be there, and a black shape obscured the view out of the scope.

Segal would later wonder how long it took for his mind to accept what happened next. It was probably a second or less before he snapped back to the reality of the moment. The sniper seemed in no hurry to take a shot, but as the gun moved into place, Segal saw the crow dive, landing on the rifle just in front of the scope.

The man jerked the muzzle up at the same time Segal dropped to his knees. The gun went off, the bullet whizzing by well over his head. Segal reached for his own gun, even though the man was out of his effective pistol range. There was nothing for it. He lowered his firearm. The scene was so bizarre he could only stand and watch.

The crow was not thrown off when the sniper raised his rifle, nor when the rifle went off. In fact, it jumped forward toward the man's face. The man turned his head away and put up a forearm in defense. Segal remembered what Dinah had told him about snipers—that their talent and performance began with their eyes. The crow seemed to understand this and attacked the man's most vulnerable point. The sniper was now facing away from Segal, stumbling downhill on the other side of the hump in the mountainside. He was bent over, flailing with his arms to free himself from the relentless attack. He finally landed a blow to the bird and began to turn around. Other crows descended and were on him. There were only five or six, but it seemed like many more. It seemed like the man was covered with black, writhing feathers, and the sound was terrifying. The sniper dropped his rifle, and his downhill stumble turned into an off-balance downhill run.

He disappeared over the crest. Segal broke out of his trance and followed, his own gun at the ready. He caught sight of the man for only a second. The sound of the crows stopped. He heard a human scream and then a sound more awful. Segal stopped to listen. There was nothing further except for the light breeze through the grass and shrubs. The crows rose, spiraled silently up, dipped, rose again, and trailed away, over the hillside single file.

Segal realized he was about at the point where the sniper had been standing. He saw the long rifle with the big scope lying in the grass. Beside the rifle was the body of a large crow, limp and lifeless. He picked it up and saw the headset and also the wounds from a few days earlier. There was no doubt. *Richard.*

Segal knew what had happened but had to see for himself. As he advanced, the downward slope became steeper and steeper. He was inching along by the time he came to the lip of the abutment where the vertical cut had been made in the mountainside for the road and the entrance to the tunnel.

There on the pavement far below lay the body of the sniper, posed as though in midstride, a pool of blood forming beside his head on the pavement.

Segal held the still-warm body of Richard tucked under his left arm. He felt a bolt of sadness work its way across his insides. Struck by an inspiration, he held Richard aloft. If anyone was watching, the crow cam would send them the most dramatic picture of the day. He felt he was helping a combat hero. The great winged crow, given one more chance to join the fight.

CHAPTER 40

Punch and Counterpunch

For the first time since he had them under his control, the colonel seemed unhappy.

"Three, come in," he said into the mic for the fifth or sixth time. Three was the guy who was supposed to keep an eye on Emily Elah and the girl. Three had not responded for some minutes now. It was the easiest assignment and also probably the least crucial for the success of the operation. After all, what could those two possibly do to change the course of events? Still, it was an irritation.

"One, report," the colonel said. One was the sniper, the real operative, the main functionary. As long as this guy was in place, everything else could be dealt with. Three was primarily on the team as their electronics tech and was not as disciplined as the others. One was the best of the best. There was no response from him either.

"What's the matter, colonel, no one wants to talk to you?" Mattie said over her shoulder.

"Just keep moving," he said. "It doesn't matter. We're almost there, and we can talk to the man in person." They were in an open field now, mainly low brush and coarse clumps of grass on the crest of the mountainside.

Into his mic, the colonel called his remaining man. "Two," he said.

"Two here," came the voice in his headset.

"Are you at the inn yet?"

"Close," the man answered.

"Report status there ASAP." It was Two who had climbed Mount Pisgah and disabled the cell tower. When the colonel lost contact with the man at the inn, he had ordered Two down to check it out.

Meanwhile, he and his captives were approaching the sniper's nest, only there was no sniper. The colonel shouted, "Halt" and swore under his breath. He looked around, checking their position. They had to be close. They were on the crest of the hill that gave the best view. In front of him was the long, lazy curve of the road as it approached the tunnel, which, according to his understanding, must be right in front of them, just out of sight. There was no place for the sniper to be out of sight, not that he could tell, since the guy loved to hide and then appear out of nowhere—loved to pull that stuff to demonstrate his camouflage skills.

"Stay here," he said to Francis and Mattie. There was literally nowhere for them to go, nowhere they could run and take cover from the machine gun that hung from a sling over his shoulder. He advanced a few steps over the crest toward the place where the tunnel entrance was cut into the hillside. "What the hell?" he muttered under his breath.

Standing there in front of him, looking the other way, was that Asheville cop, holding the sniper's rifle in one hand and a dead crow in the other.

"Drop the rifle and that stupid bird," came a voice from behind Segal.

Segal turned around slowly, at the same time moving away from the drop-off, lest he join the unfortunate sniper on the road below. He looked up the hill. A few yards away was the lead Cormorant guy, the one they called "the colonel." Segal recognized him from the photo from the VA hospital. The colonel had his finger on the trigger of a lightweight machine gun. The weapon was pointed at him but could also be easily and quickly swung to cover the other two people he saw, Mattie and Francis Elah. He had figured he might get to meet Francis Elah before the day was over, but seeing him standing there in the flesh after seeking him so intently still made an impression. And Mattie, what the hell? He stood gawking.

"Drop the rifle now," the colonel said, more insistent this time.

Segal snapped back to the present. He let the rifle drop, still trying to work out the implications.

"Now, empty your other hand."

"It's just a bird," Segal said. "A dead bird." He held the bird aloft, making sure the camera, if it was still functioning, would take in the scene. He looked apologetically at Francis. "It's Richard," he said in a low voice.

"Put it down anyway," the colonel said, "then put your hands behind your head and walk slowly this way." He motioned with the muzzle of his gun.

Segal bent and placed the body of Richard on the ground with as much reverence as the situation allowed, then complied. He realized that for the second time that day, a dangerous man was pointing a gun at him and he was not freaking out. This was something he could tell Dr. Gold the next time he saw her, if there was a next time.

When he got near, the colonel relieved him of his pistol and motioned for him to join the others. "What were you looking at over the edge there?" the colonel asked.

"See for yourself," Segal said.

The colonel edged over the crest toward the place where the tunnel entrance was cut into the hillside. He peered over and saw the body of his sniper in the road below. "Shit," he muttered under his breath. He studied the picture for a moment, then pulled himself from the frightening drop.

His earpiece crackled. He listened. "Go ahead, Two," the colonel said.

"I'm at the inn. At the designated room. No sign of our man. No sign of captives. Do you want me to search the rest of the inn?"

"Negative, no time. Disable the cars in the parking lot and bring the van north. Pick us up at the north end of the tunnel. We're reverting to backup operation, the IED plan."

"Copy."

CHAPTER 41

Plan B

D inah walked through the dining room at the Pisgah Inn, deserted now. She checked the building and parking lot for any sign of activity and saw none. She held the earpiece she'd taken from the guard. She'd heard someone identified as "Two" check in earlier and formed the impression he was headed toward the inn, so she'd moved everyone out of the room.

Lucile called from the entrance to the kitchen. "Dinah, come here and look at this."

Dinah took care not to silhouette herself against any of the windows of the dining room. Lucile leaned against a counter studying the iPad, which she showed to Dinah. It was the view from Richard's camera. Dinah said, "Hold that. I'm going to check on our guy." She made sure the prisoner was still secure. He said nothing.

Emily Elah was at the stove in the kitchen making Suzie a snack. "Don't worry, we're keeping an eye on that knucklehead," she said.

Suzie seemed to like that word, laughing and trying it out for herself: "Knucklehead."

Dinah turned her attention to the iPad. "My God, it's Francis and Mattie!"

Emily and Suzie came over. They all saw Francis and Mattie and the man with the gun.

"How are we even seeing this?" Dinah asked. They had already watched the other events transpire. They had seen Segal and the sniper and then the confusing, jostled sequence of the crow attack, ending with a view of the sniper on the road and then nothing but sky and grass. Now, this.

"Segal," Lucile said. "It's got to be Segal. He must be holding the camera, or holding up the bird with the camera." As soon as she stated that conclusion, the image was jarred and came to rest, showing nothing but blue sky with some blades of grass in the foreground.

"What does that mean?" Dinah asked.

"I'm afraid that means R.I.P. Richard," Lucile said.

Dinah let that sink in. It bothered her plenty, as much as the death of Gloria and of Chickey. More maybe. After all, she knew Richard better than the other two and thanks to Francis Elah Richard had jumped the spark gap between animal and human. Perhaps for the first time she felt the magnitude of what Francis had accomplished.

The earpiece crackled. The others leaned in to hear it. "Two reporting, colonel."

"Go ahead, Two."

"I'm at the inn. At the designated room. No sign of our man. No sign of captives."

There was a pause. Dinah understood what it meant. She put a finger to her lips and pointed at the man handcuffed in the back. Emily moved quickly to him and stuffed a dishrag in his mouth.

More crackling. "Do you want me to search the rest of the inn?"

"Negative, no time. Disable the cars in the parking lot and bring the van north. Pick us up at the north end of the tunnel. We're reverting to backup operation, the IED plan."

"Copy."

Dinah waited. No further communication. Emily Elah wiped her eyes with her forearm. Suzie jumped a bit in her wheelchair, her face flush. "Mom," she said, and then Emily went to her daughter, kneeled down and held her close.

How long had it been since they'd been with Francis, Dinah wondered. Weeks now. Too long for a family to be apart and under these circumstances.

Dinah put her finger over her mouth. Footsteps in the parking lot. Hard to make out through the wall, like cotton in her ears on a big airplane.

"Stay here," Dinah said. She slipped out her gun and moved to the front of the building. When she peeked around the doorjamb, she saw a man trotting toward the white van at the far end of the parking lot. He had an assault rifle slung over one shoulder and in one hand a bundle of thick black wires. He got in and pulled out, turning north onto the parkway, speeding away.

Dinah stepped out. The first thing she noticed was that the hood of her car was up, and likewise, that of the little

Honda that belonged to Mattie. She walked to her car and looked at the engine compartment.

"What did he do?" Lucile asked. She joined Dinah, scanning the engine from the other side. "I have no idea what I'm looking at."

"He took most of the ignition wires," Dinah said. She pointed to the empty space between the coil and the distributor, as well as the bare spark plugs.

"The car won't run without them?"

"Not even a little," Dinah said. She put her hands on her hips and visually scoured the open lot, as though some spare ignition wires might be lying on the ground somewhere.

"What do we do?" Lucile asked. "I think we can assume Mattie, Francis, and Segal are in deep-shit trouble."

"They're not the only ones," Dinah said. "I think the president is headed this way to go hiking with the first lady today. I got a look at the itinerary."

"The president and first lady?" Lucile repeated. "Good lord."

"We thought the terrorists were looking for Francis and Richard, which they were. Francis because he wouldn't help them on a mission. I think we know what that mission was."

"Killing the president and the first lady?" Lucile's eyes widened.

Dinah nodded.

"Where do you think they're heading in the van? They can't be returning to Asheville to get close to the president. He's got Secret Service with enough firepower to stop a freight train"

Dinah's expression changed. "I don't think they have any intention of going to Asheville." She opened the door to the backseat of her car, which was a mess of various pieces of athletic equipment, including a small backpack, the kind used by trail runners. She pulled it out and found a worn and folded trail map of Pisgah National Forest. She spread it out on the hood of her car. "We're here," she said, pointing, "on the Parkway." Then she ran her finger along the heavy black line on the map. "A little north of here, the way we came, is an overlook where they could pull the van off the road."

"Plus, it's just after a sharp curve, so anyone coming from Asheville wouldn't have much warning before they saw it sitting there," Lucile added.

"Look at this, too." Dinah moved her finger off the heavy black line and onto a faint dotted line beside it. "This is a hiking trail. It comes right up to the parkway at that point. That could be a getaway route for them."

"You don't think they'll drive away in the van?" Lucile asked

Dinah looked at Lucile. "I don't think there will be a van when they're done. Remember they said something about a plan with an IED? That's military-speak for a homemade bomb. An improvised explosive device. I've got to stop this."

"How are you going to get down there?"

"Getting down there will be the least of my problems," Dinah said, reaching into the backseat again. She strained for contact and came up with two hard objects that empowered and freed her in more ways than one.

"That's a waste," the colonel said. His face flamed red. "One of the finest military assets I've ever known."

He glared at Segal as if he wanted to execute him then and there.

Segal stood with Francis and Mattie on the Blue Ridge Parkway at the entrance to the tunnel. The colonel had bound the threesome's hands in front of them with plastic pull ties and marched them down the mountainside. It had not been an easy descent, especially for Segal. His leg was about to burst with pain.

On the road, the fallen man lay absolutely motionless. The colonel knelt and removed his dog tags, placing them in his own shirt pocket. He checked the man's pockets and found no other ID, just a small packet of origami paper. This he replaced in the man's pocket and patted it flat.

To Segal, it seemed the most sentimental move the colonel was prepared to make. From a holster at the man's waist, the colonel removed a pistol, which he placed in his own pocket.

The sniper had flecks of blood around his eyes and numerous cuts on his neck and the backs of his hands. "Look what your crows did to my man," the colonel said, glaring at Francis.

"Those weren't my crows," Francis said. "Those were from that flock your guy was running. Those were the genetically modified ones your guy was working with. My crows would never have attacked like that."

"Except for Richard," the colonel said.

"Richard was the exception to a lot of rules," Francis said this flatly. Segal caught a glint of sadness in his eyes.

"If you're right, how did the other crows get here? If not under your direction?"

"They probably decided to follow Richard. Crows do that. They follow powerful leaders. Richard killed their leader, leaving a void, so they took up with him. Anyway, check the wounds. You'll know I'm right. Normal crows can't do damage like that. Your guy put those reinforcements, the ones made with metal-diamond composite, on the tips of their beaks and their claws. You know this." Again, Francis talked in a calm, matter-of-fact voice.

The colonel seemed to think about this, then shook it off. "Doesn't matter," he said. "Doesn't change anything. They can't do anything to us now." Nevertheless, he looked briefly skyward.

Segal heard a sound in the tunnel and stepped back when the white van came up. It swerved at the last moment when the driver saw the body on the road. The driver got out and came around to see his fallen comrade for himself. From the look on his face, he was more disgusted than upset.

"Get these three in the van," the colonel said.

"What about him?" the man asked.

"Leave him. It will add to the general confusion. Shock and awe."

The man opened the side door and they climbed in with difficulty. Segal's bound hands hurt. The guy helped boost Mattie with a hand to her butt, which got him a nasty look. Segal ended up on a bench seat, pressed between Mattie and

Francis. He became aware of the smells in the hot, enclosed space. There was something he could not identify. He leaned toward Mattie and picked up the faint herbal fragrance of her shampoo. He leaned toward Francis, smelling mint, tobacco, and sweat. That wasn't it.

As the van took off, they were jostled, without the benefit of seatbelts. At one point, Segal was turned sideways and got a glimpse of the cargo area. Various objects were packed in, but the one that got his attention was a cube covered with canvas sitting on a wooden pallet. It was securely strapped to grappling points on the wall of the van. From the back of the cube, two wires ran to a metal box. Then he understood. That's what he smelled. Those were explosives. The van was a bomb.

He turned around, his skin on fire, sobered even more than before, if that was possible. "Colonel, I never took you for a suicide bomber," he said.

The driver laughed. Mattie and Francis seemed to stop breathing.

From the front passenger seat, the colonel said, "I'm not a suicide bomber. I have no intention of dying today."

The van pulled off to the right. It was a scenic overlook. On the other side of the road was a vertical cut in the granite, leaving no place to go. Beyond that point, the road made a sharp turn. A car approaching from the opposite direction would come upon this place with little warning and no opportunity to turn around.

As Segal expected, the van slowed and pulled over, and they were ordered out. Under different circumstances, they could have enjoyed the view. Segal walked to the guard rail and saw a sheer drop on the other side. Beyond was a view over the valley. To his left, fifty or sixty feet away, was a steep trail with steps cut into the dirt and rock. This, Segal knew, led to the Mountains-to-Sea Trail, from which hikers could descend to the road that followed the river. *That's how they're planning to escape*, he thought.

"That's far enough," the colonel said, and Segal moved away from the guard rail.

The driver made a motion with the muzzle of his rifle, and Segal walked over to Francis and Mattie, who were beside the van. To Segal, it felt like a firing squad, but then he thought of the explosives in the van and realized they would not be firing into it. He was getting accustomed to people pointing guns at him today.

The colonel walked to the guard rail to confer with the driver. At first, he kept his eye and his gun on them, but as he got into the discussion, he stared directly at his man.

"They have explosives in there under the tarp," Segal whispered out of the side of his mouth. "The van is a bomb."

Mattie and Francis blanched, glancing frantically from Segal, to the van, to the colonel.

The driver nodded to the colonel. Apparently, they had worked out the details of their plan. The driver moved along the guard rail to a higher position a few yards away. From there, Segal assumed, he had the best vantage around the curve in the direction from which their target would approach. At the same time, he could easily cover the captives. The colonel moved to the rear doors of the van, slung his weapon over his shoulder, opened the doors, and reached inside. Segal assumed he was arming the detonation device.

Whatever his task, it wasn't long before he closed the doors with a gentle click.

He walked toward Segal. His machine gun was still slung over his shoulder, but from a pocket, he removed a pistol, the one he had taken from the sniper's body. The colonel locked eyes. "Step away from the van," he said. "Not you two. Just the cop." He made a motion with the pistol for Segal to step toward the railing.

"You're forgetting your roles in this drama," the colonel explained. "You're the two international terrorists." He motioned to Francis and Mattie. "Lieutenant Segal here did not originally have a part in this drama, but since he decided to join the cast, we wrote him in." He smiled a benevolent smile. "Didn't we?" He looked at the driver, who smiled and nodded. "He is the local cop who's been on your trail for the last week for the two murders you committed. It will be apparent in the aftermath that you were responsible. Just to tie things up, the bullet they find in Lieutenant Segal, the one fired from this gun, will match the one used to kill the poor secretary at Creatures 2.0. Pretty neat, huh?"

"Let me guess the final scene," Francis said shifting forward. "The van blows up when the president's motorcade comes by. We perish in the blast as well, being either fanatical suicide bombers or just not that good with explosives."

The colonel nodded. "I like the first interpretation myself. Better storyline. More jihad-like. I'm sure that's the one the press will go with."

Segal stood by the guard rail and the drop on the other side. He was thinking of making a dash for the stairway path a few yards away. He thought with clarity and precision, almost with detachment. Gone were the panic and confusion that had plagued him these past months. His mind was focused. He could breath.

"Unfortunately, the lieutenant tracked you down. You shot him before he could prevent the tragedy. Not with anything as crude as an assault rifle, but with a pistol." The colonel raised the weapon and pointed it at Segal.

He held the gun for a moment, taking in a slow breath. Segal heard a whirring sound coming from the road.

CHAPTER 42

The Jammer

"You've got to be kidding," Lucile said when she saw what Dinah was doing. Dinah had pulled her bag containing her skating gear from the car. She was leaning on the hood, pulling off her shoes, and pulling on first her pads and then her skates.

"If I remember right, it's all either downhill or level between here and the overlook," Dinah said. She pulled the laces tight and tied them. She slid off the hood of the car and took a step and a glide and a turn, checking her equipment.

"This is insane," Lucile said, but Dinah just held out her hand for the helmet Lucile was holding.

"I have to stop this. No one else can," Dinah said. After a moment of hesitation, Lucile let her have the helmet. Dinah strapped on the familiar headgear with the jammer's star. "Stay with the others and make sure the knucklehead is tied up till we return. Whatever is going to happen will happen pretty quick."

With no further words, she was off, using long pow-er-kicks to get her momentum up. She looked over her shoulder and saw Lucile still watching.

It didn't take long to build up as much speed as she dared, and then she settled into a rhythm of long kicks and glides. She kept an eye out for debris on the road. Hitting a rock or a crack in the pavement was her biggest concern. When she entered the tunnel, it took a second for her eyes to adjust to the low light, but she had no trouble spotting the body of the sniper on the other side. She didn't slow to look but never-theless got a clear glance. It was enough to confirm what she suspected. This was indeed the guy she had followed through downtown Asheville.

From there, she simply skated, clearing her mind and settling her nerves. In her fight with the guard at the inn, she had enjoyed the luxury of planning out a series of moves in advance. Not so now, since the scene she was skating into was unknown. She would have to rely on instinct and reflexes, but these she had honed with years of training and practice. Anyway, like she told Lucile, whatever was about to happen would happen fast, and then it would be over and she would be okay or some degree of not okay, and then she would deal with that. *That's how we roll*, she thought. She knew she was on point now, and it was not the first time. She accepted it with calm and focus.

As she expected, it was mostly downhill. All she had to do was glide and maintain speed with an occasional kick. Then she hit a section through a narrow pass that was slightly uphill with enough momentum to carry her through. When she came to the crest, she saw a steep downhill section in front of her. At the bottom was a hard curve to the left, and on the right, in a pull-off for the scenic overlook, was the white van. She saw a large man standing with an assault rifle. *The others must be blocked by the van.* The man was by the guard rail and was looking the other way. He would have to be her first target. If he turned and saw her too soon, he could shoot, if he was fast. Really fast. She would have no time to go for her own gun. She gave a couple of kicks, then tucked into a low crouch and let gravity take her.

By the time Segal heard the whirring of her skates, Dinah was on the guy.

The man had time to spin toward her and put up his arm in a futile blocking motion.

Segal watched Dinah pull a notorious move she was famous for with big skaters on the roller derby track. She straightened enough to give the guy what he thought was an easy target, then at the last split second—faster than seemed possible—she ducked under his arm and came up quickly for impact. She hit him like a cannonball. In a roller derby competition, she would have let her arms contact the opponent's chest. She would hit her target hard enough to knock her off balance but not hard enough to hurt. For this killer, she spared no energy, planting her starred helmet under his chin and pushing up with both arms. Then came a horrific sound of breaking bone as the helmet struck and the man flipped in an awkward cartwheel over the guard rail. Segal heard him crashing through branches far below but no scream or any other human sound.

"That's my partner," Segal whispered. He raised his bound hands and rushed the colonel.

With little remaining momentum, Dinah spun off the rail and headed toward her second target. *She'll make it before I do.* Segal hurried.

The colonel spun toward her, pointing his pistol. He fired and missed. As she came in, he squeezed off a second shot when Segal hit him from behind. It was an ungainly blow with his hands bound together but it made the shot go wide. Dinah hit the colonel with weakened speed but hard enough to knock him down. Segal stepped on the colonel's gun hand, and Dinah pulled her own gun.

Segal heard Mattie and Francis behind them. Mattie yelled, "Oh, shit!" The smell of acrid fumes filled the air.

Dinah said, "Bullet hole."

The colonel's stray shot had entered the van. A lazy yellow flame was curling up from inside it.

Segal wasted no time. "Over the side!" he yelled. He grabbed Dinah and pulled her to the end of the railing, where the trail of steps was cut into the mountainside. He grabbed her belt, lifted, and jumped. Mattie and Francis were right behind them, the four of them tumbling on the trail steps. Brush and twigs cut and flailed Segal's skin. Rocks smashed him. Finally, he came to a stop. Dinah was near; Mattie and Francis too.

He covered his head, expecting the detonation blast. It did not come. He looked up to see the colonel standing above them, taking calm aim with his machine gun. And that was when the explosion came with a deafening concussive *whump* and a mass of flame and smoke, propelling the colonel like a flying shadow, into the air, across the skies, jettisoning him far off the side of the mountain. Debris and dust rained and Segal covered his head tight.

CHAPTER 43

All In

When the storm of debris subsided, Segal raised his head. He checked his body for functional parts with his bound and scraped bloody hands, and he was okay except for a hollow ringing in his ears. Segal shouted. "Okay? Everyone okay?" The others stirred, and apart from bruises and scrapes, they were in one piece and basically unharmed. Dinah freed their hands. They climbed up the steps of the trail, Segal's hip giving him trouble. Talking was out of the question.

Mattie held her ears. Francis followed, shaking his head side to side.

When they reached the top and got over the guard rail, Segal thought the blood pushing through his brain might be too much for him. He had to sit down. Mattie and Francis sat nearby.

Soon, several black SUVs pulled up. The head of the Secret Service got out. Segal watched him look at what was left of the van, which was not much, glance at the charred pieces of jagged metal, then eye the four of them, his gaze settling on Dinah, her helmet now off. To Segal, she looked smaller in her stocking feet, holding her skates. The agent walked over and addressed Segal and Dinah.

"Status of suspects?"

"One dead on the road. About a mile up that way." Segal blew out a breath.

"One in custody at the inn," Dinah said.

That was news to Segal. He would have to hear that story himself.

"One over the side. Presumed dead. At least incapacitated," Segal pointed. "And the leader is right there."

The Secret Service men went to the rail. Segal got up and joined them, painful as the effort was.

There he saw the body of the colonel. Clothes torn to rags. Burnt from the blast. He was lodged in the twisted limbs of an oak. As Segal closed his eyes and then opened them, two crows circled in the air before alighting on the branches beside the body, one on each side.

Mattie walked over. "As if the crows are stationed there to make sure the colonel's spirit will not reenter his body and bring him back to life."

"Yeah, I've got to hear the story behind this," the Secret Service man said.

Another black SUV pulled up. Four more Secret Service men got out. The head guy sent a couple of them to the inn and the others to look for the man who went over the side. It didn't take long for them to find him and confirm he was no longer a threat to anyone.

Segal relaxed as much as possible. Dinah sat there without speaking. Francis walked over. "Hello," he said and smiled weakly. "My name is Francis Elah. Thank you for protecting my family."

The Secret Service man spoke to the air. "They want to know if it's clear to bring POTUS up for the hike," he said, and nodded toward Segal.

"I think it's clear," Segal said.

The Secret Service man hesitated.

"After what everyone has been through, I think we'd like to see him take that hike," Dinah said.

The Secret Service man must have seen the same thing Segal saw in Dinah's face. Into the radio, he said, "Give us fifteen to clean some things up."

Later, at the Pisgah Inn, the Elah family—Francis, Emily, and Suzie—enjoyed their reunion on the porch outside the restaurant. The little girl would not let go of her father. As a group of black SUVs pulled up, Mattie played a few bars of "Hail to the Chief" on a little squeezebox. Segal and Lucile stood from their rocking chairs where they were holding hands. The president and first lady emerged from the third SUV, dressed for hiking. Before they got on the trail, though, they walked over and greeted the small group on the porch, which was how everyone got a chance to shake hands with the president. When he reached Francis, the president held his hand longer, leaned in, and said, "Thanks for everything." The takeaway photograph of the visit, the president and first lady kneeling by Suzie in her wheelchair with the panorama of Pisgah National Forest in the background, would be picked up by the press worldwide. Suzie was wearing Dinah's helmet with the white star.

After the president and first lady left for the trail, accompanied by several Secret Service men, the head man came up on the porch, signing off a call on his cell phone. "Got cell service back and found out about your buddy, Andrew Roche," he said to Segal. Dinah came over to hear as well. "He was with Cormorant, all right-they—threatened him—but still in the country. We got him out of there, and he should be home in a day or two, after we debrief him as part of the investigation."

The president and first lady labored up the trail and turned into a switchback, where the view unfolded below them through an opening in the trees. They paused and took it in for a moment in silence, catching their breath as they did.

They were about to move on when they heard an odd sound from the trees. They turned to see the source, and the first lady said in a barely audible whisper, "Oh, look, a deer. Can you believe how cute it is?"

The president looked at the animal and tilted his head. He was not so sure. He was a city guy and certainly no expert on deer, but this one did not strike him as cute or good looking in any way. In fact, now that he looked more closely, he thought it might be cross-eyed. "The ears seem really big," the president said.

"You're going to talk about big ears?" she said.

The first lady shook a little trail mix into her hand and took a step toward the deer, offering the treat on her open palm.

The deer said, "AAAAA, BEEEE, CEEEE."

The president and first lady screamed in unison and jumped back. From ahead and behind on the trail, Secret Service men converged, guns drawn. One of the men tackled the deer. From the ground, the deer raised its head slightly, said "DEEEE," and collapsed with its tongue hanging out to one side.

The incident was not reported to the press.

Jerome Guilford struggled to consciousness in the recovery room of the VA hospital on the east side of Asheville. After the hikers sent a runner ahead for help, he had endured a painful journey by stretcher and ambulance to the VA, where he was moved almost immediately into surgery for his bullet wound and other injuries.

As the effects of the anesthetic waned, his memory of events began to float into place piece by piece—the shots, the wreck, the plummet down the mountain. Then he remembered the reason he had been doing all of this. He grabbed the sleeve of a nurse as she passed his bed.

"The president. Is he all right?" he asked.

The nurse took his hand and put it on the bed. "The president is fine. Now, you take it easy and let me know when you want a drink of water." She looked at the monitor and moved on.

As the Crow Dies

Jerome Guilford lay back, relieved. But as he began to doze off, another half-memory drifted into his mind. It was a memory from the operating room.

It seemed there was a moment just after the surgery when he had regained a foggy awareness. He had raised his head and seen the surgeon pulling off his gloves and taking the mask off his face. And beside the surgeon was another, much smaller figure, also dressed in surgical gown and mask. When a nurse pulled tiny gloves off its hands, Guilford saw agile, little jet-black fingers ending in black claws. The small figure held its hand up, and the surgeon gave it a high five, after which the surgeon took out two bite-sized Snickers bars, one for himself and one for his assistant.

Or then again, maybe it was just the drugs playing tricks with his mind.

CHAPTER 44

Epilogue— Six Months After

Dinah had been out of town for a few weeks on a training course in Raleigh. It had been a while since she'd seen Segal. There was no doubt she was on the track for bigger and better things in law enforcement. It was her first night back in Asheville and Segal said why didn't they get together at the New Belgium brewery. Sit on the porch and watch the river roll by.

He was already sitting there when Dinah arrived. She hung back and looked at him. She liked what she saw. His back was straighter. Something about the way he held his head and shoulders seemed more robust. He still looked more like a college professor than a cop though. There was a book on the table in front of him, of course, but it just lay there. He wasn't doing that nervous fiddling thing with the pages.

He must have sensed her gaze because he looked up and smiled. She ran to him and they hugged. He held it a beat or two longer than she might have expected.

"Missed you," he said. "You get them all straightened out in Raleigh?"

"Not even close," she said. She slid into a seat at the table. They ordered their beers, took the first sip, took a deep breath and decompressed. She gazed down the hill. The view of the river was just as he said it would be. She looked upstream to the right.

"That's where it started," she said. They could just make out that place in the river bank where the body had been found.

Segal nodded. "You hear 12 Bones is moving?" he asked.

"No way," Dinah said. Twelve Bones seemed like too much of an institution to change.

"Not far," Segal assured her. "Maybe a quarter-mile upriver. Still in the Arts District."

She found that strangely reassuring.

"Everything tied up on the case?" she asked. "I still feel bad leaving you with the loose ends and paperwork."

Segal dismissed this with a wave. "Part of the job. But we're pretty well wrapped up, at least on our end. The murders are down to the sniper, who of course is dead. The DA is not bringing charges against the surviving member of the Cormorant team. Can't put him actually at any of the scenes. Don't worry. He'll answer for federal charges of conspiracy."

"And the Cormorant company as a whole?"

Segal reclined a little. "The colonel was right about one thing. In the aftermath, it comes down to who can tell the best story, or maybe who can tell the story people want to hear. In this case, the story that's least embarrassing for the powers that be is that the colonel and his little group went rogue and no one else knew what was going on. I suspect that some version of that will be the official history. At the same time, I heard Nancy Lund has her eye on them, so they're not completely off the hook."

They took a couple of drinks in silence and watched the river flow, complete with its kayaks and canoes and paddleboards.

"I heard Lucile is gone," Dinah said, more as a question than a statement.

"Like a turkey in the corn," Segal said.

Dinah felt a rush of sympathy.

Segal smiled. "It's OK. Lucile was exactly what I needed at the time, but it was not destined to last. She's out on the West coast now working with sea otters. Some project funded by that internet billionaire who funded the mule deer thing." He took another drink. "What about you?" he asked. "After your performance, in this case, I expected the Secret Service to recruit you. You made quite an impression on Straus and the others."

She grinned. "I may have gotten a call. Washington isn't Asheville, Segal. Maybe someday. I'm not done here."

He nodded. "Good."

Dinah reached out and picked up the book from the table in front of him.

"Cormac McCarthy? This is new for you, isn't it?"

"I decided it's time to branch out."

"Well tell me this, Segal. With Cormac McCarthy, does everyone get exactly what they deserve in the end?"

Segal grinned and downed the rest of his beer. " I'm going to have to get back to you on that."

Dinah drank too. The river was extraordinary with wind and trees. When she put down her glass, a touch of winged air brushed her cheek.

About the Author

 **Kenneth Butcher** is a materials engineer and researcher with sixteen U.S. patents. He was born in Washington, D.C., and grew up mostly in Ohio, where he was raised on a strict diet of science fiction, mystery novels, and classics. His first novel, *The Middle of the Air* (2009), received Ben Franklin and Independent Book Publishers awards. His second novel, *The Dream of Saint Ursula* (2014), is a mystery set in the Virgin Islands. Butcher lives in the mountains of Western North Carolina, where he continues to write and to research novel materials. He also publishes a podcast called The Middle of the Air, which concentrates on interviews with authors and artists who live or travel to the area. The podcast can be found at themiddleoftheair.com. His website is kennethbutcher.com.